FR

Trina Bahati

My Last

Fling

Isla Drake

Isla Drake

For anyone who's ever been lost and trying to find themselves.
Don't overlook the benefits of having toe-curling sex with a younger man. Even if you don't find yourself, you'll have fun trying.

Before you start

This book is a low angst romance with a happily ever after at the end, but it does contain some things that may be upsetting to some readers.

They include: foul language, detailed consensual sexual content, mentions of parental death, mentions of death by a drunk driver, mentions of cancer, alcohol consumption.

As always, happy reading!

CHAPTER 1

Fourteen months ago

Cole

Other people would probably avoid their workplace on their night off. But, since Peach Fuzz is the most popular bar in this little town, it's the best place to spend a Friday night without driving to Savannah. Besides Luke wanted to get out of the city, and Linc only has a babysitter for my niece until 10pm. So, Peach Fuzz it is.

I don't mind, though. I love this place. I love the comfort of looking around the room and recognizing the staff and most of the patrons. I love the friendly smiles and waves from people I've known most of my life. I know small-town life isn't for everyone, but it suits me. It's the main reason I opened my restaurant here instead of someplace like Savannah where it might have made more money or been more successful. I wanted to build something lasting in the town where I grew up. I wanted to plant my roots here. And I'm damned proud of what I've accomplished in the last few years.

This old building stood empty for years before I scraped together the last of my money to buy it. Then, I'd worked my ass off at a construction job my brother had helped me get while I'd thrown every spare penny into the renovations. Linc helped me as much as he could when he wasn't working himself or taking care of Ella. He's always been there for me, and I know I owe him more than I could ever repay. I don't think Peach Fuzz would be what it is today if not for my big brother standing beside me every step of the way.

When I walk into Peach Fuzz, it's already starting to fill up with the dinner rush. I try to act like any other patron of the restaurant, but it's difficult to stop looking at it with a critical lens, wondering who needs a drink refill or whether a table has been waiting too long for their appetizers. As I make my way through the restaurant toward the bar, I scan the tables, smiling greetings at familiar faces. When my gaze lands on an unfamiliar dark-haired beauty who's looking around the room as if she's sizing up the place, I pause to study her.

She's gorgeous with long, dark hair tumbling down her back in waves. She's sitting ramrod straight in one of the booths that run along the dance floor and separate the restaurant side of the room from the side that's more of a bar. She looks more than a little uncomfortable here. I'm guessing this isn't her normal choice of dining establishment. I don't take offense, though. If there's one thing I've learned since opening Peach Fuzz, it's that you can't make everyone happy. Damned if I don't want to try with her, though.

There's another dark-haired woman seated across from her who looks vaguely familiar, but I can't quite place her. There's a resemblance between the two women that makes me think they're probably sisters. They both have the same dark hair and high cheekbones. The other woman is a little shorter than the one who first caught my eye. She's also not as deliciously curvy. Not that I'm checking out her curves or anything. It's just one of those things a guy notices. That's all.

I watch them talk for a few seconds, wishing I could hear their conversation. I know I can't walk over and eavesdrop. That would be not only rude, but downright creepy. If there's one thing I pride myself on, it's not being one of those creepy dudes that women cross the street to avoid. I want to be the guy that women can count on to protect them from that guy. But now I'm staring at a woman I don't know and wishing I could hear her conversation. I'm not sure where this falls on the scale of creep.

I glance at my watch, realizing that my brother and Luke will be here any minute. If I'm going to do anything, now is my chance. Studying the two women again, I see that their table is empty of food or drinks, meaning they haven't had a chance to order yet. And none of the servers has walked over to greet them since I've been watching. An idea forms in my head.

"Fuck it," I whisper under my breath as I start walking toward the table.

I cue up my best smile—the one that shows my dimple and has made more than one female resident of Peach Tree blush—and turn to the curvy brunette.

"Welcome to Peach Fuzz," I say, injecting all the charm I can muster into those four words. "Is this your first time here?" I ask, though I know it is. I'd definitely recognize this woman if she'd been here before.

To my delight, her cheeks go pink, and she averts her gaze. That blush is adorable and has me wondering if I can make it happen again. I wait for her to respond, but when she doesn't, the woman across from her does.

"Yes," she says. "First time."

I reluctantly drag my gaze over to the other woman and give her a small smile that she returns.

"Do you have any questions about the menu?" I ask.

She shakes her head. "I don't think so. I'll have a peach margarita."

I give her another smile that's less forced. "That's one of our most popular drinks."

She grins up at me. "Can't imagine why."

I laugh, suddenly remembering where I know her from. She's the owner of the new coffee shop in town. I've been meaning to stop in and check the place out, but it keeps slipping my mind. I can't remember the name of the shop, but I've driven past it plenty of times.

"We have a friend joining us too," she says, pulling my attention briefly back to the present. "Can we get a margarita on the rocks for her?"

I nod. "Absolutely." I turn back to the other woman, my smile growing again. "And for you?"

It takes her a few seconds to look up at me. When she does, I'm caught off guard by the directness of her gaze. What happened to the woman who'd blushed at me less than 5 minutes ago?

"I'll have an old fashioned," she says, her full lips curving up slightly.

I grin at her. "A bourbon girl. Nice."

I hear someone call my name and look in the direction of the voice. Luke waves at me from the bar and I hold up a hand to stall him. When he nods at me, I turn back to the ladies.

"My name is Cole," giving my mystery woman another full-wattage smile. "If you need anything at all, just let me know."

I know she can hear the flirty tone in my voice. I'm laying it on thick, I know. But I can't help it. Something about this woman intrigues me. It's not just that she's so obviously not from Peach Tree. It's also not that she looks just a little out of place here in my bar. There's something else about her that's captured my attention and I can't quite put my finger on it. But damned if I don't want to find out what it is.

"Okay," she says, giving me a small smile.

I can't stand here any longer without these two women thinking I'm a creeper. So, I turn and walk to the bar, replaying every second of the brief interaction in my head. I give their order to the bartender before walking over to join Luke at the other end of the bar. He greets me with a smile and hands me a beer.

"I thought you had the night off?" he asks.

I shrug. "Can't slack when you're the owner."

Luke just shakes his head. "You can't work 24/7."

I laugh before taking a sip of my beer. "You're one to talk," I say. "The blueprint for workaholic."

He smiles ruefully. "I'm getting better these days."

I've got to admit, he's right. Since he found out he has a half-sister, Luke has made a point to take more time off from his dad's company. My brother Linc and I were shocked when he took an unplanned two-week trip to

North Carolina last month when his sister gave birth to his niece. It's the most time he's taken off from work since he was still in college. Knowing what I know about Luke's dad, I'm sure he's paying for it now.

My eyes stray over to the women in the booth. A server is delivering their drinks and I watch as they smile their thanks.

"Where's Linc?" Luke asks, pulling my gaze back to him.

"Oh, he should be here any minute," I say. "He had to wait for the sitter."

"I'm glad he gave in and decided to come out tonight," he says.

"Me too. He works too damned much too."

My gaze drifts back to the booth where I see the two women have been joined by a third woman. This time, it's someone I know. Harlow St. James. She went to high school with me and Linc. She moved back to town a few years ago and opened a beauty shop on Main Street.

"Who's the girl?" Luke's voice pulls my attention away from the table of women and I turn to face my best friend, a guilty flush creeping up my cheeks.

"Huh? Who?"

Luke laughs, but I'm saved from having to answer by the arrival of my brother.

"What did I miss?" he asks.

"Nothing," I say at the same time Luke says, "Your brother has a crush."

"Fuck off," I say with a laugh.

Luke nods in the direction of the booth and Linc turns to follow his gaze. When I see the slight stiffening of my brother's shoulders, I turn to look at the women too.

That's when I remember that Harlow and my brother were in the same graduating class. And that he had a massive crush on her back then. I almost tease him about it before I remember two things. The first is that he'd made me swear to never tell a soul about his crush on Harlow. I might have been 15 when I made that promise, but I've kept my word this long. I won't reveal his secret now. The second thing I realize is that if I were to tease him about Harlow, he'd immediately tease me about my newfound infatuation with Harlow's friend.

"Interesting," Luke mutters beside me. "Let's go say hi."

"Why?" Linc asks, turning back to Luke.

He just grins. "Because that's my new girlfriend."

A pit opens in my stomach when I realize what he just said. Luke is my best friend. After Linc, that is. Ever since my brother brought his college roommate home for Thanksgiving during their freshman year, the three of us have been inseparable. And now I've been daydreaming about what it would be like to kiss Luke's new girlfriend. That's an epic violation of the guy code. I tamp down the surge of irrational jealousy I feel at the idea of Luke and her together. It's ridiculous. I don't even know her name. I don't have any right to feel jealous.

"Wait," Linc says, holding up a hand. "I thought you didn't have a girlfriend. Isn't that your biggest problem right now?"

Luke's smile grows wider. "That was before Piper agreed to be my fake girlfriend. Come on. I'll introduce you."

Piper. Is that her name? I think back to the conversation with Luke the other night and how he'd originally stood this woman up for a date after they'd met on a dating app. Which means they'd liked one another enough to schedule a date, even if the date hadn't actually happened. Which means there might be something there that I can't interfere with, no matter how attractive I find her.

I follow Luke and my brother over to the table of women, a mix of dread and excitement coursing through me. Excitement, because I want to talk to this gorgeous woman again. And dread because I don't want to find out she's got a thing for Luke. All this runs through my head as we walk, and I don't even notice we're already standing next to the table. And we've been standing there for long enough that Luke is already introducing me and Linc to the table of women. I smile when he points to me. It's not until one of the women introduces herself as Piper that I realize I was wrong.

"And this is my sister Layna," she says, gesturing to the woman I can't seem to stop staring at. "She's in town visiting me for the weekend."

Layna. I almost smile as I repeat the name in my head. So, that's her name. I risk a glance at her and realize she's already studying me. I can hear my brother talking, but I'm not paying him any attention. All my focus is on a pair of brown eyes and full lips that are curved into a knowing smile. If I didn't know better, I'd think Layna was issuing me a challenge with that look. This is a far cry from the woman who'd blushed so prettily only 15 minutes earlier. It makes me realize that I know nothing about this woman. Testing the waters, I hold her gaze and raise one brow. I don't even know what sort of challenge I'm issuing to her, but when she downs the rest of her drink in one quick gulp, I feel my lips twitch into a half-smile.

"You guys should join us," Layna says, her eyes still on me.

When Piper nods her agreement and makes room for Luke to sit next to her, I feel my heartbeat speed up. Instead of taking the empty seat beside Layna, I look pointedly at her empty glass before meeting her gaze again.

"I'll go get us another round of drinks," I say.

Layna stands before I realize her intent. Smiling up at me, she says, "I'll go with you."

If I thought my heart was pounding before, it's nothing compared to what it's doing now. Not to mention the way my dick is rapidly hardening in my pants at her nearness. I catch a hint of her perfume and inhale deeply through my nose, trying to memorize the scent.

"After you," I say softly, gesturing toward the bar.

Layna dips her head in the faintest of nods and leads the way to the bar. My gaze strays down to her ass as she walks. She's wearing a pair of jeans that hug her hips and thighs and have my hands itching to reach out and grip those curves. I watch the sway of her hips as she walks before realizing that everyone can probably see me ogling this woman. Not that any of them can blame me for looking. She's got the best ass I've ever seen. When we reach the bar, Layna turns to face me.

"Enjoy the view?" she asks, raising a brow in challenge.

A laugh escapes me before I can stop it. "Guilty," I admit. "I'm sorry."

Her lips curve into a smile. "Don't be. I'm not."

Her gaze travels slowly down the length of my body before coming back up to my face. If I'd wondered whether she was interested before, I have my answer now with that one lingering look. I lean a little closer to her.

"Enjoy the view?" I whisper.

"Not as much as I could if we were alone," she whispers back.

Holy shit. My cock stiffens in my jeans, and I have the primal urge to drag her off to my office right now. Which is insane, right? I just met this woman. I know nothing about her aside from her name and the fact that she doesn't live in Peach Tree. That, and she's clearly a bold woman who's not afraid to speak her mind. That fact is almost as sexy as her ass in those jeans.

"Is that what you want?" I murmur. *Please say yes. Please say yes. Please say yes.*

"Maybe," she says with a smile. "But I'll settle for another old fashioned."

I grin at her, my mind reeling with all the possibilities that lay before me.

"Your wish is my command," I say before waving the bartender over.

"Careful," she murmurs as the drinks are placed before us. "I have a vivid imagination."

With a wink, she picks up two of the drinks and turns to walk back to the booth, leaving me to bring the other four drinks. I watch her walk away, my gaze dropping to her ass again as I smile. If her imagination is anything like mine, I'm in for a wild night.

When we rejoin the others, I do my best to pay attention to the conversation flowing around me. I even manage to chime in here and there. But most of my focus is on the brunette seated beside me, even though she doesn't seem to be nearly as affected by my presence. Since we returned from the bar, she seems almost indifferent to me. Which is unfortunate when her mere scent in my nose is enough to drive me wild. I wonder if the others can tell how distracted I am by her nearness. By the time I order a round of shots and Layna starts interrogating her sister and Luke about their fake relationship, I'm on the verge of throwing her over my shoulder and carrying her back to my office.

I can't seem to figure her out. She'd definitely been flirting with me earlier at the bar. But now that we're sitting with the others, she's practically ignoring me. Is this some sort of game for her? If so, I'm not sure I want to play it. I prefer being direct and honest about what I want. Most of the women I've been with have appreciated that fact about me. If I get a chance to talk to Layna alone, I'm going to be direct and tell her all the dirty fantasies I'd like to reenact with her.

Just when I'm starting to wonder if I imagined the entire encounter at the bar, I feel a hand on my thigh. I nearly jump at the unexpected contact, but I somehow manage to keep my composure. I risk a glance down and see Layna's manicured hand resting on my jean-clad thigh. The sight alone is enough to send the blood rushing straight to my dick.

I look up and realize that Piper and Luke are no longer seated at the table with us. When had they left? I didn't notice them leaving, but after a quick glance around the room, I spot them on the dance floor. Layna's hand inches higher up my thigh and I feel myself go rock hard.

Harlow and Linc aren't paying us any attention. In fact, they both look like they'd rather be anywhere else. With the party split up, I decide to test my luck with Layna.

Smiling over at my brother, I say, "I forgot, there's something I need to handle in my office."

I gesture in the direction of the back hallway that leads to my private office. Linc nods and leans forward over the table.

"It's getting a little late," he says. "I think I'm going to head home soon."

I know I should feel guilty for the relief I feel at the idea of him leaving. This means less witnesses to my potential hookup with Layna. Speaking of, her hand has now traveled even higher to rest on my hip. I do my best to give my brother a look of disappointment, but I'm not sure how believable it is.

"Don't leave yet," I say. "I'll be back in no time."

Linc looks slightly annoyed, but he nods and picks up his beer again. Harlow smiles and nods in my direction, but then immediately looks around in search of Piper. I'm not totally certain, but I think the addition of three men wasn't what Harlow planned when she came out with the girls tonight. I feel a little bad about crashing girls' night, but then I remember the feel of Layna's hand on my thigh and the promise of more. The guilt is quickly overtaken by lust and anticipation.

I lean close to Layna and whisper, "I'm going back to my office now. If you want to come, it's down that hallway. Last door on the left."

I don't imagine the little shiver that runs over her at my words. Without waiting for an answer, I turn and walk away from her and the booth, hoping no one can see the hard bulge pressing against the front of my jeans. I'm also hoping she follows me. If I had to wager a bet on it, I'd say the odds are in my favor.

I'm not stupid. I know I have a reputation in this town. Ever since high school when I had a major growth spurt one summer and returned to school looking more like a man than the gangly boy I'd been, I haven't had a difficult time finding a date. I took heavy advantage of that fact in high school and college. But for the past two years, I've been too busy with Peach Fuzz to focus on dating. I haven't had time to do much more than have a quick fling here and there. But I've always been up-front about what I want. I've never lied to a woman or pretended there was a future with me when there wasn't. Whatever might happen with Layna tonight is no different. If she wants to have a little fun while she's in town, I'm game for that. But she lives on the other side of the state. There's no way this can go beyond a casual hookup.

I feel a little guilty for abandoning my brother and my best friend, but I know they'd understand. Besides, Luke looked cozy with Piper out on the dance floor. And it's not like Linc and Harlow are total strangers. They've known each other since we moved here when we were kids. I don't know if they were friends, but I didn't sense any animosity. Linc will behave, I'm sure.

Once I'm in my office with the door closed, I turn to face the door, leaning a hip against my desk to wait. I feel a flutter of nerves as I wonder if Layna will show up. It's possible I read her all wrong, but I doubt it. I'm usually good at reading people, and she'd been somewhat obvious. At least to me. I don't think anyone else was paying close enough attention to notice her behavior. Not that it matters to me, but I got the idea that she didn't want everyone to know. Which is fine by me. I can keep a secret. If she shows up, that is. That hand on my thigh seemed like a clear sign, though.

Anticipation courses through me, making every nerve ending in my body spring to life. My cock is already hard as iron in my pants, and I reach down to adjust myself against the restricting denim. I'm just starting to think she's not going to show when I see the doorknob turn. I watch the door open silently and smile.

CHAPTER 2

Present day

Layna

"Yes, I tried it on," I say, letting my sister hear my exasperation through the phone. "Just like you told me to."

"I know. I know," Piper says. "I'm sorry I'm being such a bridezilla."

I smile. "You're not being a bridezilla," I assure her. "You're just nervous about the big day. It's totally normal."

"I don't know why I'm so nervous," she says on a sigh. "I love Luke and I can't wait to marry him. It's just that, I hate being the center of attention."

I laugh. "You're the bride. That's kind of your role on your wedding day."

"Don't remind me," she grumbles.

"Look," I say, sitting up in bed as if that's going to somehow make my words sound more serious. "You're having a small ceremony. Less than 100 people. And every person there loves you already. You're going to be so distracted by how handsome Luke is in his tux and the whirlwind of wedding stuff that you won't have time to feel nervous. Trust me. This is supposed to be a happy day. Don't let the nerves ruin that."

Piper's wedding is still over a month away, but somehow, she's managed to call me almost every day this week with some new crisis that isn't really a crisis. Not that I don't understand her nerves. I do. She's never really been a fan of being in the spotlight. Even when we were kids, she always got stage fright when it came to those elementary school programs. She'd nearly tripped over her own shoes when she walked across the stage at her high school graduation.

Today, she's panicking because she had a dream last night that it was the day of the wedding, and her dress didn't fit. So, she called me to make sure mine does. And to beg me not to change my food intake in any way. I want to laugh at the absurdity of the whole situation, but she's my baby sister and it's clear she's full of anxiety. It's my job to talk her down.

"Piper, breathe," I say, injecting calm order into my voice. "You're going to be fine. This is the happiest day of your life, remember? You're marrying the man of your dreams."

"I know," she says, but her voice still sounds off.

"What is it?"

She sighs and when she speaks again, her voice is quieter. "I just wish Mom could be there."

The sharp stab of pain laced with guilt hits me as it always does when I think about our mother. She's been gone for more than a decade, but some wounds never seem to heal. After her death, I'd had to pick up the pieces and be there for Piper. I'd traded in my big sister role for something more motherly, even knowing I'd never fill the void our mom left when she died.

"I know you do, Pipes," I say, softly. "I miss her too. Every day. But you know she'd be so proud of you. So happy you found someone who loves you as much as Luke does."

"You're right," Piper says, blowing out a breath.

She still sounds a little off, so I try to inject a little humor. "Besides," I say. "You know she'd kick your ass if you used her as an excuse to not be happy on your wedding day."

She lets out a little laugh and I smile. I don't know if I even believe what I'm saying, but that doesn't matter. I just need her to believe it.

"You're right," she says again. This time she sounds more convincing. "Besides, I still have 6 weeks to convince Luke we should elope."

"Don't you dare!" I say. "If I don't get to see my baby sister walk down the aisle in her wedding dress, I'll never forgive you."

"Fine," she grumbles. "But if I faint from nerves, you better catch me."

"As the maid of honor, I delegate that task to your other bridesmaid," I say.

"Harlow's too short," Piper says. "She'd get squished."

"What does height have to do with anything?" I argue.

"I don't know," she says. "But I think you have a better chance of catching me."

"We'll make it a team effort," I concede. Glancing at the clock, I wince. "But I really do need to get off the phone if I'm going to be on time for work."

"Shit," Piper says. "Sorry I kept you so long! Thanks for talking me off the ledge. You're the best."

I ignore the twinge of guilt I feel at my lie. "What are sisters for?"

"Love you!"

I try to inject the right amount of cheer into my voice. "Love you, too!"

I end the call with a sigh before setting my phone on the nightstand. I love my sister. She's honestly my favorite person on the planet. But lately, I've found myself struggling to be the reassuring presence she needs. And since she's constantly stressed over the wedding these days, it seems all I've been doing is reassuring her. Which means I constantly feel like I'm failing her.

"Everything okay?" says a male voice from the foot of the bed, pulling me out of my musings.

Opening my eyes, I look up to meet the intense gaze of the man standing naked before me. I'd tried to ignore his silent presence while I was talking to Piper, but looking at him now I don't know how I managed. The sheer sexiness of this man never fails to surprise me. I've seen him naked more times than I can count over the last year or more, and I'm still obsessed with his body. My eyes track over him, taking in the messy dark hair, muscled chest covered with a light dusting of hair and those sculpted abs that I know for a fact feel as good as they look. Dragging my gaze lower, I take in the impressive erection that's angling toward me. I drag in a shaky breath as desire coils tightly within me.

Nodding, I say, "Yeah. My sister is just stressed about the wedding."

He studies my face in that way that always makes me a little uncomfortable. "Is there anything I can do? Do you need to go?"

I immediately shy away from his offer. That's not why we're here today. I shake my head and grin over at him, making it clear that my sister is the last thing I'm thinking of right now.

"The only thing you can do is put that to use," I say in a low, flirty tone, my gaze going down to his massive cock.

He grins and reaches out to grip my ankles in his hands. "Yes, ma'am."

A startled laugh escapes me as he drags me down the length of the bed until my ass is just at the edge of the mattress. It's on the tip of my tongue to tell him not to call me "ma'am", but then he drops to his knees in front of me and drapes my legs over his shoulders. Then his mouth is on me, planting open-mouth kisses on my inner thighs. *Oh, shit.* My eyes fall closed as his mouth moves to my center, licking and kissing my wet slit. It should be a crime for him to be this good at eating pussy.

My thoughts immediately scatter, and I can only focus on the pleasure radiating up from where his mouth caresses me. I love this moment. The moment where I can let go of everything and just be. No one is looking to me for advice or to fix things. No one expects anything of me. Nothing else matters when I'm hovering on the verge of orgasm. And the orgasm is a sure bet. If I know anything about this man, it's that he takes pride in making women come. We've had sex dozens of times since we started this thing, and he's never left me unsatisfied. Not once.

I gasp as his tongue circles my clit. My hands fist in the sheets and my eyes fall closed. I can feel desire coiling tighter inside me, pushing me closer to the sweet oblivion I crave. I focus on the sensations spreading outward from my center where his lips and tongue are turning me into a writhing ball of need.

"Please," I gasp.

He growls against my clit, sending fresh shivers through my body. It's an acknowledgement of sorts. This man knows my body so well; knows what I need almost better than I do. At least, when it comes to sex. He's so attuned to my needs. It's always been like this between us, even if what we have doesn't go beyond sex. Since our first time together, he and I have been so in sync with each other's bodies. It's almost eerie the way he's able to play my body like an instrument. But I've given up analyzing the why of that. It's easier to just go with it. At least, it's more fun.

I feel his fingers as they spread me open, allowing him better access to my clit. *Fuck, that feels good.* I'm so close to coming all over his face and he knows it. My body feels like it might combust if I don't release this tension in me. That's when I feel him slide two fingers deep inside me, thrusting in all at once. It's just what I need, and I cry out as my body clamps down tight against those two thick fingers.

"Oh, god! I'm coming!"

He keeps licking and sucking my clit as I pulse around him, squeezing his fingers through my orgasm. My legs move with a mind of their own, clamping down on his head. Eventually, his tongue slows and gentles against me as I come down from my climax. His fingers slow, moving lazily in and out of me until the flutters finally stop. Turning his head, he kisses my inner thigh, sending another shiver through me. I sigh.

"It should be illegal to be that good at that," I say, giving voice to my earlier thought.

He grins up at me, his teeth white in the dim light as he crawls up the bed over me.

"Lucky for me, it's not against the law to make a beautiful woman come on my face," he says.

He lowers his head to take my nipple into his mouth. He sucks hard, sending a new jolt of arousal straight to my core. The sharp sting of pleasure mixed with pain has me gasping as I bury my fingers in his dark hair, holding him to me.

"Stop bragging and fuck me," I gasp.

That stupid, sexy dimple is there when he raises his head and grins down at me.

"Yes, ma'am," he says as I feel his hard length slide against me.

I can feel every ridge of his cock as it slides against my clit. My mouth drops open, and a groan escapes me as I hand him a condom. He tears the package open with the help of his teeth and reaches down to sheath himself while bracing his body above me with one hand. It shouldn't be hot, but it absolutely is. I squeeze my thighs against his body as I wait for him to fill me with his hard length. When he finally notches his head at my entrance, I feel the butterflies in my stomach go still. But more importantly, I feel my mind settle and go blank.

This is what I need. What I crave. This is the reason I've kept this going with him for as long as I have. He quiets the anxiety in my head. He makes all the noise go silent. When I'm with him I can't think of anything else. I don't feel stressed or anxious. I don't feel angry or irritated. I don't worry about my sister or my career. I just experience. It's exactly what I need.

"Yes," I gasp. "Fuck me!"

His eyes lock on mine as he plunges into me, filling me all at once, stealing my breath. He lets out a low groan as he hits home, and I stop thinking altogether. I forget who I am and where I am. I forget about tomorrow or my sister or my job. All I can focus on is this moment, this connection. Him. I don't care why. It doesn't matter. All that matters is this moment, him inside me, filling me, thrusting into me. He feels so good. So long and thick and hard. He hits the very end of me with every thrust, making my mouth fall open in a silent gasp.

He brings his hand up to grip my jaw, pulling my gaze to his just before he lowers his head to kiss me. His kiss is hard, demanding. It takes. But it's not anything I'm not willing to give him. I taste myself on his lips as our tongues tangle. I shouldn't love it as much as I do. But just like every time before, he seems to know what I like better than I do. I dig my heels into his ass and meet him thrust for thrust. My fingers grip his shoulders, holding him to me as he fills me with his hard length again and again. Every thrust of him inside me draws another gasp from my lips. I can already feel another orgasm building inside me.

"Oh, god," I moan, locking my legs around his back. "Yes!"

"You gonna come for me, baby?" he grunts as he pounds into me. "I need it. Wanna feel that pretty pussy clamping down on my cock."

My eyes roll shut. His dirty talking has never failed to make me hot. Today is no exception. His deep gravelly voice sends molten heat through my body. That, combined with the rhythmic thrusting of his thick cock inside me has my body reacting. I feel myself clench tight around his length as my orgasm slams into me.

"There it is," he groans, still working his hips between my legs as I unravel. "Come on this cock, baby. Fuck, you feel good."

A shout is wrenched from me as I dig my nails into his back. I clamp down on his hard length over and over as he continues to work his dick in and out of me. He takes my mouth in another searing kiss, our tongues battling. It's more intimate than I'd like, but I know he loves to kiss me at the exact moment he loses control and comes, so I can give him this.

I feel him groan against my mouth as he pulses inside me. He grips my jaw tighter, his hold just this side of painful, but I don't mind. It's like his hold on me is the only thing keeping me grounded as my body floats on a cloud of ecstasy. Bombs could explode outside my window, and I wouldn't notice. Not with him buried deep inside me, his mouth on mine, his hand gripping my face. My entire world slows down and centers on me and him, this moment.

Now.

Damn, I love a good orgasm.

CHAPTER 3

Present day

Cole

I roll onto my back, gasping as I try to catch my breath. My heart is pounding so hard it's a wonder she can't hear it too. It's always been like this with her. Amazing. So intense. Fucking mind-blowing. But I don't say any of that to her. I know she'd hate it. We both agreed that this is just sex. It might be fucking phenomenal sex, but it's just sex. That's all it can be. And that's enough for me.

"Fuck," I gasp, reaching down to pull off the condom.

Rolling over, I climb out of bed and make my way to the bathroom to toss the condom and grab a washcloth for her. When I turn back toward the bed and see her sprawled out, boneless and panting, I can't help but smile. Her breasts rise and fall with every heaving breath. Her dark hair is spread across the pale gray sheets, making me want to run my fingers through the soft strands. She's so fucking gorgeous. I've known it since the first night I met her. She'd been sitting in a booth at my restaurant, silently judging the place with those assessing eyes. I hadn't minded though. She'd been too beautiful for me to be truly annoyed.

When I'd walked over to talk to her and her sister, I'd felt that spark immediately. She flirted back as I flashed her my best smile. And it paid off. That night she'd let me fuck her on the desk in my office at Peach Fuzz. Let? Hell, she'd practically demanded it. Not that I'd minded. It had been the most mind-blowing sex of my life up to that point. She had me bend her over and pound into her from behind until I felt her quiver around me. I'd exploded inside her as I gripped her full hips, my fingers digging into the soft flesh of that amazing ass. I'd known then and there that it wasn't the end of things with me and Layna Brooks.

Granted, we'd ultimately decided that we were better off as friends with benefits than anything serious. And since she didn't live in Peach Tree, it made sense. So, I agreed to her terms without too much of an argument. We hooked up whenever she came into town to visit her sister, and kept it quiet, since that's the way she wanted it. Not that I put up a fight over it. I was willing to do just about anything to keep her in my life and to keep me in that tight pussy of hers.

But it's been more than a year since that night in my office and she's since moved to Peach Tree. Which means we see a whole lot more of each other than we did before. And I've had time to do a lot of thinking. I know I agreed to her terms. At the time, it made sense. She and I barely knew each other and neither of us wanted anything serious. I hadn't even considered the idea that we might still be doing this over a year later.

I figured Layna and I would fuck a few times when she came into town, then she'd move on. Or I would. Either way, I figured one of us would get tired of the other sooner or later.

At the time, it had been exciting. Keeping what we were doing secret from our friends and the rest of this town. But lately, I've grown sick of lying and pretending. Over the last month or so, I've started looking at her differently. I miss her when she's not around and I want more than just a few stolen hours here and there. The truth is, I don't want to hide the fact that she and I are, whatever we are. I don't want this to be a secret anymore. I want to make this thing real. I want to take her on a real date. I want to spend more time with her with our clothes on. That last part is hard for even me to believe. But the more I get to know Layna, the more I want to make her mine. And not just her body. I want all of her. I just can't quite find the nerve to tell her.

Right now, I want to crawl into bed beside her and pull her against me. I want to hold her while we sleep. I want to cuddle her to my side and talk about our plans for the day. But I know I can't. For starters, I know she'd push me away if I tried. She's made it crystal clear that she's not looking for anything serious. We're just having fun. We're not ready to settle down. We both agreed to that. But it's okay. I've waited this long. I can wait a little longer.

Layna cleans up with the washcloth and tosses it into the hamper before disappearing into the bathroom. By the time she returns, I've tugged on my boxers and jeans. She's wearing a pair of black, lacy panties and a matching bra that makes her cleavage look mouthwatering. I let my gaze wander over her body as she moves to her closet for her clothes. Her round ass sways from side to side as she walks, making me want to pull her back against me and fuck her from behind. Instead, I reach out and give her delicious ass a light smack. When she jumps and lets out a startled laugh, I shrug.

"I couldn't help it," I call out as she disappears into the walk-in closet. "That ass was too tempting not to touch."

"You're incorrigible," she mutters as she walks back into the room carrying a pair of black dress pants.

"Next time, I want to fill you up from behind," I say, wrapping an arm around her waist and pulling her back until she's flush against me. Lowering my head, I plant a kiss on the side of her neck.

"I want to watch that sexy ass bounce on my cock," I whisper against her skin.

Layna shivers as she lets out a shaky breath. I know how my dirty talk affects her. She loves it when I tell her exactly what I want to do to her body. I feel my dick stir as I imagine what I just described. It's easy to picture. I've had her bent over so many times before that the image is practically branded into my mind. If she weren't already running late, I might be able to convince her to go for round two. But, since I know she'd be pissed if I made her late for a meeting, I let her pull away from me.

"There isn't going to be a next time," she says, pulling away from me before tossing my shirt at me.

I huff out a laugh as I pull the shirt over my head. "Yeah, you've said that before."

She shrugs. "This time I mean it."

"You've said that before, too," I say.

"I'm serious this time, Cole," she says, turning to look at me fully. "This was the last time."

I sit on the edge of her bed and pull on a sock. I search the floor for the other one, trying to remember where I might have tossed it. I don't even remember taking my socks off. I'd been too preoccupied with getting Layna naked.

"On the dresser," she says.

Glancing over, I see that she's right and my missing sock somehow ended up on the dresser.

"Thanks," I say, making my way across the room to retrieve it.

"Why now?" I ask, turning to watch as she buttons a white blouse, covering those amazing tits I'd been feasting on only a half hour earlier. I feel my dick twitch at the memory.

"Because it's time," she says vaguely.

"That's not an answer," I insist, pulling the sock onto my foot. "Tell me why."

She sighs. "Fine. I've decided I need to get serious about my future. With Piper's wedding coming up and seeing Harlow settled with your brother, I've realized I'm too old for flings. It's time for me to find the right guy, too. I can't do that if I'm still sneaking around with you."

I try to ignore the sting of that comment and deflect with humor. My specialty.

"What am I? Chopped liver?" I say with a grin.

Layna rolls her eyes, but she's smiling. "You don't want to settle down," she says. "You've said so yourself. Besides, you're too young for me."

I scoff. "You make it sound like you've been robbing the cradle or something. Eight years isn't that big of a deal."

"Almost nine," she corrects.

Now, it's my turn to roll my eyes. "Whatever. We're both consenting adults. I don't see what the big deal is."

"That's because I'm older and wiser."

I laugh because it's clear that's the reaction she wants. But inside, I'm starting to worry. She's really ending things. She's tried it before, but she always changed her mind. Something about her tone today and the way she won't meet my gaze makes me believe her this time.

"You're serious?" I ask. "You really don't want any of this anymore?"

I gesture down at my body, wiggling my eyebrows at her suggestively. She finally looks at me, a smile playing on her lips. But it's what I see in her eyes that makes me finally believe her words. There's a hint of sadness there, but it's mixed with resolved determination. She really means it this time. She's finished with me.

"We both knew this was temporary," she says, her voice softer than before.

It's that softness in her tone that feels like a stab to the chest. It hits me harder than any sharp words could have. She's right, I know. We've always agreed that this thing between us wasn't serious. It was temporary. Two friends scratching a mutual itch. But when it kept going for a year with no signs of stopping, I'd started to wonder if maybe it could be something more. It's on the tip of my tongue to ask her to reconsider. To ask her on a date. To see if we could try this for real.

"I have a date," she says, her voice loud in the quiet room.

It takes me several seconds to understand the meaning of her words. When I do, something twists painfully in my chest. A date? She hasn't dated anyone since we started sleeping together. It was one of the rules we made back in the beginning. If either of us was ever ready to start dating, we would end this. No hard feelings. No repercussions. Back to friends. No benefits. Those four words do more to prove she's serious than any other explanation would have. I give her a single nod.

"Okay," I say. I force myself to smile.

She studies me for a moment as if waiting for me to say more. When I don't, she goes on.

"It's this Friday night," she says. "I met him at a bookstore in Savannah. We talked for a while, and he asked for my number."

I nod as she explains how she's only been talking to him for a week, and he asked her on a date only yesterday. Which means she'd planned to end things with me before she'd texted me to come over this morning. That stings more than it should. But I know I don't have any right to be upset. It's not like we're a real couple. She's never lied to me or pretended we were more than we were. It's not Layna's fault I got too attached. That's all on me. Though I am a little annoyed that I didn't know before we fucked today. If I'd known it was the last time, I would have given her more than two orgasms.

"Okay," I say again when we're both fully dressed. I give her a smile that I hope is unbothered. "I hope your date goes well." The words taste like ash on my tongue, but I hope they're convincing enough.

She gives me a smile that doesn't quite reach her eyes. "Thank you, Cole," she says. "For understanding."

I shrug. "It's what we agreed to, right? No hard feelings."

She nods. "Right."

"If you change your mind, you know where to find me," I say with a playful wink.

She smiles, but it's far from the laugh I expected. Then she leans forward and kisses me on the cheek, her lips barely a whisper against my skin.

"Bye, Cole."

CHAPTER 4

Present day

Layna

I watch as Cole turns to leave, clenching my jaw shut against the urge to call his name, to ask him to stay. To come back to bed and forget about the last 10 minutes. If I asked him to stay, I know he would. It would be so easy. It wouldn't be the first time I've tried to end things and changed my mind. But I don't do it. I know better. It wouldn't be fair to either of us. Not this time.

I meant what I told him. It's time to move on from this thing that started the night we first met. We're too old for friends with benefits. Well, I am, anyway. Cole's still young enough to find it fun and exciting. And it was fun and exciting. I enjoyed my time with him more than I ever thought I would. But I'm ready for something more serious and I can't find it if I'm still having a fling with a man nearly a decade younger than me.

When the door closes softly behind him, I blow out a breath and swallow hard against the lump in my throat.

The tension eases between my shoulder blades even as I feel a painful squeeze in my chest that I do my best to ignore. It's better this way. I know it is. Cole and I had our fun, but that's all it was. A good time. Nothing serious. We'd always planned to end this eventually. Now's as good a time as any.

We both knew from the beginning that this thing between us was temporary. It's why I've never broken my rule about sleeping with him. We hang out occasionally. We fuck a lot. But we don't do sleepovers. I didn't want to blur the lines between us. I knew, even when we first started this thing, that I could easily get used to having Cole Prescott in my bed. And not just for his skills when it comes to sex. He's funny and charming and sweet. He turned out to be an amazing friend. Which is why I'd known I needed to have boundaries. To his credit, he never pushed back at me for my rule about sleeping together. Now that it's officially over, I'm glad I never broke that rule. Even if part of me wonders what it would be like to wake up next to him. I immediately veer away from that dangerous line of thinking and focus on getting ready for work. It won't do any good to dwell on what might have been. It's best to focus on reality. And the reality is I need to hurry or I'll be late for work.

Since I quit my job in Atlanta and moved to Peach Tree, I've been working as a public defender in Savannah. It pays a lot less than my old job, but I finally feel like I'm doing something good with my law degree. I'm not just making rich people richer. Instead, I'm helping defend people who can't afford an attorney. I'm not blind. I know that many of my clients are guilty but that's not for me to decide. It's my job to provide the best legal defense possible. It's stressful and mentally exhausting. It's also thankless most days. But the truth is, I love it.

I think it might be my dream job. Sometimes I'm shocked that I once worked as a corporate lawyer. Looking back, I'm not sure why I ever thought that was the epitome of success. I'd made an insane amount of money, but I'd been miserable for a long time before I finally mustered up the courage to quit that job and leave the city. Looking back, I'm so happy I made that decision when I did. I can't imagine my life if I were still there. These days, I'm happy with my life and my choices, even if I'm a little lonely at times.

I catch sight of the massive peach-shaped water tower as I walk past the front window of my little apartment and shake my head. Part of me still can't believe I live in Peach Tree, Georgia. It's even more surprising that I'm genuinely happy here. I think seeing my little sister happy and settled in this tiny town is what spurred me to finally acknowledge how unhappy I was with my big city life. But there's no denying that I'm happy here. I love my job and my cozy apartment above Harlow's salon. I'm even growing to love this little town, though that fact continues to surprise me.

I rush downstairs and make my way out the side door to my car. I hadn't exactly been lying to Piper earlier. If I don't hurry, I'm going to be late to meet my new client. I hate being late and I absolutely refuse to be late to a first meeting with a new client. It's not only unprofessional, but it sends the message to the client that they're not my priority. A lot of my clients have already been failed enough. By authority figures, lawyers, their family, or the system itself. I never want to be one of the people who fails them.

I spent last night reading over the file for my new client. He's 19 years old with an arrest history already. This time he's being accused of petty theft, which wouldn't be a big deal on its own. But since he has a history of trouble with the law, the judge isn't likely to look favorably on him. I'm hoping I can keep him out of jail.

I manage to make it to work on time. I even have a few minutes to look over my notes about the case before my new client arrives. He's a skinny kid with a mop of dark hair and an obvious chip on his shoulder. But I can see in his eyes that he's scared and trying to hide it. When he takes a seat in the chair across from my desk, he slumps in it, averting his gaze. He looks like he's annoyed to be here. Like I'm wasting his precious time. Part of me wants to laugh at his antics, but I don't. I've seen his type before. They've learned that authority figures can't be trusted, and they count me as one of them.

"Good morning, Will," I say giving him a smile. "Thanks for meeting with me."

He rolls his eyes. "Like I had a choice."

Yep. Definite chip on his shoulder.

"I looked over your case file and I think we can make it so you don't do any jail time," I say. "We can cut a deal for probation if we plead guilty—"

"What's this 'we' shit?" he cuts in. "I don't know you."

I bite back a sigh, keeping my expression pleasant. "I get it. You don't know me, and I don't know you. You don't want to trust me. I get that, too. But you don't have a lot of options here, Will. The evidence against you is strong. A plea is your best option."

"I didn't do shit," Will says, his voice rising with anger. "I'm not sayin' I did."

I know this part too. Most of my clients argue their innocence until I lay out the facts and explain that there's no way they'll win if we take it to trial. Granted, there are the occasional few who really didn't do what they're accused of. But those are rarer than I care to think about. I know some public defenders would look at a kid like Will and write him off. They'd look at their caseload and talk him into a plea so they could move on to the next file. But that's not why I took this job.

"Why don't you tell me what happened that night," I say. "Everything you can remember."

Will looks at me for a long moment like he's trying to decide if I'm tricking him. I guess he must be satisfied with what he sees because he blows out a breath and sits up a little straighter in his chair before he begins to speak.

CHAPTER 5

Present day
Cole

I walk away from Layna's apartment, taking the side street that leads to my house. I keep replaying those last few minutes in my head. How did I not realize she was going to end things? It's not like she hinted at it. She's been a little distant lately, but I just figured she was busy with her sister's wedding. I didn't think she'd actually end things.

I don't know why I'm so surprised. Someone like Layna doesn't do flings. I'm shocked it went on as long as it did. Hell, I'm shocked she ever let me touch her in the first place. She's a lawyer and I'm the owner of a bar in Peach Tree, Georgia. What did I think was going to happen? I tell myself it's for the best that we ended things now before one of us got too attached. That might have made things awkward between us. Especially since her sister is marrying my best friend. It's not like we'd never see each other again.

This is for the best, I decide as I let myself into my house. It's quiet, as it has been ever since my brother and my niece moved in with his girlfriend. I'm happy for Linc, even though it took me a while to get used to the house being so empty. The three of us lived here together for so long that I'd grown used to the company. Come to think of it, I'd never lived by myself before Linc and Ella left. I went from my parents' house to the college dorm, to living with Linc and Ella.

Now that I've had time to get used to the silence, I think I like living alone. Not that I don't miss having them nearby. But in a town as small as Peach Tree, it's not like I need to go far to visit. Plus, I volunteer to hang out with Ella any chance I can. I pretend it's just to give Linc and Harlow time alone, but really, I just love being Ella's fun uncle. It's a role I take seriously. And it has the bonus of annoying the shit out of my big brother.

I have a few hours before I need to go to work, but I don't want to spend them in this big empty house all alone. I could go to the gym, but I'm not in the mood for a workout. If I'm honest with myself, I'm not in the mood to be alone with only my own thoughts for company. The thing about living in a small town is that there are limited places to socialize with other people, especially at 8:30 in the morning. Luckily, I know just the place. Smiling, I turn and walk back out the front door and to my truck.

I make the short drive to Piping Hot Brews, Peach Tree's most popular coffee shop. The coffee is amazing, but that's not the main reason I like to go. The blueberry scones are the best I've ever had. If I'm lucky they'll still have some left from the morning rush. The shop also happens to be owned by Layna's sister, Piper. The joys of small-town life.

When I arrive at Piping Hot Brews, I'm surprised to see not Piper behind the counter, but Luke. I've known Luke since he and my brother met their first year of college and he'd come home with Linc for Thanksgiving. At the time, I'd wondered why he didn't go home to his own family for the holiday, but it seemed rude to ask. Eventually, Luke told us that holidays with his parents were typically miserable affairs and he'd much rather experience them with a loving family. He usually couldn't get out of Christmas with his parents, but he spent every Thanksgiving after that with us. Not that my folks minded setting another place at the table. They adore Luke. If he weren't a grown man, I think my mom would have tried to adopt him.

"Hey, Luke," I call as I make my way to the counter.

"Hey," he answers. "Let me guess. Blueberry scone?"

My eyes scan the glass case where the pastries are stored, searching until I see that I'm in luck. The blueberry scones haven't sold out yet.

"You know me well," I say when I reach the counter. "Iced coffee and a blueberry scone, please."

Luke shakes his head at me, but he's smiling. "You know it's possible to become addicted to sugary pastries."

I shrug. "If these blueberry scones are wrong, I don't want to be right."

I look around for Piper while Luke works to make my coffee and plate the scone. I don't see her anywhere. The shop isn't overly busy right now, but there are enough patrons in here that one person shouldn't be working alone.

"Where's Piper?" I ask.

He hands me my coffee and rings up the sale on the register. "She needed a few minutes to relax," he says. "She's stressing about the wedding. I sent her back to her office with some noise-canceling headphones and a calming playlist."

I nod as if I understand. I don't know the first thing about planning a wedding or the stress that goes into it. But I know Layna was on the phone with Piper earlier and she was definitely talking her down over something to do with dresses. Not that I can tell Luke that. No one knows about me and Layna. We've kept it a secret from everyone we know.

"I'm sorry, man," I say. "Is there anything I can do to help?"

He shakes his head. "I don't think so. I hired a wedding planner last month. It's last minute because we thought we didn't need one. But it's a friend of Mya's. She's doing us a big favor taking us on."

I nod as I bite into the scone. I groan, my eyes rolling back in my head as I chew. I point to the scone and talk with my mouth full.

"This is just what I needed," I say.

Luke rolls his eyes and tosses me a napkin. "Chew with your mouth closed. Heathen."

"Don't scold the customers," Piper says, walking up behind Luke and wrapping her arms around his waist.

Luke shifts so he can put an arm around her shoulders and kisses the top of her head. "Cole doesn't count as a customer."

"Hey!" I protest. "I paid."

Piper frowns at Luke. "I told you not to charge him."

"How many times have I told you?" Luke says. "That's no way to run a business."

She shrugs. "He gives me free loaded fries."

"And shots," I say with a grin.

Luke rolls his eyes. "Neither of you know how to run a business. You can't give everything away."

"Hey, Cole," Piper says.

"Yeah?"

"Out of curiosity, did Luke charge you for his marketing of Peach Fuzz when you first opened?"

I grin as I pop the last bite of scone into my mouth. "Nope."

Luke rolls his eyes. "That was different."

"I don't see how," she says. "Marketing costs more than scones."

"Look at you two," I croon. "Already bickering like a married couple."

"Don't you have somewhere to be?" Luke asks. "Somewhere not here?"

I clutch my chest dramatically. "Ouch. That stings." Picking up my coffee, I take a big sip. "But no, actually. I've got a couple of hours to kill before work, so I figured I'd come have some coffee and the world's most delicious pastry."

Piper laughs and rolls her eyes. "Stop it. You'll make me blush."

"He's not allowed to make you blush," Luke says. "That's my job."

"You two are disgusting," I say, only mostly teasing. "Piper, if this man ever treats you badly, you know where to find me. I'll marry you for these pastries alone."

She laughs and Luke glares at me.

"You? Married? That'll be the day," he says.

"What's that supposed to mean?"

He laughs before noticing that the question is a serious one. His brows draw together in confusion.

"Seriously?" he asks. "Cole, you don't want to settle down. I know you, remember?"

What the hell? He's the second person to tell me that today. Does everyone think I'm some man-whore who'll never have a serious relationship? Not that I've ever been in a serious relationship. I mean, there was one girl in college, but that was a long time ago. But I have been sleeping with the same woman for more than a year. Not that I can tell them that. Besides, I don't think that counts when Layna and I established in the beginning that what we were doing wasn't serious and would never be.

"Maybe I'm turning over a new leaf," I say.

My words don't even sound convincing to my own ears. Is this what everyone in this town thinks of me? Probably. It's not like I've given them any reason to think differently. Is this what Layna thinks of me? Yes. It's why she didn't consider me for a second when she was deciding to start dating again. I'm not boyfriend material. The realization stings, but I shouldn't be shocked by it.

"Really?" Luke asks, clearly skeptical.

I wonder for a second if it's worth trying to convince my best friend that I'm not the kind of man I used to be.

I haven't been that guy for more than a year—not since Layna and I made our rules and agreed to only sleep with each other for as long as we both wanted it to last. It's true that I'm not that guy anymore, but I can't explain to Luke why. The idea of going back to the old me who was content with casual hookups that meant nothing no longer appeals to me.

I force a laugh. "Nah. Not really."

Piper rolls her eyes, smiling, and walks over to help a customer at the counter. Luke just smiles at me.

"One of these days, man," he says. "Some woman will come along and sweep you off your feet. Then you'll be ruined for all the others. Just wait."

I roll my eyes at his words because I know that's what he expects me to do. But I secretly think he may be right. Only I don't need to wait for it to happen. Because I think Layna Brooks has ruined me for all other women.

CHAPTER 6

Eleven months ago

Layna

"Holy shit," I gasp, trying to calm my racing heart.

I'm sprawled naked across Cole's muscular chest, my entire body boneless from the intensity of the orgasm I just had.

"I can't move," he mutters. "Just bury me like this."

I huff out a laugh.

"Put on my tombstone, 'Cole Prescott: He came himself to death.'"

I laugh again and push myself up enough to look at his face. His eyes are closed and he's still panting. There's a fine sheen of sweat on his neck that holds my gaze. It's ridiculous how good looking this man is. I think I could stare at him for years and not get tired of it. At that thought, I feel something stir deep inside me and shake my head to clear it.

"Your brother won't put that on your tombstone," I say, moving to climb off him. "Ella can read, you know."

Cole laughs and his arms come around me to pull me back down on top of him.

"Oh no, you don't," he says. "Just a few more seconds."

Alarm bells ring in my head even as I let him pull me to him. He wants to cuddle? That's not allowed. This thing between us is just about sex. It's new and we've only done it a few times, but cuddling is definitely not part of it. He should know that, right? Reluctantly, I ease myself a few inches off him and pat his chest.

"No cuddling."

He doesn't try to stop me when I roll off him this time. I move to sit on the edge of the bed, my back to him. I take a few deep breaths as I work up the nerve to say what I've been meaning to say after each of the last four times we did this.

"This isn't serious," I say. "This thing we're doing. It's just sex."

He's quiet for so long that I turn back to look at him. He quirks his mouth in that grin I pretend not to love.

"I know," he says. "Giving yourself a reminder?"

I roll my eyes. "I'm reminding *you*. Because snuggling isn't part of the arrangement."

"What arrangement? We never made one."

I pull the sheet up to cover my naked breasts and shift to fully face him. "Fine," I say. "Let's make some ground rules."

He sits up and leans back against the headboard, making no move to cover his nudity. I know I shouldn't, but I let my eyes stray down the length of his body, taking in every ridge of muscle, every dusting of hair, every delicious inch of him. How is one man so damned gorgeous? It's not fair.

"My eyes are up here, counselor," he says in that teasing tone that he knows annoys me.

"Sorry," I say, directing my gaze up to his amused expression. "I can't help it you're so fun to look at."

He grins and flexes one bicep. "Oh? You see something you like?"

I cut my eyes downward. "I'm more of a thigh girl," I say, running a fingernail over one of his toned thighs.

"That's funny," he says. "Because I was just thinking about your thighs."

His hand is suddenly under the sheet and on my bare leg, sliding higher.

"What about my thighs?" I ask.

"Just how I like to be between them."

His voice is low and husky and dripping with innuendo. Even though we just finished having amazing sex where I came so hard I saw stars, I feel a little sliver of desire coiling low in my belly. What is it about this man that turns me into a horny teenager? If I'm not careful, I could get addicted to him. That thought is enough to pull me back to my senses. Briefly.

"We need to talk about the rules," I whisper, even as I trail my fingertip higher on his thigh.

"So, talk." His fingers lightly squeeze my leg, making me shiver.

"No sleeping with other people," I say.

His hand stills on my leg and his eyes dart to my face. His expression is no longer playful.

"Layna, I know I have a reputation in this town, but I've never cheated on anyone. Ever. I don't sleep with more than one woman at a time."

"I just figured that since I don't actually live here..."

I trail off, realizing that no matter what I say, it will likely sound insulting to him. And that's not how I meant it. I'd only meant to reassure him that I wasn't sleeping around when I go back to Atlanta.

"I'm sorry," I say. "I didn't mean it that way."

He grins and his fingers begin their lazy movement once more.

"Good. Now that we understand that, what's your next rule?"

"We can't tell anyone," I say.

He studies me for a long moment, but I can't read his expression. If the secrecy bothers him, he's not letting on.

"Can I ask why?" he says.

I lightly scrape my fingernail over his thigh, moving higher. "I don't want my sister to ask questions or to worry about me. It's not like me to have a casual fling, so I know she'll want to talk about it. And I don't want to."

"Fair enough," he says. "But you know things like this are hard to keep secret in a town this small."

I've had the same thought already, but I'd still like to keep it quiet for as long as possible.

"I know," I say. "But we also don't need to broadcast it. If only you and me know, the odds are better that we'll keep it quiet."

"If that's what you want," he says. "What else?"

I eye him for a moment. "You're awfully agreeable. Don't you have any rules?"

He grins. "Not if I can help it."

I roll my eyes. "Be serious for one second, please."

His hand trails higher, skimming my hip now. "I thought this wasn't serious. That's the whole point, right? It's supposed to be fun."

"You know what I mean," I say.

He sighs and meets my gaze. "Fine," he says. "Honesty. That's my rule. No matter what happens, we don't lie. If you want to end things, tell me and there will be no hard feelings. But no lying. If we're keeping secrets from the rest of the world, we can't keep them from each other too."

I nod, but something in his words feels more serious than the situation warrants. "Okay," I say. "But who's to say you won't be the one to end things?"

He grins as his fingers slide between my legs, brushing lightly against me. "I'm never getting enough of this sweet pussy," he says, pushing slowly into me without breaking eye contact.

"Cole," I gasp.

"No more talking," he says, pushing deeper into me. "The only rule for today is, when you come, you do it loud and messy."

Desire curls low in my belly and I feel myself grow wetter. He leans forward, his lips barely brushing mine.

"Make me," I whisper against his mouth.

CHAPTER 7

Present day

Layna

With my work schedule and case load, it's not always easy to make time for myself. It's why my sister and I decided to make time once a week or so to have lunch or dinner together. We realized how much we missed each other when she moved from Atlanta to Peach Tree nearly two years ago and all her time was taken with getting her business up and running. For almost a full year, I barely got to see my baby sister. It felt strange. For so long, we were all we had. It's hard to let that go. That's when I'd decided to move to Peach Tree. It wasn't only so I could be closer to Piper, but I won't lie and say it wasn't a deciding factor.

After I'd moved out of the house she shares with Luke, Piper and I decided we should make time to see each other. So, we meet up once a week for a meal and to catch up. It hadn't taken long at all for us to bring Harlow in on our outings. Even though I've only known Harlow for a year, she fits into our sisterhood like she's always been there. Now, the three of us have a standing date for dinner or drinks once a week, no matter how busy we all are.

Tonight, the three of us are sitting together at a booth at Peach Tree. I'd wanted to go to the Mexican restaurant or to the diner across town. I'd wanted to go literally anywhere else, if I'm being honest. But I hadn't been able to come up with a solid reason for avoiding our favorite bar and I'd quickly been outvoted by the others. The truth is, I wasn't sure I was ready to run into Cole tonight. I haven't seen him since the other morning when I'd told him we needed to end things. I'm worried things will be awkward, despite our agreement. But thankfully, he's not working tonight.

We sip our drinks while Harlow fills us in on the renovations that she and Linc are doing on her new house. Well, it's not new. It's actually her childhood home that she'd had to sell after she lost her mom to cancer. Linc bought it as a surprise for her and is working hard to restore it to its full glory. Which okay, is pretty damned romantic. Not that I'll ever admit that aloud.

"You should see the floors," Harlow gushes. "Original hardwood is so hard to match, but Linc somehow did it. You can't even tell which areas were damaged."

"Hardwood floors, huh?" I say. "Is that the new diamond necklace?"

Harlow laughs. "It is for me. He can keep the diamonds. Just give me a spa shower with multi-function rainwater showerheads and I'm a happy girl."

Piper eyes her. "Let me guess, big enough for two?"

Harlow just grins. "Obviously."

"Showers are just more fun with a partner," Piper says as if it's the most logical statement in the world. "It's good to have someone to wash your back."

"Or any hard-to-reach areas," Harlow says with a wink.

We all laugh, but there's a small part of me that's envious of the two women. I've never showered with a man. The idea feels more intimate and personal than anything I've ever done with previous boyfriends. And what Cole and I had was strictly physical. Showering together felt like crossing a line, though I'm not even sure why.

I shake off thoughts of Cole. That's in the past. It's time for me to look to the future. Isn't that why I agreed to go on a date? To see if I can find what Harlow and Piper have?

"In the interest of full disclosure," I say, leaning forward across the table.

"You're such a lawyer," Piper interrupts with a shake of her head.

I roll my eyes. "Yeah, yeah. Shut up. As I was saying, in the interest of full disclosure, I have a date Friday night."

I pick up my drink and take a sip. There's a split second of stunned silence before Piper lets out an excited squeal that nearly pierces my eardrum and causes everyone within thirty feet of us to look our way. Harlow smiles and claps quietly, thankfully showing her excitement with a little less enthusiasm than my sister.

"Stop it," I say, waving a hand at my sister. She's acting like I just told her I won a billion dollars in the lottery and bought us a private island to retire on.

"People are staring," I say through gritted teeth. "Besides, it's not that big of a deal."

"Oh, it's a big deal," Piper says. "You haven't dated anyone since you left Atlanta."

I haven't dated anyone since well before I moved to Peach Tree. I haven't dated anyone since I met Cole and we started hooking up. It was one of our rules. No sleeping with other people while we were sleeping with each other. There were other rules as well, but that was the big one. It's why he gave in so easily this morning when I told him I had a date. He knew I was serious about ending things and he respected my decision. I've got to admit, I respect him even more for adhering to the rules so steadfastly for so long. It's admirable. Not that I ever truly doubted that he would. He might be a sexual deviant behind closed doors, but he's always been a gentleman in all other respects.

"Why now?" Harlow asks, interrupting my musings. "You didn't seem like you were interested in dating."

I shrug. "I don't know. I'm not getting any younger. And I'm forced to listen to you two bragging about your hot boyfriends and your amazing sex lives. Maybe I want to be able to brag, too."

"Well, you could have had just about anyone in town if you'd acted interested," Harlow says. "You just never gave anyone the time of day."

That's because I was too busy sneaking around with Cole. I never really noticed anyone else in town. Not that I can tell them that. That would mean telling them I've been lying to them both for over a year. It's times like this that I hate the lie Cole and I have been keeping for all this time. Not being able to tell Piper and Harlow about our arrangement has led to even more lies while I've tried to justify my lack of interest in the male species. It would be so much simpler if I could just tell them why I haven't been pursuing anyone. But telling them the truth would just lead to a whole lot more questions. Not to mention some awkward attempts at matchmaking. I don't know if either of them would believe that Cole and I are just friends with benefits. I doubt they'd let it go without at least trying to get us to date. And I don't need to hear Cole say it again to know that he's not interested in settling down for good.

I shrug. "I was settling into a new town and a new job. Finding my rhythm. Now, I think I'm ready."

Piper drops the subject, but part of me wonders if she fully buys my excuse. If not, she doesn't press the issue. Instead, she starts peppering me with questions about my date. By the time the food arrives, I'm already exhausted from fielding a million questions while maintaining my huge secret. Sometimes I wonder if all the rules Cole and I came up with are even worth it. There are times like tonight when it would be easier if everyone knew about our little fling.

"Do you think he could be the one?" Harlow asks.

For a split second I worry that my face betrayed some of my thoughts. Then I realize she's asking about my date. I push aside thoughts of Cole Prescott and tell them all about the guy I'm having dinner with on Friday.

"It's way too early for that," I say. "He's cute. But not like over-the-top. He's funny and has a nice smile. He works in finance, I think."

"Finance?" Piper says. "Like accounting?"

Her tone makes it clear how she feels about that. I roll my eyes. Piper worked as an accountant before she decided to move to some small town no one had ever heard of and open a coffee shop. She'd secretly hated her career as an accountant and probably still harbors some ill will toward the profession. She's much happier now than she was before. Looking back, I'm surprised I never noticed it before. Or maybe it wasn't that she was unhappy back then. It's just that she's so much happier now that the difference is impossible not to see.

I shake my head. "Like investments, I think. I don't know all the details."

"Sounds boring as hell," Harlow says.

I laugh. "It's not *my* job. If he likes it, I don't care."

"Yeah, but if you date him, he's going to want to tell you about his day," Piper says. "All the exciting investments he's making."

It's obvious how she feels about the idea of listening to someone talk about investments. She's not wrong, though. I really don't know if I can pretend to be interested in investment talk. But that's what the date is for, right? To see if Dillon and I are compatible.

"It's a first date," I say. "It's not like we're making plans to spend our lives together. I'll worry about how boring his job is once I figure out if I even like the guy."

"Makes sense," Harlow says. "You can't tell much about someone from the first meeting, anyway."

"That's true," Piper agrees. "When I first met Luke, I was convinced he was a womanizing jerk."

"I think he was before he met you," I joke.

She shakes her head, smiling. "I don't care about his past. As long as I'm his future."

"Aw," Harlow gushes. "You two are sickeningly adorable."

"You're one to talk," I say. "You and Linc can't keep your hands off one another."

She just grins. "I can't help it if the man is madly in love with me."

"The feeling is clearly mutual," I say drily.

She sighs. "It really is."

We spend the next hour laughing and talking while we demolish a pitcher of margaritas and three different plates of appetizers. By the time we're ready to call it a night, I feel a strong urge to open the top button on my jeans. I love these nights with Piper and Harlow, but my waistline has noticed the effects of so much delicious food. Not that I'm complaining. I love my body the way it is. And so has every man I've ever been with. I know Cole never had any complaints.

I wince internally. Why am I thinking about Cole right now? I should be thinking about my upcoming date. Or my heavy caseload. Or my sister's wedding. Anything but the man I stopped sleeping with only 48 hours ago. I can't seem to help myself, though. I wonder if he's upset that I ended things. If so, he didn't show it. Maybe I should talk to him. I could clear the air and make sure there are no hard feelings. But what would I even say? *Hey Cole, sorry I decided we can't have toe-curling sex anymore. We cool?*

"Earth to Layna," Piper says, pulling me out of my musings and back to the present.

From the looks on the faces of the two women, I'm guessing they've been trying to get my attention for a while now.

"What's up?" I ask, pasting on a smile.

Piper's brow furrows. "We were talking about wedding hair. Do you want your hair up or down?"

"Oh," I say, thinking quickly. How long had I been zoned out? "I think down would be more comfortable. But up definitely looks more elegant. It's your wedding, Pipes. How do you want your photos?"

She rolls her eyes. "I told you already. I want to elope."

I point a finger at her. "You shut your mouth, missy. No more talk of eloping."

"Ugh," she says. "Fine. But I'm not deciding how my bridesmaids wear their hair. I've already made a million decisions about this wedding. From flowers to tablecloths and the freaking forks. The forks! Why is that my decision? They're forks!"

I want to laugh, but I'm worried my sister is spiraling into anxiety attack land and I need to rein her in before it gets that far.

"Piper, chill," I say. "I can handle those kinds of trivial things if you need me to. And Harlow and I will sort out our own hair if you truly don't care what we do. But try to relax and enjoy this. You're marrying a man you love who adores you. This is a good thing."

She sighs. "You're right. I'm being ridiculous. Besides, Luke has helped me so much with the planning. He's the one who found the wedding planner for me. It's one of his sister's new in-laws. She's been amazing."

"I'm sure if you told her you don't want to be involved in the minute details like silverware, she'd be happy to make those decisions for you," I say.

"Oh, this was before we hired Hannah," Piper says. "Actually, I think the fork thing was the final straw. When

Luke witnessed my meltdown, he called Mya right away and asked for Hannah's help. She's been a godsend. Even from two states away. But she'll be there the entire weekend of the wedding. I know I'm going to need all the help I can get to keep it together."

"Everything is going to be perfect," Harlow says. "Even if it's not, it doesn't matter. Because the important thing is that you're marrying the person who's perfect for you. All the other stuff doesn't matter."

"You're right," Piper says. "I need to trust that. Even if everything else has me anxious, I know I've got one thing right."

I smile at my sister, wishing I could find a way to take away the worry and stress she's feeling. I'd gladly take on all the wedding planning duties if I could. But she's already found someone to do that, and she's still stressed. I wonder if I can come up with something to help her relax before she forgets that her wedding is supposed to be fun. As we hug goodbye and I walk to my car, I add 'Help Piper de-stress' to my mental to-do list.

CHAPTER 8

Ten months ago

Cole

I take extra care with my appearance tonight, knowing Layna's back in town. It's been a month since we fucked. Which means it's been a month since I had more than my own hand to satisfy me. It's been a long month. Layna was here two weeks ago visiting her sister, but we couldn't find a way to sneak away together. This time, I'm determined to find a way to get back between those pretty thighs. Even if it's just a quickie in my office.

By the time Linc and I get to Peach Fuzz, the place is packed. I'd known it would be. It's a weekend night, after all. But Linc hasn't left the house except for work in weeks, so I decided to drag him out with me for at least one drink. If Layna happens to be here with her sister, that's just a convenient coincidence.

Several people greet me and Linc as we walk in and make our way up to the bar. I get the attention of Alex, one of our newest bartenders. She nods in my direction before grabbing two beers from the well under the counter and handing them to me.

"Thanks, Alex," I say.

"No problem, boss," she says with a smile.

I roll my eyes. "Just Cole."

"Whatever you say, boss."

I decide to let the 'boss' thing go, for now. Some of my employees think it's funny to fuck with me. They tell the new hires that I only like to be called boss and that I'll get angry if they call me by my first name. I look over and see my other bartender Tony watching my interaction with Alex and laughing. I glare at him, pointing two fingers at my eyes and then back to him. But he just laughs harder. I sigh, turning back to my brother to hand him one of the beers.

"Thanks, boss," Linc says, grinning.

"Don't."

He shrugs. "I think it suits you."

"Shut up."

I turn and survey the room. To anyone else, it probably looks like I'm just checking on my place of business and making sure nothing is amiss. And I am. Mostly. If I'm also scanning the room looking for a certain tall brunette with fuck-me eyes and a mouth made for kissing, no one needs to know. I spot her almost immediately. She's sitting in a booth talking animatedly with Piper and Harlow. I'm not shocked to see her here. It's common for the three of them to come here for drinks whenever Layna comes into town. Still, something about my first sight of her threatens to steal my breath. I try not to focus on that feeling as I direct Linc's attention to the table of women.

"Look who it is," I say.

Linc goes still beside me as he looks in their direction.

"Let's go say hi," I say.

"Why?"

I shrug. "They're our friends, right?"

Linc looks hesitant. "Piper's engaged to our best friend," he says. "But he's not here."

I shrug. "We're just saying hi."

He sighs as I begin to walk toward the table. I know he'll follow me. He'd never leave me hanging. Linc's usually the quieter brother. He's a little standoffish at times, but I know it's just because he's not very outgoing. He's not big on crowds and he doesn't always like meeting new people. But these aren't new people. We've hung out with these women plenty of times since Piper and Luke started dating. This is nothing new. We won't interrupt girls' night. We'll just say hi and see if they need a round of drinks on the house. It'll be quick. And if Layna gives me that look that says she wants to meet up later, so be it.

The three women are laughing as we approach the table, but I didn't hear what was so funny. I wait for them to notice the two of us standing there, but to my shock Linc speaks before they can.

"Do I get to hear the joke?"

The three women go quiet and turn as one to look at Linc. It takes Layna a second to notice me standing on the other side of my brother, but I can see the exact moment when she does. She smiles my way before lowering her gaze to the drink on the table before her. I smile at the other two women, making sure to keep my expression neutral. It's far from the first time I've had to pretend in front of our friends that I'm not desperate to touch her. I can be casual.

"Just an inside joke," Harlow says.

When Linc doesn't say anything else, I decide that's my cue to pick up the slack.

"Ladies," I say, flashing them my best smile. "I trust you're having a nice night out?"

They all nod, and Piper asks us if we want to join them for a drink or two. I do my best to hide my excitement at the prospect. This puts me that much closer to getting in Layna's panties. Linc takes the empty seat beside Harlow, and I slide into the seat next to Layna. She does her best to act like she's unaffected by my presence, but I fight back a smile when I hear her sharp intake of breath.

A server comes over and I order a round of fresh drinks for the table while we all catch up on one another's lives.

"How long are you in town, Layna?" I ask as I hand out the drinks.

Piper speaks before Layna can open her mouth. She's so excited she's practically bouncing in her seat.

"She's moving here!"

The shock of that statement hits me like a punch in the gut and I nearly spill my beer. Thankfully no one notices. My mind reels. Layna is moving here? Since when? She never mentioned she was even thinking about it. She was just here two weeks ago. What the hell. What does this mean for our fling? Will she want to end things? Take them to another level? I have so many questions and I can't ask any of them right now.

"Really?" I say, turning to look at Layna. She doesn't quite meet my gaze. "I didn't know that was your plan." The words are pointed, but I hope no one else notices.

She shrugs, unaffected. "It wasn't at first. It's a recent decision."

A recent decision? Sounds impulsive to me.

As if she heard my thoughts, Piper echoes the same sentiment. The two women go back and forth for a few minutes with Layna arguing her decision and Piper expressing concern for her sister's impulsiveness. She's right, though. This kind of rash decision doesn't sound like Layna. I wonder what made her decide to do it now. I wonder again what it means for me and her.

If she wants to keep things going, this works out well for me. It means I can have Layna whenever I want instead of waiting for her to come back into town and stealing her away from her sister. This will make things far more convenient. If she wants to keep things going, that is.

"What did I miss?"

I look up to see Luke standing next to Piper, smiling down at her. Harlow accuses her of inviting boys to girls' night. Piper points to me and Linc.

"They're here," she says, defensive.

"That's different," Harlow says. "We didn't invite them."

"Hey," I say. "We're right here. We can hear you."

The girls roll their eyes as Linc and I laugh. Suddenly, everything is back to normal. Luke slides into the booth next to Piper which puts Layna even closer to me. I suppose I could move to the other side and even things up, but then I wouldn't be close enough to Layna to smell her subtle perfume or to hear her low laugh when Luke says something funny.

"Next round of drinks is on the guys," Layna says. "Since they crashed our girls' night."

I don't point out that I got the last round. Truthfully, I don't care. I'll buy all the drinks if it means I get to sit next to Layna for a little longer. When Linc asks Piper and Luke about wedding plans, I take advantage of the focus being on the two of them to lean closer to Layna.

"You didn't tell me you were moving here," I say in a voice only she can hear.

"I didn't tell anyone," she murmurs, not looking at me. "But now you know."

I concede this with a nod. "You want to meet me in my office?" I murmur.

"Might be obvious," she whispers.

I put a hand on her thigh, careful to make sure it's not visible to anyone else.

"Then be stealthy," I whisper, letting my fingers slide under the hem of her skirt to brush against her through the fabric of her panties. "Unless you don't want to."

I can hear her sharp intake of breath. "I do."

"So, make it work."

Linc is the first to leave, citing his early morning tomorrow. After that, it's not long before Harlow decides to leave. I make the excuse of finishing up some work in my office and make my goodbyes. It's more obvious if Layna and I are the last two people at the table and we don't leave with the others. And judging by the way Piper and Luke can't keep their hands off one another, it's only a matter of time before they go home.

I make my way to my office to wait. The anticipation of wondering if Layna is going to show up feels familiar. Just like the first time, I feel myself grow more excited with each passing moment. I'd been at half-mast the entire time I sat at the table with the others, but now my cock is straining against my pants. It's been too long since I've had her. I can't wait to sink balls-deep into that sweet pussy of hers.

Thankfully, it's not long before I see the door begin to open and Layna's dark hair as she ducks quickly inside. She looks at me, her eyes bright with excitement. I don't give her time to talk or to think about it. I pull her against me and plant my lips on hers. She lets out a startled sound that melts into a sexy little moan as I back her up against the closed door with my body.

Her hands are everywhere, touching me as if she can't decide which part of me needs the most attention. If she'd ask, I'd tell her it's definitely my cock. But I'm so caught up in kissing her and the feel of her soft curves against me that I don't care right now.

"Moving to Peach Tree, huh?" I ask as her hands slide under my t-shirt, smoothing over my abdomen.

"Yeah."

Her mouth goes to my neck and she delivers a little stinging bite before soothing it with her tongue.

"Is that a problem?"

Her voice holds a slight challenge that makes me grin. I'd be an idiot to challenge this woman.

"Not at all," I whisper. "I just wonder what this means for us." I take her mouth in another searing kiss that sends all the blood rushing straight down to my cock.

"Nothing," she says, tilting her head to allow me access to her neck. "The rules stay the same."

"Why?"

"Because it's fun," she says, running her hands over my chest. "Neither of us wants serious, remember?"

"Fair enough," I say, cupping her breast through her shirt.

"Are we going to talk or fuck?" Layna asks, her breath catching as I pinch her nipple lightly.

I take her hand and guide it to the front of my pants, letting her feel how hard I am.

"What do you think?"

She smiles as she gives me a squeeze.

"We need to be quick," she whispers. "Piper's going to wonder why I didn't come home right away."

I slide my hands under her skirt to squeeze her ass. "Baby, if you were expecting me to be anything other than quick after a month of missing this sweet pussy, you're going to be disappointed."

She laughs softly, still gripping me through my pants. "You'd better not disappoint me. I've been looking forward to this for weeks."

I pull her leg up around my hip and grind against her hot center, making her mouth drop open in a silent gasp.

"Yes, ma'am."

Her hands move to my pants, and she makes quick work of undoing the button and zipper before reaching in to grip my length.

"Don't call me ma'am."

I grin. I love it when she's bossy.

CHAPTER 9

Present Day

Layna

This has got to be the worst date I've ever been on. And I once had a frat boy puke on my feet on our second date before trying to kiss me. I also broke a tooth on my date's braces at my junior prom and wound up at an emergency dentist. I didn't even get to dance. So, I know a thing or two about shitty dates. This is somehow worse.

Dillon seemed like a perfectly normal guy when I met him in the bookstore. He'd been cute and charming. He had kind eyes and a nice smile. We talked about books and art. I'd even felt a hint of excitement when he'd asked for my number. But tonight, it's like that man disappeared and he turned into a different man altogether. One who can't stop talking about his mother and keeps invading my personal space. As if those two things alone weren't enough of a red flag for a first date, there's the fact that he keeps doing them *simultaneously.* Piper had been worried about me being bored by him talking about his job. I wish that was the problem.

The third time he runs his hand down my bare arm in what I assume is meant to be a seductive maneuver while waxing poetic about how soft his mother's hair is, I'm ready to run for the hills. If I don't get out of here soon, I'm worried I'll end up as a pet in this man's basement. Why did I think it was a good idea to start dating again? Oh yeah, because I was trying to settle down and find a partner in life. Right now, dying alone sounds appealing.

I push my food around on my plate a few more times before smiling and excusing myself to use the ladies' room. Dillon admonishes me to hurry back to him and I assure him I will. I do my best not to run from the dining area. I try to come up with a plan as I walk to the back of the restaurant where the bathrooms are located. I'm starting to regret not meeting Dillon at the restaurant tonight. Instead, I'd let him pick me up from my sister's coffee shop. At least I didn't let him pick me up from my apartment. The last thing I need is this weirdo knowing where I live.

Since I don't have a car, my options are limited. I consider sneaking out and using a rideshare app to get home, but I can't get outside without passing directly in front of the table where Dillon is currently sitting. He'd easily spot me. Especially since the restaurant isn't overly crowded for a Friday night. Maybe I can text Harlow or Piper to come get me. But no. Piper is on her mini getaway with Luke this weekend. She needs this relaxation. I won't interrupt that.

I type out a quick text to Harlow as I duck into an empty stall. I don't really need to use the toilet, but I need the illusion of privacy the stall provides. I lean against the wall of the stall, willing Harlow to text me back. When 5 minutes pass with no response, I know I've been gone too long already. Dillon is going to wonder what I'm doing in here. There's only one other person in town I might be able to call. But I really don't want to call him. Besides, he's probably working. I chew my thumb nail absently, staring at Cole's name on the screen.

I type out a text before deleting it. I reword the message and read it back before deleting it again. Finally, I sigh and give up on texting. Before I can chicken out, I hit the button to call him. I'm not even sure he'll answer a call from me after the way things ended the other day. I'm only a little surprised when he picks up on the second ring.

"Layna, what's up?"

Cole's voice is casual, but I can hear a faint note of surprise in his tone. We haven't spoken since the other morning when I broke things off. At first, I wasn't sure how to be around him without the added layer of our sexual relationship. Then, I felt awkward that he would know I was avoiding him. But I tell myself that he hasn't reached out to me, either. So, maybe he felt the same way.

"Cole?" I whisper, trying not to be heard by the other women in the bathroom. "I need your help."

"Are you okay? Where are you?"

The worry and urgency in his voice is unmistakable. I feel a tinge of guilt.

"I'm fine," I hiss. "Just listen."

"Okay," he says, drawing out the word.

"This date is awful," I whisper. "I need your help."

I hear a snort of what might be laughter before he speaks.

"What do you want me to do about it?"

"Get me out of here!" I whisper-shout into the phone.

"Just sneak out," he says.

"I can't!" I hiss. "He'll see me. Besides I don't have my car."

"You let a stranger see where you live on a first date?" His voice has lost its humor now. He sounds pissed. "Layna, do you know how dangerous that is?"

I roll my eyes. "I'm not an idiot. I had him pick me up at Piping Hot."

"Good," he says, clearly relieved. "So, tell me what's so awful about this date?"

I close my eyes, bracing myself for ridicule.

"He keeps talking about his mother," I say, trying to be tactful.

"So?" he says. "He loves his mom. That's a good thing. They say you can tell a lot about a man by how he treats his mother."

"I think he loves his mother a little *too* much, if you know what I mean."

I hear another snort. This time I'm certain he's laughing and trying to hide it from me.

"Seriously?"

"What?" he asks. "I sneezed."

"You forget I've heard your scream-sneeze before. That wasn't it," I say.

"I do not scream," he argues. "It's more of a manly shout."

"Whatever. Are you going to come get me, or not?"

"I'm not sure I should," he says. "What if he's just nervous? He might be your soulmate. You should give him more of a chance."

I resist the urge to let out an exasperated screech. "Cole, he's definitely not my soulmate," I say.

I'm beyond whispering at this point. I don't care if every woman in the bathroom hears my conversation at this point. If it means Cole will come and get me out of here, it's worth a little embarrassment.

I sigh. "He's getting really touchy. I keep moving away, but he's not getting the hint."

"He touched you without your consent?" Cole's voice has lost all humor now. He sounds almost angry.

"It's nothing I can't handle," I say. "And it's more that he keeps crowding me, invading my personal space. I don't get rapey vibes if that's what you're worried about."

"You know vibes can lie, right?" he says. "Even the nicest seeming guys can be pieces of shit."

"I know that, too," I say. "And I appreciate your worry. But I get the feeling he's the type who needs to ask his mother permission first."

He barks out a laugh, not even attempting to hide it this time. I can't help it. I smile.

"Stop laughing," I say, glad he can't see my smile.

"Oh, come on," Cole says. "This shit is hilarious, and you know it."

"Fine," I say. "It's funny. You happy now?"

"A little," he says. "How do you want me to play this?"

"What do you mean?" I ask.

"You said you want me to come get you, right? That's why you called."

"Obviously," I hiss. "I can't let him take me to a secondary location. That's how they get you."

He laughs. "Okay, no more true crime for you."

"It might be saving my life tonight," I say.

"Do you want jealous husband or distraught family member?"

I roll my eyes. Of course, he'd go for something dramatic. "How about a work emergency?"

He sighs. "Fine. It's not as sexy, but I guess I can manage it."

I can't stop the laugh that slips out. "Thanks, Cole."

"What are friends for?" he says.

I smile, feeling a warmth slide through me as I end the call. Cole and I might have started out as just a fling, but somewhere along the way he became one of my closest friends in Peach Tree. Despite how hard I tried to fight it. It's not what I expected when I hooked up with him in his office that first night. Looking back, I still don't know what pushed me to follow him down that hallway, but I can't regret it now. It may have been the beginning of my first and last fling, but it was also the start of a friendship that I don't know that we'd have if things had played out differently.

CHAPTER 10

Eight Months Ago

Layna

Cole groans dramatically as he lowers the cardboard box he's carrying to the living room floor. I know for a fact that box isn't heavy because I loaded it into my car myself just last night. Which is how I know he's exaggerating its weight.

"That's the last of it," he says. "Thank the gods."

"That one goes in the bedroom," I say.

He narrows his eyes at me before bending down to pick the box up again.

"What happened to 'Thank you, Cole. You're amazingly kind and selfless to give up your whole day to help me move into my new apartment.'"

I roll my eyes at his back as he walks down the hallway to the bedroom.

"Thank you, Cole," I say sweetly. "You're amazingly kind and selfless to help me move into my new apartment. And so strong, too!"

He returns to the living room without the box and narrows his eyes at me once again. "Did you doubt me, woman?"

I open one of the boxes on the kitchen counter and peer inside.

"Not even for a second," I say. "I've seen those muscles in action, remember?"

Strong arms encircle my waist and Cole's lips brush the back of my neck. "You want to see them in action again? We could break in your new place."

I feel a shiver run up my spine as I lean back against his hard body. Common sense wars with my libido. I know what I need to do, but what I want to do is let Cole use those sexy muscles to do unspeakable things to my body. Common sense wins out, though. Barely.

"I have too much to do," I say weakly. "I need to unpack."

"Do you need to unpack right this moment?" he whispers, his hand sliding up to cup my breast.

My eyes fall closed, and I suck in a breath. I know I should stop him, but I can feel myself on the verge of giving in. Not that I'm putting up much of a fight.

"I'll tell you what," Cole says, kissing the back of my neck. "For every box we unpack, one of us loses a piece of clothing. And then, when we're both naked, we take an orgasm break."

I know what he's doing. There's no way I'll ever get unpacked if we stop for sex after every five or six boxes. And I know that we won't stop at one orgasm. Cole's never given me less than two orgasms any time we've had sex. Not that I'm complaining about that. The man takes sex seriously.

"I promise you everything will be properly put away," he says, as if reading my mind.

"To my specifications?" I ask, pushing up against the hand on my breast.

His lips move to the shell of my ear. "I swear it."

I can feel him hardening against my lower back and it turns me on more than it should. Knowing he's this affected by my nearness does something to me. And knowing exactly how amazing sex with him can be doesn't make it easy to resist him.

"Fine," I say. "But I get to pick which boxes we open."

He gives my nipple one last squeeze before releasing me and stepping back. I do my best to pretend I don't immediately miss the contact.

"I figured you'd say that," he says with a grin. "Which one is first?"

I take a calming breath and try not to look at the obvious bulge in the front of Cole's pants as I move to one of the larger boxes in the kitchen. After reading the label, I smile.

"This one."

I expect him to complain about the contents of the box, but he just shakes his head.

"Stalling, huh? That's okay. Anticipation will make it that much better."

I suppress a shiver at the promise in his words as I cut the tape open to reveal dozens of objects individually wrapped in white paper.

"Let me guess," he says. "You want to wash all these dishes before putting them away?"

I smile. "How did you know?"

"Because I know you," he says, lifting one of the dishes from the box. "Is it too much to hope these are dishwasher safe?"

His voice is so hopeful that I can't help but laugh. "Actually, yes. They are. I don't have the patience to buy dishes that can't be put into the dishwasher."

He grins. "Something we agree on."

Cole unwraps dishes while I stack them in the dishwasher. We methodically work our way through the box, paper piling up around our feet as we go.

"You never told me why you decided to move to Peach Tree," he says, handing me a bowl. "Is it just about your sister?"

"What do you mean?" I ask. Turning to face him, I gaze directly into his eyes, my expression deadly serious. "I moved here to be closer to you."

There's a moment of stunned silence as Cole's eyes widen and his mouth drops open. I hold my gaze for as long as I can before I break into laughter. He looks absolutely terrified.

"Holy shit," I gasp. "You should see your face!"

"I knew you were kidding," he says, moving to gather up the discarded paper.

"You did not," I tease. "You were two seconds away from running for the door."

He tosses a piece of paper at me, and I catch it before it can hit my face.

"I wasn't going to run," he insists. "More like a light jog."

I look at him with raised brows, making it clear that I don't believe him for a second.

"Sorry," he says sheepishly.

I shake my head, still laughing. "Relax. I'm not stalking you, Cole. I just needed a change. That's all."

"I never said stalking," he mutters, defensive. "Besides, you're the one who came up with the rules, remember? Just friends who have sex. No strings."

"I remember. And I meant them. Besides, I really was kidding. I didn't move here for you."

"That's a relief," he teases.

"Shut up," I mutter.

"Seriously, though," he says. "Why did you move here? It's a big change from Atlanta. It can't just be about Piper."

I shrug, wondering how much to tell him about my reasons for leaving my life in Atlanta behind.

"There were lots of reasons," I say, keeping my focus on stacking dishes in the dishwasher rather than looking at Cole.

"You don't have to tell me if you don't want to," he says, his voice gentle.

Maybe it's that gentle tone that has me wanting to open up to him. Maybe it's the fact that he can't tell anyone else what we talk about because everything about our 'relationship' is a secret. I don't know the reason, but I find that I'm not opposed to telling Cole things I've never said aloud.

"It's okay," I say, busying myself with cutting open another box. "I don't think I was happy there. Not really. It took me a long time to realize it. I think I was just going through the motions in Atlanta. Not really living my life. It wasn't until I started coming here to visit Piper and I could see how happy she was here that I realized how empty my life in Atlanta was. Somehow this little town has more character and life in it than the massive city I lived in."

I shrug. "I don't know. It got so I was making up excuses to come out for the weekend. My apartment started to feel suffocating. Piper said something to me once. She said, 'I can breathe here.' It took me a long time to realize what she meant. And it wasn't just about the lack of smog. There's less rush here. Less worry about getting to where I need to go or trying to be someone I'm not. I can just be me here. That probably sounds crazy."

I trail off, surprised at how much I just revealed to Cole. I wonder if he thinks I'm crazy. It's not like we've spent a lot of time talking about ourselves when we're together. We mostly just try to get one another naked as quickly as possible. He's really good at getting me out of my clothes. Not that I've ever complained about that skill. It's served us both well over the past few months. But this conversation feels bigger than any of our past interactions. It feels like more than simple friendship. Which is not at all what either of us wants.

Hadn't he just freaked out when I let him think I moved here for him? He's clearly on the same page when it comes to this friends-with-benefits situation we've got going. I'm not about to ruin it by bringing up serious issues.

"Hey."

Cole's voice pulls me out of my rambling thoughts, and I look up to see his brown eyes locked on mine.

"It doesn't sound crazy," he says. "I get it. When I left for college, I thought for sure that was my ticket out of this town. I wanted to be more than Peach Tree's golden boy. I thought I couldn't wait to get as far from here as possible. But I don't know. It never felt right. College life, city life. None of it felt right. It was like I was wearing a pair of shoes that was half a size too small. I could fit. I could make it look like I belonged. But I knew I'd never be comfortable."

He shrugs and his mouth quirks up into that sexy grin. "So, I came back home. To my family. To this little town and all its eccentric folks."

"And the peaches?" I tease.

A small laugh escapes him. "And the peaches."

I pick at a corner of tape where it's peeling up from the box nearest my hand, unable or unwilling to look at Cole when I ask my next question.

"Did it make you happy? Coming back home?"

I hear him exhale with a sigh. "Maybe," he says. "Sometimes. But I don't think uprooting your life is a magic cure for anyone's happiness. Sometimes we need a reset switch, sure. But ultimately, I think we all need to work for it. Every day. Some days I work harder than others."

I look at him, brows drawn low in confusion. "You need to work to be happy? You seem like the most well-adjusted person in this town."

He laughs. "No one is happy all the time. But I try to focus on the good things in my life. When I'm having a shitty day, I focus on those instead of the bad things. I've got a healthy family, a thriving business, killer dimples, and the body of a Greek god."

His hands go to my hips. "Plus, I've got this sexy woman who lets me do all kinds of filthy things to her. And now she's living just down the street."

I smile and let him pull me against his body. "That's certainly convenient."

"Isn't it, though?" His hands slide down to cup my ass. "You know what else?"

"What?"

"Since we finished unpacking a box, it's time for you to lose a piece of clothing."

"Is that what we agreed?" I ask, my hands sliding up to the back of his neck.

"Mmhmm," he whispers, pressing his hips against mine until I feel the hard bulge there. "And I get to pick which one."

"I don't remember that rule," I say, grinding against his erection.

I can feel my desire growing with every second I spend touching Cole. It's why I tried to insist we unpack before doing anything physical. I knew he'd be able to distract me if I let him near me. And I was right. I'm thoroughly distracted right now.

"Pants off, Miss Brooks," he says.

There's a hint of challenge in his voice, like he thinks I might back down. The old Layna might have. She would have been in a hurry to get unpacked and put everything in its proper place. But I'm trying to turn over a new leaf. Isn't that the whole reason I moved to this town?

"My pants for your shirt," I say, raising a brow in challenge.

He grins and takes a small step back. Holding my gaze, he reaches for the hem of his t-shirt and pulls it up over his head. I let my eyes trail over the newly exposed skin, my body already humming with desire. I take in the pecs and the defined abs leading to a pair of jeans that sit low on his hips. The vee of defined muscle leading down to his waistband has me wanting to trail my tongue over it, but I resist the urge. When I bring my gaze back up to Cole's face, I see a hint of amusement in his eyes.

"Pants?" He reminds me.

I keep my gaze on his as I unbutton my jeans and slide them over my ass and down my legs until I can step out of them. Picking them up, I toss them in Cole's direction. He catches the garment easily and drops it onto the arm of the couch, his gaze never leaving mine. The air feels cool on my exposed legs, and I can't help but feel a little naughty standing here like this with him.

"Shit, Layna," he says, his eyes dropping to my panties. "Is that a thong?"

I smile. "Yep."

"You're going to make it really hard for me to follow the rules if you're walking around here with your sexy ass on display all afternoon."

I just shrug. "Sounds like your problem. Not mine."

I turn away from him and walk over to another large box filled with more dishes. Keeping my back to him, I bend over and peel back the tape holding the box closed. I know how I must look right now. I'm wearing a sheer lace thong that leaves my entire ass uncovered. And right now, my ass on full display for Cole as I bend down to pull a carefully wrapped coffee mug from the box. He hasn't said anything, but I know he's watching me. I can feel his gaze as though it was his touch on my skin. My heart pounds as I straighten and place the mug on the counter.

I'm not surprised at all when I feel Cole's hand on my bare hip, but the anticipation has me jumping slightly at the contact. His fingers curve around my hip, gripping me lightly.

"Let's take a break," he says in that low, commanding tone I love.

"Not yet," I say, trying to sound unbothered. "No orgasms until we finish at least 4 boxes."

His lips brush the back of my neck. "How about, I give you an orgasm each time we finish putting away a box? That sounds fair."

The idea is more tempting than I want to admit. But I try not to show how badly I want to give in.

"How is that fair?" I ask. "What about you?"

"I love making you come," he says. "It's the hottest thing I've ever seen."

Holy hell. That's hot.

How does he always know exactly what to say to turn me on? Not that his mere presence doesn't have the same effect. His hand slides around to my stomach, sliding under the hem of my shirt. His fingertips slip just beneath the waistband of my panties and go still. He's so close to touching me where I want him, but I know what he's doing. He's letting me decide.

"Besides," he says, "If I do my job right, you'll be coming on my tongue shortly."

His tongue traces along the shell of my ear. "Trust me when I tell you that having your taste on my tongue is even better than watching you come. When your thighs grip my head and your fingers tangle in my hair. Your back arches and I can feel that little flutter right before you cry out. It's almost as sexy as when I feel you come on my cock."

"Such a filthy mouth," I whisper.

"You love my filthy mouth," he growls.

That type of arrogance from anyone else would bother me, but we both know he's right. I love the dirty way he talks when we're alone. His words and that gravelly voice are enough to make me wet, and he knows it.

"I bet if I slid my hand lower, I'd find that pretty little cunt of yours soaking wet right now," he says.

When I don't say anything, he begins to move his fingers in little teasing circles directly above my pubic bone.

"Tell me I'm wrong, Layna."

I let my eyes fall closed, wishing he'd make good on his threat and touch me. But I won't ask him to. It would mean letting him win, and I hate admitting defeat.

"Wouldn't you like to know," I whisper.

"You have no idea how badly I do," he admits. "I want to feel you all wet and slippery under my fingers. I want to taste you on my tongue."

I feel his hard length against my back, and I can't help but press back against him. I want him. We both know it.

"But only if you want it, too," he says.

As if he believes for one second that I don't want this? He knows better than that. There's no way my actions could be construed as anything but willingness on my part. But I know what he wants. He wants me to ask him to touch me. It's not that he wants me to beg. That's not it at all. He doesn't get off on making me beg. He gets off on making sure I'm fully present in every moment of what we do together. He gets off on hearing me say the words. I made the rules for this little game today and he wants me to be the one to change them or throw them out the window if I want to. And I want to. God, do I want to. So, why am I hesitating?

"It's okay to bend the rules, Layna," he whispers. "No one needs to know. It can be our little secret. Just say the word and I'll have my face buried between those pretty thighs in a heartbeat."

I can picture the scene he's describing. His head between my legs. His mouth on me. I want it so badly. He knows it, too. But he won't do anything unless I say the words. It's frustrating, but it's also sexy as hell. It makes me feel powerful. No man has ever given me so much control in the bedroom. Hell, most of the ones I've been with have barely concerned themselves with whether I came. But Cole? He's so focused on my pleasure that I don't have a doubt that he could have me coming in less than two minutes if he wanted to. He knows my body that well. So, why am I hesitating? These boxes will still be here in an hour. Or even two.

"Let me taste you, Layna."

That one sentence is the final straw. What woman could hold out against that? Not me, that's for certain.

"Cole," I whisper.

"Yes?"

"Okay."

"Okay, what?" he asks. "Tell me."

I let out a little frustrated sigh. He's going to make me say it. Fine.

"Make me come, Cole. Please."

"I thought you'd never ask."

His hand immediately moves lower, sliding down between my legs. He lets out an appreciative growl when he finds me wet and ready.

"So wet, counselor. Is this all for me?"

"You know it is," I whisper, turning my head to capture his lips with mine as his fingers slip inside me.

Cole's other hand comes up to hold my jaw, keeping my face turned toward his as he kisses me. His tongue tangles with mine as his fingers slide in and out of me, filling and stretching me before spreading the wetness up over my sensitive clit. I gasp against his mouth at the zing of pleasure from that simple touch. His fingers slide over my clit over and over, driving me closer to the edge with every stroke. I'm so turned on I know it won't take long for him to make me come.

I moan against his mouth, reaching one hand up to tangle my fingers in his hair. Before I can completely lose myself in Cole's kiss and what he's doing with his fingers, he pulls out of me and spins me around to face him. With his hands on my waist, he walks me backwards until I feel the kitchen counter at my back.

"What—"

But I don't get a chance to finish my question before Cole lifts me up and sets me on the counter. He sinks to his knees and looks up at me, a devilish grin on his face.

"I said I wanted to taste you. So, let me."

As if I would stop him.

I expect him to pull my panties off, but instead he hooks a finger under the lace and yanks them to one side before lowering his mouth to plant an open-mouthed kiss on my exposed flesh. I gasp as I watch his tongue dart out to lick me. He's almost casual about the gesture, as if he's got all the time in the world. I want to urge him on, to beg him to focus on my clit and make me come. But I can do nothing but watch his slow, languid movements.

It's clear that he's enjoying himself. Each time his tongue brushes my clit, I shiver, and a small gasp escapes me. And each time, Cole's mouth quirks up into a little grin. He's loving this. He's getting off on teasing me. And I can't help myself. I love it, too. Normally, I'd be impatient. I'd want to come as fast and hard as possible. But right now, I can't look away from Cole's face between my legs, his mouth on me.

It's the middle of the afternoon. Sunlight streams through the open curtains and casts a golden glow on him where he kneels between my thighs. He looks like some sort of wicked angel, sent down to pleasure unsuspecting women with his impossibly skilled mouth. I have the ridiculous thought that if my old coworkers could see me now, they wouldn't recognize me. The Layna I'd been before would never have stopped in the middle of a task to let someone eat her pussy on the kitchen counter. It feels so deliciously wrong and dirty, but in the sexiest way possible. I gasp again as his tongue brushes my clit. This time, he doesn't stop at a quick flick of his tongue. He circles it, starting up a rhythm that has me moaning and my eyes falling closed.

"Oh, god," I moan.

His mouth leaves me, and my eyes shoot open to glare at him.

"Don't stop," I gasp.

"Eyes on me, Layna," he says. "I want all of you."

The intensity in his gaze is almost overwhelming, but I keep my eyes on his. Unable to speak, I just nod my understanding. I can give him this. I can do whatever he demands as long as he doesn't stop. When he's sure he has my entire focus, he lowers his head again. His tongue moves faster now, sliding and swirling against my clit in tight little circles until I'm gasping. Every muscle in my body is tense and I can feel myself ready to break. It feels like every nerve ending in my body has come alive and is centered on that single spot between my legs.

"Oh, fuck," I moan.

My body is wracked with tiny tremors, and I can see the determined light in Cole's eyes as he grips my thighs, spreading me open so he can feast. He wants this as much as I do. That knowledge spurs me on, sending me closer to the edge of oblivion. The pleasure in my center builds higher, coiling tighter, ready to detonate. That's when I feel Cole slide two thick fingers inside me, his attention on my clit never wavering. He pumps his fingers in and out, in time with the rhythmic slide of his tongue against my clit. That's all it takes.

I cry out as my world explodes into waves of pleasure so intense, I almost shy away from it. The pleasure is nearly too much. Too intense. My inner walls clench, squeezing against Cole's fingers as they continue to pump in and out of my body. My back arches and I can barely keep my eyes on his. His focus is entirely on me, his brown eyes locked on mine as I come on his tongue, and he drinks every drop of my release. By the time he eases his fingers out of me, I'm gasping for breath and my muscles ache like I just had an intense workout.

The look of pleased satisfaction on Cole's face as he plants a kiss on my inner thigh borders on cockiness, but I don't care. He has a right to feel cocky after what he just did. I've never come so hard in my life. I collapse onto my back, boneless as I lie on the kitchen counter, surrounded by the still-full boxes I've yet to unpack. I don't even care about that right now. The boxes can wait. Everything can wait. Right now, I need to figure out how to go on living with the knowledge that my sex life has peaked. Because I know, without a doubt, that I'll never have an orgasm like that again.

"Holy shit," I breath, raising my head to look at Cole.

He's standing between my legs wearing a smirk that would normally annoy me. But I can't find anything but intense satisfaction in me right now. With gentle hands, he slides a finger under the fabric of my panties, sliding it over to cover me once more. The back of his finger brushes my clit as he does, and I shiver. That only turns his smirk into a full-blown grin.

"You ready to unpack another box?" he asks.

I can't help but laugh.

CHAPTER 11

Present Day

Cole

I end the call with Layna, a smile still on my face. She called me to save her from a shitty date. I'm not stupid enough to think I was her first choice. Piper would have been number one on the list, after all. But I know Luke took her out of town for a relaxing spa weekend to help with the wedding stress. Harlow would have been her second choice. But clearly, she wasn't available. Which left me. Some men might be irritated that they weren't at the top of the list, but I know Layna. It's hard for her to ask for help. The fact that she called at all is a big deal.

We haven't spoken since I left her house the other morning when she ended things between us. I know we both agreed there would be no hard feelings and there truly aren't. I'm not angry with her for ending it, even if I don't completely understand her reasoning. But I've been struggling with how to act around her now that we're not sleeping together. Not that we've ever acted like anything but friends in front of others or in public.

But I can't deny that I've been avoiding her. When Linc told me Harlow was meeting Piper and Layna for drinks at Peach Fuzz the other night, I'd changed my mind about going in to help with the dinner rush. Not that they'd needed me. I wouldn't have abandoned them if they had. But I'd still let the fact that she'd be there dictate my actions and that's just stupid. This is Layna. Regardless of whether we're having sex or not, she's still the same person she's always been. I've never felt awkward or uncomfortable around her. Not since the night we met. Granted, we'd started having sex the night we met. It's occurring to me that maybe I don't know how to act around her now because we've never known one another in a non-sexual way.

I should just treat her the same way I treat Piper or Harlow. Except I've never felt the smallest hint of desire when it comes to the other two women. It's always been different with Layna. Since the night we met, there's been a spark of attraction. A spark that quickly became an inferno. How do I pretend that doesn't exist anymore? I don't know if I can. But none of that matters right now because she needs my help. She needs me to be her friend tonight, so that's what I'm going to be.

I make the short drive to the restaurant and park near the front door. I'm not sure it's a legal parking space, but I won't be here long enough for a ticket. I hope. I run my hands through my hair and try to decide what I'm going to say when I see her. I know we settled on a work emergency as our cover story, but the truth is I don't actually have a plan as I walk inside. I'm just going to wing it. That never goes badly, right?

I spot her as soon as I walk into the restaurant. The hostess smiles at me, but I point toward Layna's table and shake my head.

"I'm meeting a friend," I say. "She's right over there."

I walk past the hostess' stand, eyes locked on the beautiful brunette with the leering man seated entirely too close to her in the booth. Why is he even seated on her side of the booth? Who does that on a first date? Her hair is falling in waves over her shoulders and she's wearing a dark navy dress that shows more of her thigh than this guy has a right to see, in my opinion. But I remind myself that it's not my place to think about what she's wearing or who she's wearing it for. It never has been. But especially not tonight. I need to focus on the task at hand.

"Layna!" I say, injecting a hint of worried relief into her name. "There you are!"

She looks up at me and I can see the immediate relief in her brown eyes. It's that single look from her that tells me how uncomfortable she really is with the man seated next to her. I know I teased her about it, and she even laughed with me on the phone earlier, but it's obvious she can't wait to get away from him. Seeing that look in her eyes and knowing who put it there sends a swell of anger through me. Part of me wants to haul her out of that booth and tell this jackass to stay the hell away from her. But that's not what she wants. It's not why she called me here. So, I try to remember the plan.

"I'm so glad I was able to find you," I say, walking toward the table with purpose.

I intentionally ignore her date who I can see is looking from Layna to me with a confused expression.

"Who are you?" he asks.

But I keep my gaze on Layna as if I didn't hear him. "The Reynolds case is a complete disaster," I say. "My computer crashed, and I lost all the work I was doing on that motion. I need your help, or it won't be ready for court tomorrow."

"Is everything okay?" the creep asks.

I glance at him. "Client/attorney privilege," I say with all the haughtiness I can muster. "In other words, none of your business."

I turn back to Layna. "I hate to ruin your Friday night, but the entire case hinges on this."

"Oh, wow," she says, finally getting on board. "I can't believe you didn't have a backup. That was rather careless of you."

I bite back a retort. She's messing with me. I can see the hint of amusement in her eyes. She's lucky I'm not an asshole.

"You know what," I say. "You might be right. Maybe I do have a backup. No need to take you away from your dinner."

"No, no," she says, scrambling from her seat. "I should go with you and make sure you didn't screw it up."

She turns back to her date. "I'm so sorry to cut this short. But you know how hard it is to find good employees these days. You practically need to hold their hand through everything."

I give her a small pinch on the back of her arm, pleased when she flinches the tiniest bit.

He waves a hand. "I understand completely. Can I call you next week?"

"Definitely," Layna says with a smile.

She drops some cash on the table and waves before turning and walking with me to the door.

"Don't look back," I say. "I think he's sniffing your napkin."

A small laugh escapes her as we walk out into the night.

"You're such an ass," she says, but she's grinning.

I shrug. "You like it."

"Your ass?" she leans back to look at it. "It's not bad."

This playful banter is something I worried would be lost after the other day. It's something we've always been good at, and it's one of my favorite parts of our friendship. I'm happy to see I was wrong.

"It's amazing, and you know it," I say, opening the car door for her to climb inside.

I run around to my side and climb inside. A snort of laughter escapes me as I pull out of the parking lot.

"Stop laughing," Layna grumbles from the passenger seat.

I do my best to stifle the laughter I've been battling since I dragged her from the restaurant. It's clear that guy isn't exactly a catch.

"I'm sorry," I say. "I'm trying. It's just so funny."

"Try harder," she says. "I'm glad my suffering amuses you."

I glance over at her as I pull to a stop at a traffic light.

"Oh, come on," I say. "You have to admit, it's a little funny."

She rolls her eyes, but I can see a smile tugging at the corner of her mouth. "Fine. It's a little funny."

"I'm guessing no second date with that guy?" I ask.

"Definitely not," she says. "And what was that shit about a motion? Do you even know what a motion is?"

I shrug. "Nope. But I've seen cop dramas. Some lawyer is always filing a motion to dismiss or an appeal or something."

"Not on a Saturday," she says.

"Good thing your date didn't think about that," I say.

"I guess so," she says, shaking her head. She sighs. "Back to square one."

"What do you mean?" I ask.

"Just that I thought he was a decent guy, and it turns out I was way off base. Now I need to regroup. Why does dating need to be so hard?"

I want to tell her it doesn't need to be so hard. I want to tell her I'm right here and ready to date her. But she's made it clear that's not an option. As her friend, it's up to me to help her. Even if it kills me.

"You should try online dating," I say.

She makes a face before shaking her head. "I don't think so."

"Why not? It's a good way to meet people you wouldn't otherwise meet," I say. "Technically, Piper and Luke met online. And they're getting married soon."

She sighs. "Piper and Luke are a special circumstance. They probably would have met eventually even without the dating site."

I acknowledge this with a dip of my head as the light turns green and I start driving again. "Maybe so. But the dating app sped things along."

She sighs, turning to look out at the night as it passes by her window. "I wouldn't even know what to put on a dating profile."

I perk up. "I can help with that," I say. "We can set it up together and I can help you weed out the duds."

What the hell? What am I saying? Why would I offer to help her find dates? I don't even like the idea of her dating. The fact that tonight's date turned out to be a disaster brings me more happiness than it should. But I can't let her know that. I'm the supportive friend, remember?

"You want to help me find a boyfriend?" The disbelief in her voice is obvious.

"Unless you want to go back to our mutually beneficial relationship," I say, waggling my eyebrows.

She smiles, but it's clear her heart's not in it.

"Just kidding," I say. "I know you said you wanted to find something serious. And since I'm not that guy for you, I figure why not help you out."

"You're serious?"

My immediate reaction is to say, 'Hell no, I don't want to help you find a boyfriend unless that boyfriend is me.' But I can't say that. She's made it clear that I'm not on her list of boyfriend options. I'm not going to set myself up for more rejection by offering again. But helping her find a potential future husband? Can I really do that? Can I not only watch her date someone else, but help her find that someone else?

I think back to the disappointment in her eyes when I'd picked her up at the restaurant and how upset she'd been that this guy had turned out to be a creep. I realize that yes, I can do this for her. If I can help her avoid feeling the way she felt tonight, I'll do it. No matter how much I'll hate it. When it comes to Layna, it seems I can't deny her anything.

"Yeah," I say. "That's what friends are for, right?"

The words feel dry as dust in my mouth, but I force a smile without taking my eyes off the road.

"It's early," I say. "Let's go back to my place and work on your online dating presence. It'll be fun. Plus, having a guy's perspective will help your profile attract more potential dates."

She scoffs. "I think me being female and reasonably attractive will do the job. I've seen how you guys are. You're not at all picky."

I laugh. She's not totally wrong. There are plenty of guys who aren't picky about the women they hook up with. But she's dead wrong about being 'reasonably attractive'. She's fucking gorgeous.

"The kinds of guys you're hoping to attract aren't looking for a casual hookup," I say. "That's the kind of thing I can help you spot. I can weed out the jerks who are just looking to get laid and help you figure out who's looking for something real. Trust me. I'm an expert on this."

She laughs. "Why does that not surprise me?"

"Because you know I'm an excellent judge of character?"

"Or because I know you've been that guy looking for a casual hookup," she says.

I shrug. "You were, too," I remind her.

"True."

"One more thing? You're not reasonably attractive. You're beautiful, Layna. And anyone who doesn't see and appreciate that isn't worth your time."

I don't know why I added that last part. I just couldn't stand the idea of someone as amazing as Layna not having confidence in herself. Maybe I didn't tell her enough when we were still sleeping together, but she deserves to know how gorgeous she is. She deserves to hear it every day.

"Thank you," she says in a soft voice. "That's really sweet of you to say."

I shrug, feeling uncomfortable now. "It's just the truth. You deserve a guy who will tell you every day how amazing you are. Don't settle for less than that."

"Okay," she says. "Let's do it."

I glance over at her to see that she's looking at me. "Yeah?"

She nods. "Yeah. You can be my dating Yoda, or whatever, and help me find Mr. Right. I can't promise I'll take all your advice, but I promise to listen and consider it."

"Fair enough. Ice cream?"

"Like you have to ask."

We stop by Peachy Freeze, the local ice cream parlor, and I go inside while Layna waits in the car. I grab a pint of cookie dough for her and pistachio for myself before hurrying back to the car. I pass her the bag containing the two cartons of ice cream and she peeks inside before smiling.

"What?" I ask.

She shrugs. "Nothing. Just surprised you remembered my favorite flavor."

I roll my eyes as I back out of the parking spot. "I only remember it because one day I'm going to visit you in the hospital after you get salmonella from unbaked cookie dough."

She laughs. "The stuff in ice cream is safe. It's just the homemade dough you shouldn't eat raw. I looked it up."

"Says the woman who eats raw cookie dough by the tube," I mutter. "Of course, you looked it up."

She just shrugs. "If eating cookie dough is wrong, I don't want to be right."

We keep up the banter for the five minutes it takes to drive to my house. When we go inside, Layna takes off her shoes and grabs us some spoons while I go for my laptop. We end up seated on the couch together eating ice cream and laughing as we put together her dating profile. I steal photos of her from Piper's social media to use because she doesn't have photos of herself on her phone that aren't selfies. She tries to argue about some of the wording I use in the bio I write for her, but I ultimately win.

"This is crazy, right?" she asks as she studies the profile we've made.

I shrug. "I don't see why it's crazy. Lots of people use online dating and tons of people find the right person online. What's crazy about it?"

She sighs and ducks her head, not able to meet my gaze.

"Tell me," I say.

"It just feels like I'm trying too hard or something," she says. "Aren't people going to wonder why I can't meet a man on my own? Why I need to resort to an online dating site?"

I ignore the sting of those words. She did meet a man on her own. And she did hit it off with that man. Only she doesn't want to see him that way. And now I'm thinking of myself in the third person. I shake off that train of thought and try to focus on what Layna needs right now.

"Listen," I say. "You're not trying too hard, and no one is going to think that. They're going to think you're a busy professional who's spent the past several years making a career for herself, rather than focusing on romance. And there's nothing wrong with that. There's nothing wrong with you, Layna. Where's the strong, confident woman who bosses me around every chance she gets?"

She laughs and I see a hint of a blush on her cheeks. "That's different."

"I don't think it is," I say. "You're a successful lawyer and a total badass. There's some man out there who wishes he was lucky enough to be with you."

That man is me.

I think the words, but I don't say them. She won't welcome them, I know. No matter what I feel, she's made it clear that we're just friends these days. Which means I also resist the urge to kiss her.

"Thanks, Cole," she says. "You're not bad at the pep talk thing."

I grin. "If I ever need a reference, I know who to call."

"Why are you doing this?" Layna asks, catching me off-guard.

"What do you mean?"

She gestures at the computer. "This. Why are you helping me with a dating profile? Why are you agreeing to be my wing man after..."

She trails off, but I don't need her to finish to know what she was going to say.

"After we spent more than a year giving each other orgasms every chance we could?" I say.

Shaking her head, she rolls her eyes at my choice of words, but I can see she's smiling. Leaning forward, I set the laptop on the coffee table and turn to face her.

"Look, we may have started out just having fun," I say. "But we became friends. And regardless of whether we're still giving each other those amazing orgasms, I want to be here for you when you need me. That's what friends do. Layna, I care about you. I can't just turn that off because we stopped having sex."

She looks at me for a long moment as if searching for something. I shouldn't have added that last part. It was too serious. Too honest. If I'm not careful, she'll see through me. I grin at her and waggle my eyebrows.

"Just because you refuse to see how amazing we could be together, doesn't mean I can let you die alone," I say.

Her mouth drops open, and she shoves my shoulder with a laugh. "Dick! I'm not going to die alone. I'm old, but I'm not decrepit."

I laugh along with her before shaking my head. "You're not old, Layna," I say. "You need to stop getting so hung up on your age. It's not like you're 80. You're barely past 30."

She makes a face. "I'm 33."

I gasp, putting both hands on my cheeks. "Oh, no! Not 33! The horror!"

"I hate you," she mutters, but the corners of her mouth are curved into a smile.

"You're just fishing for compliments," I say. "You secretly love hearing me tell you how young and beautiful and sexy you look. But you aren't getting any of that from me tonight. Save it for your new online boy toys."

She laughs. "I don't want any boy toys. I just want someone who wants what I want."

"What's that?"

She shrugs and looks away from my gaze. "I don't know. A house. A life together. Maybe a kid or two eventually. Or a pet. Hell, I might settle for a needy houseplant at this point. I just want someone who mostly has their shit together and wants to settle down. Someone who doesn't cheat. Someone who's tolerable to look at and is a decent kisser."

I smile at her description, but inside I'm seething. Before I can stop them, the words come out.

"You deserve so much more than that," I say. "You deserve someone who thinks the sun rises and sets in your eyes. You deserve someone who will worship every inch of your body. Someone who tells you every day how lucky they are to have you. Someone who will be beside you through everything life throws at you. Because they want to be there. Because the idea of being anywhere else is physically painful. You deserve the fucking world, Layna. Can't you see that?"

We go still, our eyes locked on one another for a long moment. It's so quiet I can hear my own heart pounding. It would be so easy to lean in and kiss those full lips. I've done it a thousand times. I can see in her eyes that she's thinking it, too. We could pick right back up where we left off. But I know it would just be temporary.

And we'd only end up back where we started. Friends. Reluctantly, I come to my senses and clear my throat, turning to look at the clock on the wall.

"It's getting late," I say. "I think we got a good start on your profile for now."

She nods, turning to glance at the laptop. She smiles as she stands. "Yeah, definitely. I should head home. Thanks for everything, Cole."

I move to stand, to walk her to the door. But she waves me back.

"No, don't get up. I know my way out. I'll text you tomorrow if I think of anything else for the site."

Before I can get my bearings enough to go after her, I hear my front door open and close behind her. She's gone. I know I should go after her and insist on driving her home. Even though her place is a short walk away, I should be a gentleman and take her. But I don't. Because I don't trust myself not to keep saying things I know I shouldn't say.

CHAPTER 12

Present Day
Layna
What was that?

The question repeats itself over and over in my head as I make my way to my apartment. I replay the events of the night, starting with Cole's arrival at the restaurant. Our interaction had felt normal and natural, despite the change in our status. It had been a relief to hear the teasing tone and be able to banter back and forth with him. After everything, I'd been worried I somehow screwed it all up when I ended the physical part of our relationship. But Cole is still the same man I've always known, and that made me happier than I thought possible.

I hadn't expected him to offer to help me find a man, though. It feels wrong, somehow. Yes, we're friends and I know friends help one another with this sort of thing. But after so long spent having sex with him every chance we could, the idea of discussing my dating life with him feels almost unnatural. But he hadn't seemed bothered by the idea. He hadn't backed down from creating my profile on that dating site and he'd even given me pointers. So, why am I so irritated?

And why do I keep replaying his last words over and over in my head as I lie awake in my bed. The intensity of his gaze on me as he'd recited the list of all the things he believes I deserve had stolen my breath. For a moment, I'd wondered if there was more to his words than simply wishing good things for a friend. For a moment, I'd wanted there to be. Which is ridiculous. Cole is Cole. He's not changing his ways anytime soon. He's never given me any hint that he wants to settle down or have a serious relationship. Not that I've given it much thought.

I haven't.

At all.

Not really.

I sigh in the dark. Okay, maybe I've wondered what it would be like. But only once and that was months ago. I've come to my senses since then. And even if I did want to be with Cole that way, it's clear he doesn't want me. If he did, he certainly wouldn't be helping me find someone else. Right? So, regardless of his big speech earlier about not settling for less than I deserve, I know the truth. That was just him being a supportive friend. That's what friends do. They hype one another up. Tonight, he was kind and supportive, and gave my dented ego a much-needed boost, but that's all it was. I'd be a fool to try to read more into his words. He'd even said he's not that guy for me. If that's not a sign that he's not interested, I don't know what is.

I think about Piper and Luke, and I sigh. I've never seen two people more in love. I used to dream of having something like what they have. It took me a long time to realize how unrealistic that is. As a little girl, I grew up believing in fairy tales and happily ever after love stories. But some people aren't meant for the big love story. And that's fine. I'll be happy with someone who respects me and listens to me. Someone who has the same goals in life. I need to stop focusing on what I can't have and go after someone who's attainable. Someone who wants what I want. I may have downplayed my own wants and needs to Cole earlier, but I know the odds of finding what he described are slim to none.

So, I'll settle for someone who makes me reasonably happy and leave the falling in love to my sister. She was meant for the fairy tale life. I was meant for more practical things. Despite all that, I fall asleep to Cole's words repeating in my head.

You deserve someone who thinks the sun rises and sets in your eyes.

It's a nice dream.

CHAPTER 13

Present Day
Layna

"I swear, Piper. He wasn't even the same guy," I say, laughing. "Not even close!"

Harlow who's sitting next to my sister, covers her face to hide her own laughter. "How did you figure it out?"

I narrow my eyes at her. "For starters, the guy online wasn't white! That was a bit of a clue." I pick up my drink to take a sip. "I should have known an Idris Elba lookalike doesn't need a dating app to find a woman."

Harlow and Piper laugh even harder.

"Shut up," I mutter, taking a sip from my mimosa.

The three of us are meeting for brunch today on Peach Fuzz's back patio. It's one of the changes Cole implemented when the outdoor seating area opened. The restaurant is open for brunch on the weekends now. As the only place in town that serves mimosas flights, I think it's safe to say he's got a good thing going here. We didn't invite the guys today and I made Harlow and Piper promise me that no boys would crash our morning. Today is all about the ladies.

Piper holds out her hand. "Pull up his profile," she says. "I need to see. For science."

"His profile is gone," I say. "Serves him right for lying. This man showed up looking more like Danny DeVito than Idris Elba. And I'm not trying to be rude. I'm sure that's someone's type. But it's not mine. And it's not who I thought I was meeting."

They laugh some more at my expense before finally calming enough to talk again.

"What about the other guy?" Harlow asks. "The lawyer?"

I shrug. "I have a date with him next week. But if I get catfished again, I swear to you, I will give up. I'm going to join a convent and become celibate."

Piper rolls her eyes. "You will not. You like sex too much for that."

I laugh, but she's not wrong. All the time I spent sneaking around with Cole is proof of that. Not that they can ever know about that. It's over with now, anyway. They don't even know that Cole is helping me with my online dating. Speaking of, he totally missed the red flags on that last guy. I need to give him shit for that. But he's been accurate about most of the guys I've matched with on the app. Maybe I'll go easy on him. The few dates I've been on in the last month haven't been anywhere near as disastrous as the one with Dillon. I haven't even needed him to bail me out. I count that as a win by itself.

I'm still surprised and happy that Cole and I have managed to maintain a normal friendship after our little fling ended. It's been nice talking and laughing with him without sex hanging over us. Not that I haven't missed the orgasms. I'm only human. I just try not to think about them when he's around. It's easier that way.

"Tell me about this next date," Piper says. "What's he like?"

I take out my phone and pull up his profile on the dating app before handing the phone to my sister. Harlow leans close and they both look at his profile.

"His name is Michael," I say. "He lives in Savannah. He's an attorney at one of the mid-sized legal firms in the city."

"He's cute," Harlow says. "Not my type, exactly."

I laugh. "We all know your type is the strong, silent type with a beard and long hair."

She smiles as she lifts her glass. "Guilty."

"He seems nice," Piper says, handing me back my phone.

"Nice?" I ask. "Why doesn't that sound like a compliment?"

She shrugs. "I'm sure he's great. You won't know until the date, though. So, I'll wait to hear what you think about him."

I eye my sister, wondering why it seems like she has more to say on the subject.

"What aren't you saying?" I ask on an exhale.

She sighs. "Nothing, really. I'm sure this Michael guy is great. I hope he's perfect for you."

"But?" I prompt.

"But I think you've narrowed your sights too much," she says. "All these guys who look great on paper might not have what you need in a partner. You need someone just a little adventurous. Spontaneous. You're so serious all the time. You need someone who can pull you out of your comfort zone every now and then. And no offense, but Michael doesn't exactly scream adventure."

My first instinct is to argue with my sister. I don't need adventure or spontaneity. I need someone safe and secure. I need someone who'll be there for me. Someone comfortable. Why would I want adventure? I'm getting past the age of being whimsical about dating. I need to be more practical. But I don't tell her any of that. Instead, I just nod. That must not be good enough for Piper, because she makes me promise to give it more thought.

"How's work?" Harlow asks, as if sensing I need a change of subject.

I make a face. "Could be better."

"Are you allowed to talk about it?" She asks.

"I just have this client who looks really guilty on paper, but he swears he isn't," I say.

"Isn't that most of your clients?" Piper asks.

"Pretty much," I concede with a nod. "But I don't know. This kid has me convinced he's telling the truth. I don't think he did what they're accusing him of. The problem is I can't find a way to prove it."

"That's hard," Harlow says. "I don't think I could handle that kind of responsibility."

"Me either," Piper agrees.

I laugh. "Most of the time it's paperwork. Very boring. Not life or death."

"Yeah, but if you can't keep someone out of jail, their life could be ruined," Harlow says. "If I screw up my job, the worst thing that happens is they look bad in pictures for a few weeks."

"I don't know about that," Piper says. "I've had some bad haircuts that felt like they might ruin my life."

We all laugh, but Harlow's words hit me harder than I let on. If I can't figure out a way to get the charges dropped against Will, this will stay on his record forever. It'll follow him around anytime he tries to get a job. It could seriously impact the rest of his life. He's just a kid. He deserves more of a chance at a normal life. Especially if he didn't do it. There are times when the weight of responsibility from my job seems to weigh heavier. This is one of them.

CHAPTER 14

Seven months ago

Layna

My face breaks into a smile as I end the call. The radio comes back on as my car registers that I'm no longer on the phone. I take a few breaths as my hands grip the steering wheel. I got the job. It's not that I doubted they'd hire me, but you never know. And my background isn't in criminal law, so it would have been easy for them to dismiss me. But they didn't. I got the job.

I let out a loud screech of excitement and bounce in my seat at the red light, forgetting that I'm in downtown Peach Tree and my windows are down. Coming to my senses, I risk a glance around and see no less than 4 upstanding Peach Tree citizens looking at me like I might have lost my mind. I give a small wave and what I hope is a sedate smile as I close the windows, hoping the tint is dark enough to block their view of me.

But even their judgment can't dim my excitement. I'm finally going to put my law degree to use helping people in a way I haven't been able to since I passed the bar. A sense of fulfillment washes over me as the light turns green and I take my foot off the brake. I think of all the different ways my life has changed for the better since I left Atlanta. For one thing, my stress levels are much lower. Even before getting the call today that I'm officially no longer unemployed, I'd felt less anxiety than when I was working for the biggest firm in Atlanta and making tons of money.

I also think maybe I'm happier here. More relaxed. I know I'm happier living closer to Piper and being able to see her whenever I want. That's a major bonus. But there's something about the small-town life that I hadn't counted on when I moved here. Things move at a different pace. People seem to have more patience for minor inconveniences. Sure, it has its quirks. My eyes stray to the massive monstrosity they call a water tower and I smile. Piper was right. It does grow on you. I drive slowly through town, taking in everything around me, enjoying the autumn leaves on the trees. It really is a gorgeous day.

As I stop to let a mother with a stroller cross the street in front of me, I catch sight of Peach Fuzz to my left. Before I can stop myself, I scan the parking lot for Cole's truck, smiling when I see it. He's been working like crazy lately, trying to get the new outdoor seating area ready for its grand opening. I can't wait to see the place when it's finished. I know Cole is proud of it. On impulse, I flip on my turn signal and pull into the mostly empty lot. It's early enough in the day that the place isn't open yet. But I know some employees will be there getting ready for the coming day.

I don't text or call Cole. I want to catch him off-guard; see him in his natural environment. I'm sure the front door is locked since the restaurant isn't open yet, so I head around the back to where I know the patio is nearly completed. I pull open the gate to the tall privacy fence and enter, closing it behind me. When I turn around, my mouth drops open in surprise.

I don't know what I'd expected, but it's not this. Had I thought it was nearly completed? I can't see anything that doesn't look perfect and ready for the public to enjoy. There's a large wooden deck with plenty of tables and chairs spaced evenly throughout. There's a fully stocked bar at one end of the covered porch. The wide steps lead down to a grassy area with more casual seating scattered around. There's an area for outdoor games off to one side and even two large clay fireplaces for the cooler winter nights that are just around the corner. Looking up, I see lights strung throughout the trees. I try to picture this place at night, lit up and cozy with the fireplaces burning and smiling people scattered around, eating and drinking.

"Wow," I whisper.

"Employees only, counselor," comes Cole's voice from behind me.

My heart in my throat, I spin around to look at him. I know my wonder must show on my face because he grins and holds his hands out to encompass the entire area.

"Well? What do you think?"

I shake my head, gazing around at the area again before turning to look back at him. "Cole, it's amazing. I don't know what I expected. You said it was a patio. But this is an oasis."

He laughs and looks away from my gaze. I can see a faint blush on his face. It's sort of adorable.

"Thanks," he says. "I think it turned out okay."

"Don't start being modest now," I tease. "It's way more than okay."

He smiles, his gaze on mine now. "Thanks, Layna. That means a lot."

"I'm just telling the truth, Cole. You should be so proud of what you've done here."

Cole looks surprised and pleased by my praise that I wonder if he was nervous to show me this place. But that doesn't make sense. I'm sure he's just anxious for the grand opening to go well. He'd be nervous to show anyone this place for the first time. It's not about me.

"I mean, I only helped," he says. "Linc and his guys made it happen."

I shake my head. "There you go again. Being modest. It was your vision. Your plan." I smile up at him. "It's okay to be proud of it. It's your baby."

He laughs, but he's nodding. "Yeah, I guess it is. Thanks."

"Anytime."

He eyes me for a moment. "What made you stop by on this fine autumn morning, counselor?"

I smile at the hope in his voice.

"Actually, I didn't stop by for that," I say. "I've got some big news."

"I love news," he says. "Good news, I hope?"

I nod, smiling. "Yeah. I think so. Remember that job I was trying to get?"

His eyes light up. "With legal aid?"

I nod.

"Did they call you?"

I nod again, my smile growing even wider. "They want me to start in two weeks."

Cole's face lights up with excitement and he throws his arms wide. It's the only warning I get before his arms are locked around me and he's lifting me high into the air, spinning us around.

"Woohoo!" he shouts. "I'm so happy for you! You did it!"

I laugh, unable to do anything but hold onto him as he finally slows to a stop, still holding me against him. Slowly, he lowers me, sliding me down the length of his body until my feet are back on solid ground. My face hurts from laughter as I look up into his face. He looks younger than ever right now, his eyes lit with excitement and happiness. It should be a reminder of all the ways we're different or all the ways we can't really work together. Instead, I've never wanted to kiss him more than I do right now. His face is flushed from excitement. His eyes are locked on mine as he smiles down at me, his arms still holding me close. Time seems to slow to a crawl. I know I should move away. Or say something to lighten the mood. Do something. Anything instead of standing here waiting for this man I can't have to kiss me.

Cole's head lowers toward me, infinitely slow. I have all the time in the world to stop him or to move out of his embrace. But I don't. I just stand there, watching him move closer. Knowing his intent, but unable or unwilling to do anything to stop it. Luckily for both of us, divine intervention appears.

"Have you seen my impact drill?" Linc calls, snapping us out of our trance.

His voice might as well be iced water for the effect it has on me and Cole. We spring apart like two guilty teenagers who just got caught making out at a school dance. I take a deep breath to calm the butterflies in my stomach before turning to look in the direction of Linc's voice. He's not looking in our direction. Instead, he's opening the doors on a massive tool chest and peering inside. After a few seconds, he sighs and closes the chest before turning to look in our direction.

"Cole, I gotta go—oh, hey Layna," he says. "I didn't know you were here."

I smile, taking another small step away from Cole. "Hey Linc. I was just stopping by to see the progress. This place is amazing."

He nods and looks around, smiling. "Yeah. It's really coming together. Not much longer now."

"Layna landed a new job," Cole says. "She was just telling me all about it."

I blush, though I'm not sure why. Cole didn't say anything remotely flirty or sexual. So, why am I acting like a school girl with a crush right now? This is Cole. I've had sex with this man more times than I can count. I've touched, kissed, and licked almost every part of his naked body; and he's done the same to me. There's no reason to be shy around him now.

"That's great, Layna," Linc says, smiling. "Is this the one in Savannah that Harlow mentioned?"

I nod. "Yeah. Public defender with legal aid. I'll be helping people who can't afford legal representation."

He nods. "That sounds awesome. I'm sure there are plenty of people who could use that kind of help." He turns to look at Cole. "I hate to run, but I need to go get my impact drill from the house. I need it to finish installing the sign above the bar. It needs to be up to code before the inspection."

I wave a hand. "I'll let you guys get back to work. I need to go tell Piper the good news anyway. I'll see you later?"

I don't wait for them to do much more than nod before I turn and walk back out the way I came in. I still don't know what that moment was that passed between me and Cole. And I don't know why I stopped here to tell him about my big news before telling my own sister. Why had he been my first thought? Was it just because I was near him when I got the call? That's got to be it. There's no other explanation.

And that moment we had was just about sexual tension. It's been a week since we hooked up. It's clearly affecting my judgment and making me act weird in public where someone might see. That was a close call, too. Luckily Linc hadn't seen Cole holding me that way. I need to talk to him and make it clear that things like that can't happen again. We need to stick to the rules and keep anything physical private.

CHAPTER 15

Present Day
Layna

By the time Friday rolls around, I've had such a long week that I'm almost dreading my date with Michael. Part of me wants to text him to reschedule, but it's too last minute. It would be rude. Besides, I can't find the right partner if I skip out on the dates I get matched with, right? So, I force myself not to cancel. Besides, it's just meeting a guy for drinks after work. With any luck, I'll be home by 8 and in my pajamas in front of the television by 8:15.

I walk into the restaurant on River Street shortly before 6pm, still wearing the clothes I wore to work all day. Part of me wishes I'd had time to change, but it can't be helped. At least I'd touched up my makeup in the bathroom before leaving work. That's good enough, right? I sigh, realizing that if I didn't have this date tonight, I would already be home, relaxing with a glass of wine.

"Layna?"

The voice behind me pulls me out of my thoughts and I paste a smile on my face before turning and looking into the prettiest eyes I've ever seen. They remind me of photos of the ocean from places I've never visited. My gaze tracks over the rest of his face and I take in the charming smile, the dimples, the faint stubble. His photos online had not done him justice.

"Michael?" I ask, giving him my best smile.

He nods and holds out a hand. "Nice to meet you."

I shake his hand, taking a moment to notice how his hand feels against mine. His palm is warm and dry, his skin smooth. His grip is firm, but not too tight. He doesn't linger, releasing my hand after only a few seconds. He motions toward the bar.

"Shall we?"

I smile and turn to walk in that direction, wishing now that I'd brought a change of clothes. I feel rumpled and tired-looking next to this perfectly put-together specimen. It's not just that he's handsome. He exudes confidence without being arrogant.

"I'm glad you were able to make it tonight," he says as we take our seats at the bar.

"Me too," I say.

"It's been a long week," he says. "I think I needed this chance to unwind."

I sigh. "I thought it was just me, but this week feels like it's been a month long."

He laughs. "Agreed."

We study the happy hour menu in silence for a few seconds before he lowers his to the bar top. Turning to look at me, he smiles.

"What?" I ask.

"You're prettier in person," he says.

I open my mouth to respond, but a soft laugh escapes as my face heats in a blush. Unsure how to respond, I mumble something that sounds like 'thank you' and go back to studying the menu. I worked through lunch, so everything I see sounds delicious. But I don't think this gorgeous man wants to see me stuffing fries into my mouth by the fistful on a first date. I wonder what I can order and keep my dignity when it arrives.

"I don't know about you," he says. "But I'm starving."

I laugh. "I was just thinking the same thing. I skipped lunch."

"At least you have an excuse. I ate lunch and I'm still starving. I think anxiety burns calories."

I shake my head. "If that were the case, I'd be a size 2."

His gaze roams over me before coming back up to my face. "That would be a shame."

I feel my face heat again, but before I can form a response, he goes back to studying the menu.

"Right now, I think I could eat one of everything on this menu," he says.

I laugh, but I can't help but agree. It's a small menu with only 5 items, but I know they're all meant to be shared. I think about my sister admonishing me to find someone spontaneous and adventurous. I decide to test Michael to see his response.

"Let's do it," I say.

He studies my face, a questioning smile on his face. "Really?"

I nod. "Why not? We're both hungry. Why deprive ourselves?"

His lips quirk up into a half-smile and his gaze dips to my mouth briefly. I realize my words probably sounded flirty and part of me wants to call them back, but I don't. Isn't that why I'm on this date? Why I joined that stupid dating app in the first place? I wanted to find a match. I won't know if we're compatible unless I show him who I really am.

"Okay," he says, waving the bartender over.

When the cute redhead walks over and smiles at us, Michael points to the menu. "We'll have one of each, please."

She blinks as she tries to decide whether he's joking or not.

"Okay," she says. "Anything to drink?"

Michael orders a beer before turning to me.

"An old fashioned and a water, please," I say.

Nodding the bartender walks over to the computer to put our orders into the system before returning to make our drinks.

"Bourbon, huh?" Michael says. "Impressive. I don't know many women who like the taste."

I shrug. "What can I say? I'm one of a kind."

He smiles. "That, you are."

By the time the plates of appetizers arrive and fill the bar top, I'm convinced I made the right call by not canceling this date. Michael is funny, charming, and witty. The conversation between us never feels forced or stale. And he keeps peppering in compliments about me that I don't hate. We don't manage to finish all the food, but it's a close call. I hold myself to one drink before switching to water. I need to drive home, after all. I notice that Michael does the same. But even after we're finished eating, we linger, talking and laughing until well after happy hour ends. Finally, after the second time the bartender asks us if we'd like to move to a table for dinner, I decide it might be time to wrap things up.

"I should probably get going," I say, my tone making it clear that I don't really want to end the night.

He nods. "Me, too."

He calls for the check and I swear I see the bartender heave a relieved sigh. I reach for my wallet to pay half the bill but he waves me away.

"Nope," he says. "This is on me."

"Are you sure?" I gesture at the numerous plates spread out on the bar.

He just smiles. "Absolutely. Tonight was fun. It's been a long time since I've met a woman who isn't afraid to be herself."

I shake my head. "That's not totally true. There was definitely some fear."

He laughs. "Anything worth doing is a little scary, right?"

I smile as I move to stand. "In the interest of honesty and being myself," I say. "You look better in person, too."

He smiles, shaking his head and I see twin dimples appear. Damn. I'm a sucker for dimples.

"Thank you," he says.

I smile and lean down to kiss his cheek.

"Thanks for a great night," I say before walking toward the exit.

"Layna!"

I turn around at the sound of my name. Michael is standing there, still waiting for his card to be returned to him.

"Can I call you?"

I smile. "I'd be disappointed if you didn't."

His face breaks into a wide smile as I turn and walk from the bar. I somehow manage to wait until I'm back in my car to squeal like a giddy teenager. Michael seems too good to be true, but I can't help the happiness coursing through me. I'd wanted to kiss him, but it didn't feel like the right time. I replay the night in my head as I drive home to Peach Tree, wondering if maybe there's something to that dating app after all. It's too soon to tell, I know. But I'm feeling more hopeful after tonight.

Chapter 16

Cole

I smile at the server as she sets the plates of food on the table in front of us. Layna is seated across from me at a local burger joint just outside of town. It's one of Peach Tree's best-kept secrets. It looks like a dive from the outside, but locals know they've got the best burgers in the county. I can't wait to dig in.

Layna called me this morning to ask if I would meet her for a late lunch this afternoon to talk about her latest date with Michael. I'd tried to get her to give me the info through text or even a phone call, but she'd insisted we meet in person. It's not that I didn't want to see her. I do. In fact, I want to see her too much. All the time, in fact. I think that's part of the problem.

It's been a month since we stopped having sex and I think maybe I'm having withdrawals. It's not that I've never gone for this long without sex before. I have. I've gone for several months at a time in the past with just my hand for company. It's not the sex I miss, exactly. I think it's her. Layna. I can't stop thinking about being with her and mentally reliving all the amazing times we had. Sometimes with the company of my hand. Which is absurd. Our arrangement was a mutual one. We both agreed to the rules. And I hadn't even been upset when she ended things. Not really. So, what's bothering me now?

I've never been this way about a woman. Not even after my college girlfriend broke up with me. And we'd been dating for nearly a year. I even thought I was in love with her. And I still hadn't been as obsessed with her as I am now with Layna. So, why can't I seem to shake the memory of Layna in my bed? Is it just because she's the one who ended things? Is it a pride thing? Maybe it's because she's so clearly moving on without me. Maybe that's what I need to do too. I need to find someone new who can push aside the memory of being with Layna. I roll the idea around in my mind, trying to make it seem more appealing, but it's no use. I don't want to date someone else. I just want things to go back to the way they were before. But I know that's not an option.

Eventually, I push all that from my mind and focus on the reason she asked me here today. Her date. Or, I should say dates. Because she's had several over the past few weeks. None of them has been promising. Granted, none of them had been quite as terrible as her disastrous date with Dillon. I haven't had to rescue her from any of them. But they've mostly been underwhelming. I've listened to her tell me about each one and why things just weren't right. Up until the current guy. The one she went out with for a third time last night. The guy she's technically been dating for two weeks now. Michael. I try and tamp down the annoyance I feel at the thought of him. I don't even know the guy. I'm sure he's perfectly respectable. Otherwise, she wouldn't have gone on a second or third date with him. Right?

"A third date, huh?" I say.

I reach over to snag the pickle off Layna's plate and put it on my own. She hates pickles, but she always gets them anyway so I can have them.

"That sounds serious," I tease.

She rolls her eyes as she grabs a few of my onion rings to add to her plate before offering me some of her fries. This is our normal routine. She can never decide if she wants fries or onion rings with her burger, so I order onion rings, she orders fries, and we share. It's a mutually beneficial meal solution.

"I don't know if I'd call it serious," she says. "But there's potential."

Her words say one thing, but the smile on her face says something else. She looks excited and nervous. I take a bite of my burger and study her for a moment.

"Potential, huh? Is that lawyer talk for you want to bang him?"

She laughs and throws one of her fries at me. "No! It means he's cute. He's nice." She shrugs. "I like him."

Her face goes pink with a faint blush, and I feel a sinking feeling in my chest. I don't know what that blush means, but I know that the few times I've seen it are when I've said something sexual to her. And the first night we met. She'd blushed that night too. So, what does it mean now?

"Like him, huh?" I say, trying to keep my tone normal. "That's a good thing, right?"

She looks thoughtful. "Yeah." She nods. "I think so."

"You think?" I press. "What's that mean?"

She sighs. "It means I'm not sure. He seems perfect on paper. We get along. He's funny and cute. He's a gentleman. But what if all that's fake? What if he turns out to be a jerk? What if I get invested and he doesn't feel the same way about me? This is hard."

She looks so worried and nervous that my heart squeezes in my chest. I hate seeing her so unsure of herself. I'm used to the strong, confident, bold woman who spent more than a year bossing me around every chance she got. I'd be lying if I said I like hearing her wax poetic over another man. It's not an ideal circumstance, but I do my best to overlook that and instead focus on reassuring her. She's my friend and she needs a pep talk.

"That could happen," I say. "There's no guarantee in anything in life. But it could just as easily go the other way. He might turn out to be exactly what you think he is. And he might like you just as much as you like him. You're never going to know unless you give it a shot. Who knows? This guy might turn out to be the one."

The words burn my throat on the way out and I barely manage to utter them without making a face. The one? Seriously? Am I really pushing her to fall in love with another guy? I must be some sort of masochist.

"He is a good kisser," she admits in a low voice.

A rushing sound fills my ears, blocking out the noisy restaurant around me. He kissed her. The son-of-a-bitch kissed her. I try to remember what he looks like from the picture on his dating profile. When the image of his blonde hair and car salesman smile comes to my mind, I immediately envision Layna in his arms, his mouth on hers. The sudden anger that surges through me shocks me. I don't know why I'm angry. Of course, they kissed. People kiss. Especially after three dates. It makes perfect sense. So, why am I so enraged by the idea of it? Hadn't I known she'd kiss someone else eventually? Hell, I've been pushing her to date different men for weeks now. So, why am I so bothered by the idea of her kissing one of them?

Because you never thought she'd really move on without you.

The thought flits through my head briefly and I push it aside. It's ridiculous, anyway. We were never a couple. Of course, she moved on. I not only gave her permission to move on; I encouraged it. I helped her to do it. I have no right to be angry about it now. With a strength of will I didn't know I possessed; I muster up a smile that I hope is believable.

"That's great," I say. "It sounds like things are going well."

She nods, but she still looks unsure. "Yeah. I guess they are."

"Layna, this is a good thing," I say. "This guy seems like he's perfect for you."

I hate the words as they leave my mouth. I hate even more that they might be true. I've always known she would never be mine—not truly. So, why is the realization that I was right hitting me so hard right now?

I force a laugh. "Hey, maybe I should give that app a try. Since it's working so well for everyone I know."

Layna's wide eyes shoot up to meet mine and her mouth drops open. "You want to find a serious girlfriend?"

I shrug. "Maybe. Why not?"

I'd meant it as a joke. A way to steer the conversation away from her and Michael. Because there's no way I'm joining a dating site and trying to find a girlfriend. I don't want to meet someone new. I don't want to learn someone's likes and dislikes or their hopes and dreams. I've already done that. With the woman across the table from me. The realization hits me like a punch to the gut. The reason I can't see myself with another woman is because Layna is the only woman I want. And she's the one I can't have.

Shit.

When did this happen? How did this happen? I mean, I've always liked Layna. That's not a shock. I've always desired her. That didn't go away just because we stopped fooling around. But what I'm feeling right now isn't like or desire. It's a possessive need to claim her as my own. To know that she's mine. Is it just jealousy because she's moving on? Or is it something else? I don't know. And I don't know how to figure it out.

"I didn't think you wanted that," she says.

I shrug. "I didn't think I did either. But people change."

She nods, picking at her fries. "Yeah. I guess they do."

CHAPTER 17

Four Months Ago

Cole

"What about Linc and Ella?" Layna asks, peering over at me from the passenger side of my truck.

"They're at Harlow's shop," I say, pulling to a stop in the driveway. "I told them I had to work tonight."

"You lied to your brother?" she asks.

I unbuckle my seatbelt and shift in my seat to face her. "We're both lying to everyone in this town, remember?"

She sighs, looking torn. "You're sure he won't come home?"

"I'm one hundred percent certain," I say. "We've got at least two hours before he comes home."

She chews her bottom lip and I see her glance up and down the street as if my brother is going to jump out from behind a bush and catch us sneaking into his house. Well, it's technically my house too. But that's only because I moved in here a few years ago and I pay half the expenses. Not that Linc has ever asked me to. But

I wanted to be close to my niece and it was clear Linc needed the help after he split with Ella's mom. Between the two of us, we've done a great job raising that little girl, I think. But it does mean that bringing a girl back to my place hasn't happened in years. This might be the first time I've ever had a girl at this house.

I've been keeping an eye on Ella for the past few days while Linc has been working at Harlow's shop in the evenings. But tonight, I wanted to see Layna. It's been more than a week since I've had her naked, and the need is strong. I know she feels the same way because when I'd texted her dirty messages earlier, she hadn't chastised me like she usually does. She'd responded with a winky face emoji and something that might be a bomb exploding. I'm not totally sure what she meant, but I took it as a positive sign. I'd texted her to go for a jog and I'd pick her up out by the water tower and bring her back to my place. She hadn't balked at meeting me, but now she's hesitating when it comes to going inside my empty house.

"Tick tock," I say, nodding toward the clock on the radio.

She sighs. "Fine," she says. "But if we get caught, I'm kicking your ass."

I grin. "If we get caught, I'll let you bend me over your knee and spank me."

Rolling her eyes, she says, "You'd probably like it too much."

I consider that as we climb out of my truck and head for the front door. "I can't say I've ever been spanked. I've definitely smacked a few asses over the years though."

She points a finger at me. "Don't even think about it."

"Who knows," I say with a smile. "You might like it."

She just laughs.

"That's not a no," I tease.

I unlock the door and motion for Layna to enter first, then follow behind her. Then I turn and lock the door behind me. Even though Linc isn't supposed to be home for 2 more hours, I figure the locked front door will slow him down just a little. On the off chance something happens, and he comes home before I can sneak Layna out, that is. I watch her as she looks around the house, remembering that this is the first time she's ever been here. I wonder what she thinks. Is it what she expected of two bachelors? I like to think Linc and I have decent tastes when it comes to interior design, but I'd be lying if I said this place couldn't use a woman's touch in certain areas.

I watch Layna as she studies the framed pictures on the walls. She stops walking in front of one of them, smiling as she turns to look at me.

"Is this you and Linc?"

I walk over to look at the picture she's talking about, even though I know which one it is. It's a photo of me and Linc when we were kids. We were both gangly boys, all knees and elbows and grass-stained jeans. We'd gone fishing that day and when we came back, we begged our mom to take a photo of our catch. We'd both been so proud.

"Yeah," I say. "That's us."

"How old were you?"

"About 10, I think," I say, trying to remember back to that day.

Linc hadn't hit his growth spurt yet, so I was nearly his height, despite our age difference.

"That's a big fish," Layna says.

I smile at the memory. "Yeah. But I didn't catch it. Linc let me take the credit though."

"Why?"

I sigh. "Because I sucked at fishing. And I'd spent all morning bragging about how I was going to catch the biggest fish in the pond. Only I didn't catch shit. I kept losing my bait. Then I got tangled up on a log and lost my hook. That's when I decided I was finished with fishing for good. I was so mad. But then Linc got a hit on his line. He knew it was a big one. He could feel it. He was so excited, too. But he called me over and let me pull it in. I still don't know why he did it. He wouldn't tell me."

Layna's quiet for several seconds, her gaze locked on the photo.

"I think I know why," she says softly.

"Why?"

Her lips turn up in a hint of a sad smile. "He's your big brother. He's responsible for you."

I look from Layna to the photo and back again. Something about her words make me think she's talking about more than just a fish. I think about the way she and Piper lost their mother so suddenly when she was still just a girl. She'd had to grow up faster than most kids. She'd taken on the responsibility of raising her little sister when she probably still wished she had someone to look after her. I wonder how many sacrifices she made along the way. I'm willing to bet there were plenty, and all of them way more important than a damned fish.

I think about the protectiveness I've seen in Layna's gaze when she looks at her sister and I feel like I understand her a little better now. She's always so tough, so guarded. But it's because she's had to be. She's always had to be the strong one. It can't have been easy, never being able to lean on anyone else for help. I want to tell her she can lean on me, but I know what kind of reaction that would get from her.

"It must have been hard," I finally say. "Being the one who had to take care of it all."

She looks at me, confusion in her eyes.

"After your mom," I say. "That must have been so hard."

She turns back to the photo before she speaks. "It was. And it wasn't."

She reaches out her hand and brushes her fingers over the picture.

"People always act like I did some heroic thing, but I didn't. I just did what anyone would do. She's my sister. She was the only family I had left. Of course, I was going to step up. It didn't matter what I planned to do after high school. It didn't matter that I had scholarships and a class schedule. None of it mattered to me anymore. It's crazy how fast your whole life can change because one drunk idiot decided he was okay to drive home."

I feel a lump in my throat. I'd known the story from Luke, but I've never heard Layna talk about her mother's death. I still don't know all that she went through back then. I doubt I ever will. But I know she's wrong about one thing.

"I do think it's heroic," I say. "You didn't just raise your sister. You raised her to be the amazing woman she is while simultaneously not giving up on your own dreams. You did more than some people ever dream of doing. You should be proud of that."

"Piper is pretty amazing," she concedes.

I notice she doesn't say anything about being proud of herself. I wish I knew why she's so hard on herself. I wish I could convince her of how amazing she is. Before I can figure out what to say, Layna turns to look at me, all traces of sadness gone from her expression. Her expression is teasing now.

"Tick tock, Cole," she says, raising one brow in challenge.

It's clear that she's finished talking about herself and her past. It's too bad. In the past few minutes, I feel like I've learned more about who she is and why than in all the months we've been fooling around. But I can tell she's shutting down that vulnerable part of herself again. I just hope it's not the last I get to see of it. I force myself to smile as I gesture toward the stairs.

"Let's go."

CHAPTER 18

Present Day

Cole

After lunch with Layna, I'm struggling to come to terms with my newfound realizations. I sit in my truck, parked outside the restaurant for nearly an hour after she drives away. What the hell happened? All I know for sure is that I want Layna. And not just in a sexual way. Not just in a 'I wonder what it would be like to date her' way. I want her in the kind of way that has me wondering what our kids will look like. And that terrifies me. I've never thought about kids with anyone before. I've never even thought about a real future with anyone before. But now? It's all I can think about. And I can picture exactly how it would look.

We'd have a dog. Layna's a dog person, for sure. Our house wouldn't need to be too large or ostentatious. She'd want to decorate the house her way, that's for sure. And I'd be happy to let her. I'd be happy to let her direct every aspect of our lives, so long as we spend them together. And kids. She mentioned kids before. I know she wants them. And she'd be an amazing mom. I picture her holding a tiny dark-haired baby in her arms and smiling up at me. *Whoa!* My thoughts screech to a halt in my brain.

What the hell happened during that 45-minute lunch? I barely recognize my own thoughts. Kids? A dog? What the hell? Layna holding a baby? Who am I? I need to try and make sense of what I'm feeling, but my thoughts are a jumble. My brain feels overwhelmed with this new knowledge. I wish I had someone to talk it out with. Someone I trusted to be honest with me about the situation. But the only person who knows I've been having a secret fling with Layna is Layna. And I damned sure can't talk to her about it. Not while she's currently planning a way to ask Michael to be her date for the wedding. Remembering Michael has me grinding my teeth almost painfully.

I could talk to Linc. My brother has always been level-headed and responsible. He'd tell me if I was being stupid or if I was on the verge of ruining my life. He also knows me better than anyone else in the world. I know I promised Layna to keep this secret, but how much does it really matter now? It's over between us. Besides, I need to talk to someone before my head explodes and I run to Layna and beg her to date me or fuck me or just take pity on me and put me out of my misery. Besides, she never needs to know I told Linc. He can keep a secret. If anything, he owes me for keeping his crush on Harlow a secret for a decade. If I ask him not to say anything to Harlow, he won't. It'll piss him off, but he'll keep it quiet.

Before I can change my mind or talk myself out of it, I drive to the house he shares with Harlow. I'm hoping she's not home because I don't have much of a plan for if she is. I don't see her car in the driveway, but that's no guarantee. If she answers the door, I'll just ask to talk to Linc. Maybe I can get him to go for a drive with me. Yeah. That'll work.

When my brother answers my knock on the front door, I sigh in relief.

"Cole," he says, giving me a confused look. "What's up?"

"I need to talk to you," I say, pushing past my brother to get into the house. I look around for Harlow or Ella, but I don't see either of them. "Are you alone?"

Linc just looks at me as he closes the door. "Hello to you, too," he says. "Harlow took Ella out shopping. Why?"

I take a seat on the couch and run a hand through my hair. "Because I screwed up and I need to talk to someone."

He eyes me for a moment, his gaze shifting from confusion at my arrival to calm seriousness in a heartbeat.

"Tell me what happened," he says, taking the chair opposite me.

I blow out a breath, trying to think of how to start this conversation. No matter how I word it, I lied to Linc. For over a year. He's bound to be hurt by that. But I can't keep it to myself anymore. I need advice and my big brother is the one I've always been able to count on when it comes to advice. So, I need to tell him.

"There's a lot you don't know," I say, meeting his gaze.

"So, tell me," he says.

"Layna and I have been fooling around," I say, ripping the bandaid off quickly.

To his credit, Linc doesn't show much reaction to this news beyond a slight widening of his eyes. He also doesn't interrupt with any questions, so I keep talking.

"Well, we were fooling around," I amend. "Until a few weeks ago when she broke things off and said she needed to get serious about her future and try to find Mr. Right." I let the disgust in my voice tell him how I feel about that.

I stand, beginning to pace now as my words come faster. Now that I've started talking, it's like I can't stop. The dam holding it all in has broken and words just come rushing out.

"Because we always agreed it was just friends with benefits, you know? Just fun. Neither of us was ready to settle down, so we were just having a good time in the meantime. Right? Only now, she's dating again. At first, I wasn't bothered by it. Well, not too bothered by it. But now? Now, she's dating this guy and I think it's getting serious. He's a lawyer. Wears fancy suits. Comes from money. He's probably the exact kind of guy she's looking for to settle down with."

"Cole, stop pacing and sit still," Linc says. "You're making me dizzy."

I sigh and sit back down on the couch. He eyes me for a moment before speaking.

"Why does Layna having a boyfriend bother you so much?"

"He's not her boyfriend," I say, automatically rejecting the idea. "They're barely even dating."

"They've been on three dates, and she's kissed him," he says. "And it sounds like date number four is on the way. If he's not her boyfriend yet, he will be soon."

I grumble audibly. He's right, I know. But I don't want to think about that right now. I wave a hand, dismissing his words.

"The title doesn't matter," I say. "I need to know what to do now."

"What do you mean?" he asks.

I roll my eyes. "About Layna. What am I going to do."

"Why do you need to do anything? You said you were just fooling around, right?"

I meet my brother's gaze, unable to answer his question. He looks at me for a long moment and I watch as the confusion clears in his eyes and realization dawns.

"Oh, shit," he whispers.

I nod. "Exactly."

He blinks and gives another shake of his head. "I mean, I always thought maybe you had a crush on her. And now you're telling me you two were fooling around, but I didn't realize it was serious."

I hate the dismissive tone in his voice. As if what I feel for Layna is some childish crush that could be pushed aside or forgotten.

"It's serious," I say. "It started out as just a fling. Friends with benefits. But somewhere along the way, I think I started to fall for her."

"Fall for her?" he repeats. "Like, *fall* for her?"

"Yes," I say, without hesitation.

I don't know when or how it happened, but I can see it so clearly now. I've completely fallen for Layna Brooks. And she doesn't want me.

Linc eyes me for a long, silent moment before dipping his head in a single nod. That's the thing about my brother and me. We might tease one another and sometimes I know I drive him crazy, but he's always there for me when I need him. And right now, I can tell that he's trying to think of the right thing to say.

"How long has this thing between you two been going on?" he asks.

"Since the night we met," I say, feeling a little guilty at the shocked expression on my brother's face.

Linc's eyes go wide, and his mouth drops open in surprise before his brow furrows and I know he's thinking about the past year. He's probably remembering every instance when I acted strangely or left early when we were out together. He's thinking about every time I lied to him about where I was going.

"A year?" he asks. "Wow."

"I'm sorry," I say lamely. Guilt and shame wash over me and I wonder if he feels hurt or betrayed by my deception.

He holds up his hand and shakes his head. "Give me a second."

I sit back, giving my brother the time he needs to piece everything together. After a full minute he turns back to me.

"Let me see if I have all this right," he says. "You and Layna started screwing around the night you first met. You both agreed it would be just sex and no strings attached, right?"

I nod.

"But somewhere along the way, you caught feelings for her," he goes on. "Only now, she wants to end things and find a respectable man to settle down with?"

"Basically," I say.

"And since you were too much of a chicken shit to tell her how you feel, now she's dating some douchebag lawyer who's all wrong for her." He looks at me. "So far, so good?"

I nod again, shooting him a glare for the chicken shit comment.

"Yeah," I mutter.

"And you're sure she doesn't feel the same way about you?" he asks, his voice gentler than before.

I feel a sharp stab of pain in my chest at the words. "I think her having a new boyfriend is pretty compelling evidence."

"I thought you said he wasn't her boyfriend?"

"Shut up."

Linc shakes his head. "I still can't believe you've been sleeping together and hiding it all this time. Wow."

"Sorry," I say again, because it seems like the thing you say when your brother finds out you've been lying to him for more than a year.

"I'm more impressed that you were able to keep a secret like that in this town," he says. "How do you know she doesn't feel the same way?"

"She made it clear early on that we were just fooling around. Nothing serious. It was purely physical." I take a deep breath and say what I've never told anyone else. "I was attracted to her. Obviously. I wanted to be with her in whatever way I could. So, I agreed to her terms, even though a small part of me always wondered if we could be something more. But she lived in Atlanta.

"Then, when she kept coming back to visit Piper, we just kept fooling around. But we were also hanging out, becoming friends. So, then it became friends with benefits. Somewhere along the way, I stopped wanting just the physical. I wanted to be with her for real. I kept thinking if I bided my time and kept showing her that I'm more than just a fuck-boy idiot that she'd eventually feel what I feel. But then she told me she had a date and wanted to end things. And since we made the rule about no hard feelings, I decided to let her go. I didn't think she'd move on this fast."

I laugh, though nothing about this is funny.

"God, I was so fucking stupid. To think she would take me seriously." I drop my head down into my hands and dig my fingers into my hair. "She just wanted to have one last fling before she found the guy she wants to be with forever. I should have known that guy wouldn't be me. No one falls for the fling."

"Cole, stop," Linc says, interrupting my rant. "I want you to answer a question for me."

"What?" I ask, letting my misery seep into my tone as I meet my brother's gaze.

"Are you sure this isn't just infatuation? You've never had a woman turn you down before."

I feel my anger rise. Of course, he'd think that. Cole Prescott, ladies' man. The guy who's never been in a serious relationship. The guy who charms the pants off any woman he wants. Why would that guy be talking about love and settling down with one woman?

I meet my brother's gaze. "Linc, I haven't so much as looked at another woman since the night I met Layna. She's it for me. I can't explain it. I just know it. The way you know Harlow is the one. That certainty? I feel that when I look at her. I look at Layna and I can see it all. Everything that matters is right there in front of me."

Linc shakes his head, but he's smiling. "Wow. Look at my baby brother, all grown up and falling in love."

"Shut up."

He laughs. "I would tease you more, but you're already so miserable it takes the fun out of it."

I want to give him some smartass retort, but he's right. I'm pathetic.

"The thing is," I say, "she wants what I want. I know she does. She told me. She wants to settle down and start a life with someone. Start a family. All of it. She just doesn't think *I'm* capable of it."

"So, show her you are." he says with a shrug.

He says it like it's the simplest thing in the world. Like I haven't been wracking my brain trying to come up with a way to convince Layna to give me a real chance.

"How?" I ask.

My brother grins at me and waggles his eyebrows. "Woo her."

PART TWO

CHAPTER 19

Cole

I don't know how the hell my brother expects me to woo Layna. I've never wooed a woman in my life. I don't know the first fucking thing about trying to get a woman to fall for me. My main strengths have always been my good looks and my charming personality. But I'd always been aiming to get a woman to sleep with me. Not to fall for me. And a woman like Layna doesn't fall easily. If she did, I have a feeling she'd already have done it. Didn't we just spend more than a year making one another come as often as possible? If that didn't work, what else am I supposed to do?

When I'd said this to Linc, he'd laughed and rolled his eyes at me.

"You've got to do more than just give her orgasms," he'd said. "She can get those with a vibrator."

"So, what do I do? You landed Harlow, so you must know something."

He'd laughed at me again. "I think that was just dumb luck on my part. But I'll tell you one thing. In a relationship, all anyone really wants is to feel like they matter to the other person. That means listening. Paying attention to the details. Showing her that you care about what's important to her. Showing up for her when she needs you to."

That conversation took place three days ago and I'm still trying to figure out what I need to do to convince Layna that I'm right for her instead of Mr. Third Date. Linc's advice is solid, but it's also nothing I haven't been doing all along. I've always paid attention to what's happening in Layna's life. I've always tried to be there for her. Hadn't I helped her get out of that date with Dillon, the weirdo? I remember her birthday and her favorite ice cream flavor. Hell, one time she'd asked me to come over for sex and before I got there, she started her period. I'd offered to go buy her tampons. If those aren't the actions of a caring boyfriend, I don't know what is.

So, what do I need to do to convince her? The wedding is this weekend and I'm running out of time to make my move. I'm worried she's going to be all caught up in the romance of Piper and Luke proclaiming their love for one another that she'll do something rash. Like sleep with her new lawyer boyfriend. The thought of it makes me feel sick to my stomach. I know I can't be angry at her for moving on with her life, especially because I never gave her any indication that I wanted to be with her for real. Maybe that's what I need to do. Maybe I need to just tell her how I feel. Spell it out in no uncertain terms.

Just look her in the eyes and say, "Layna, I'm in love with you. What do you say we go on a date?"

I roll my eyes at my own stupid thoughts. I can't do that. Too much has happened between us. She'll think I'm just jealous of her new relationship. I think about Linc's words from the other day and wince. Even my own brother had wondered if I was just bothered by the thought of losing her to someone else. If Linc hadn't believed me, how can I expect Layna to? I can't. So, I need to find a way to show her instead of telling her. Actions speak louder than words, right?

Maybe tonight is my chance. We're all meeting up at Peach Fuzz for one last hangout before the happy couple gets married. It's the place where Layna and I met and the place we first hooked up. That's got to be some kind of good luck symbol, right? It can't hurt to remind her of all the good times we've had at Peach Fuzz. Maybe the memories of the past year will help.

By the time I walk into Peach Fuzz, I'm feeling more nervous than ever. I haven't seen Layna since lunch the other day when I realized I'm in love with her. I'm not sure I know how to act around her now. It seems so ridiculous to try and act normal around her when all I want to do is kiss her. How am I supposed to pretend everything is the same when my whole world is changed?

When Layna walks in, I can't help but stare at her. She's gorgeous, but then I've known that since the night we met. So, why does just looking at her cause an ache in my chest? Why is it so hard to look away from her? Is this what love is supposed to feel like? Because if so, I'm not sure I like it. Or maybe it feels like this because it's one-sided. If I knew she loved me too, I'm sure it wouldn't hurt so much. Right?

I'm nervous as the six of us gather at our usual table, drinks in hand. I take the seat across from Layna, making the numbers even. It also gives me the opportunity to look at her as much as I want. Besides, I don't trust myself to sit next to her. I'm worried I might do something crazy, like give in to my need to kiss her.

"You ready for the big day?" Linc asks Luke.

Luke just smiles and gives Piper an adoring look. "I've been ready to marry her for months. I can't wait."

All three women go gooey at Luke's words, the 'awws' unanimous. Linc and I just smile. Luke's a lucky bastard, being certain that Piper loves him as much as he loves her. Linc, too. He and Harlow are just as sickeningly in love. I lift my glass to my lips and take a deep drink of the dark liquor, welcoming the burn. Maybe if I drink enough of it, it'll replace the ache in my chest.

"I'm happy for you both," Linc says. "Just think, the next time we all meet here, you'll be husband and wife."

Piper smiles and leans her head on Luke's shoulder. He kisses the top of her head. They look so peaceful and happy. I'm shocked by the intense envy that hits me as I watch them. To my right, Harlow and Linc are holding hands. I've never felt more like a fifth wheel than I do right now. My gaze goes to Layna as I wonder if she feels the same, but her expression is unreadable. I know she started dating because she wanted what our friends have; what her sister has. Has she found it already with Michael? Am I too late?

"I can't believe my baby sister is getting married," Layna says.

"I know," Piper says, turning to her sister. "It feels weird to get married before you. Remember when we were kids and we used to imagine our big double wedding?"

They both laugh.

"Don't remind me!" Layna says through her laughter. "We used to spend hours daydreaming about wedding dresses. If I recall, you wanted a massive skirt like a princess. Aren't you glad you grew out of that phase?"

Piper shrugs. "I think I could still pull it off."

"Do I need to make some calls?" Harlow asks. "Last minute wedding dress change?"

"Definitely not!" Piper says, emphatic. "The dress I chose is perfect."

"I can't wait to see you in it," Luke says.

"Seriously," Layna says. "You've got to stop being such a cute couple. It gives the rest of us false hope."

Everyone laughs at her joke, but Piper shakes her head.

"So cynical," she says. "What about Michael? I thought you guys hit it off?"

"We did," Layna says. "We're taking it slow, but I really like him. It's too soon to know for sure though."

I clench my jaw against the urge to say something rude. Linc glances in my direction and I can see he's trying to judge my mood. After the other day and my big confession, he's got to know how much this conversation is eating at me. I ignore him and take another sip of my drink as the three women talk about Michael and how successful he is, how smart and funny, how great his smile is.

"Taking it slow is good," Linc says as soon as there's a lull in the women's conversation.

When they all turn to look at him with questions in their gazes, he shrugs.

"I mean, it's good to get to know a person before you rush into a relationship. Right?"

Harlow looks at him with a raised brow. "You mean for 20 years or so?"

His expression turns sheepish. "Maybe not quite that long," he mutters.

Harlow smiles and shakes her head. "Don't listen to him. If you like Michael, you should see where it goes."

She winks at Layna. "Find out if you're compatible. In all areas."

I pick up my glass and down the rest of the bourbon in one gulp before standing.

"I'm getting another round," I say, walking toward the bar before waiting for a reply from anyone.

There's no way I can sit at that table and listen to Layna's best friend and her sister tell her she should sleep with Michael to see if they're compatible. It's not like I'm a prude. I'm a reformed man-whore, after all. I'm the last person to judge someone for who they have sex with. Layna wasn't a virgin when we met and I never asked her about who she was with before me. It didn't matter. But that was before. Before I fell for her. The idea of her sleeping with someone else now makes me want to punch something. Or throw up. Or drink another glass of liquor. Though I know none of those things will change what Layna does or doesn't do. There's only one thing I can do that might have an influence on what she does. But I can't bring myself to say the words. I can't bear to hear her reject me. And I don't know why she wouldn't.

"You okay?" Linc asks from beside me. "You've been pretty quiet."

I hadn't noticed him until he spoke. I should have figured he'd follow me. He's the only one at that table who knows how I feel about Layna. He's the only one I can talk to about this.

"Not really," I say.

"You should just tell her," he says. "Get it out there. See what happens."

I shake my head. "What if she doesn't feel the same way?"

He shrugs. "So, what? At least you know you tried. You put yourself out there. You can't control what she feels. But if you never tell her, then she's going into a relationship with someone she might not really want because she doesn't have all the facts."

I think about his words. I appreciate my brother trying to be optimistic, but I think his opinion is biased by the fact that I'm his brother. Not to mention the fact that he's in a happy relationship and there's no question his girl loves him.

"Maybe you're right," I say. "But if you're not, it's going to make Luke's wedding awkward. I don't want to be responsible for that."

"So, wait until after the wedding," Linc says. "But don't wait too long. You deserve to be happy, too."

I smile. "Thanks, Linc. You know I'm happy for you and Harlow, right?"

He grins. "I know. She's amazing."

I nod. "Yeah. She's too good for you."

He laughs. "That's why I'm going to marry her before she figures it out."

Shock slams into me and I turn to stare at my brother, eyes wide. "Seriously?"

He nods, his smile wide. "I bought a ring last week. I'm taking her for a surprise trip after the wedding. Mom's keeping Ella for me."

"Holy shit!"

"I know," he agrees. "Be cool though because no one else knows. I want to surprise her."

"I can keep a secret," I say. "Trust me."

"I didn't think you could before our little talk the other day," he says. "Shocked the hell out of me."

"Wait," I say. "Were you not going to tell me because you thought I wouldn't be able to keep it to myself?"

He laughs. "Maybe."

"Dick."

"I'm kidding," he laughs. "I was always going to tell you. You're going to be the best man, after all."

I smile at my brother. "I'm honored." Something else occurs to me and I hold up a hand. "Wait, did you tell Mom? Since she's keeping Ella?"

He shakes his head. "No. But I think she suspects. She got all weepy when I asked her if Ella could stay with her for a week."

"She knows," I say. "She always knows."

"How does she do that?" Linc asks.

The bartender puts the last of the drinks on the bar in front of me and I smile my thanks.

"No idea. It's sorcery," I say.

Linc and I gather up the drinks and head back toward the table where they others are still laughing and talking.

"Thanks," I say before we get too close to the others.

"For what?" he asks.

"Talking me out of my funk. Reminding me to stop wallowing. This is a happy night and me being mopey is just going to ruin it."

Linc smiles. "Anytime."

When we return to the table and hand out the drinks, it's clear the others have carried on the conversation about Michael and Layna in my absence. Not that I'm complaining. I'm glad I missed it. I can see that Layna looks a little tense. She's probably tired of being the center of attention. I know her well enough to know she hates that.

"Well, Cole," Piper says. "That just leaves you."

My gaze shoots to hers, questioning.

"Just leaves me for what?" I ask, unsure of what she's talking about.

"You're the only one still single," she clarifies.

A laugh escapes me and I roll my eyes.

"He likes it that way," Luke says. "Right, Cole?"

I shrug, suddenly uncomfortable. I look around and see that Piper, Luke, Harlow, and Linc are all looking at me for an answer. Layna looks like she's trying not to laugh as she sips her drink. Traitor. But now I think I know how Layna felt just a few minutes ago, being grilled about Michael. Since when does everyone need to know about everyone else's dating lives? Just because the four of them are happily matched up doesn't mean everyone around them needs a partner immediately.

I shrug. "I like my life, sure," I say. "But that doesn't mean I'd turn down the right woman. I don't want to be single forever. I'm keeping my eyes open."

I force myself not to look directly at Layna as I say the last part.

"*You* want to settle down?" Luke asks, disbelief evident in his tone.

I laugh. "Is it that hard to believe that I'd want to find the right woman and get married some day? You make it sound like I've sworn off marriage or something."

"Well, no," Luke says, backtracking. "That's not what I meant. It's just that you're younger than the rest of us. You've never acted interested in marriage and kids, all that stuff."

I roll my eyes, feeling slightly annoyed. "Just because the subject never came up doesn't mean that I haven't thought about it. I don't want to be single forever. Look, it's not like I'm rushing to the altar tomorrow or anything. But yeah. If I found the right girl, the one who makes me feel that spark or whatever it is, I'd be happy to settle down and get married. I want kids one day. I want the whole thing. The only reason you guys didn't know that about me is because you never asked. You always assumed I was happy to keep being a man-whore forever. But lately I've been thinking it's time to grow up. Get serious about my future."

My gaze goes around the table, glancing at each person in turn. Harlow and Piper are both smiling, but they look like they're two seconds away from a chorus of 'awws' followed by tears. Luke's eyes are wide with surprise, but he's wearing a delighted grin. Linc is the only one who doesn't look shocked. But then he knew I felt this way for a while. And Layna? Layna looks absolutely stunned by my little speech.

Her eyes are wide, and her mouth is slightly open as she looks at me like she's never seen me before. She's still as she holds my gaze for several long moments, neither of us looking away. I don't know what she sees when she looks at me, but something between us feels like it's shifted slightly. Or maybe I'm seeing what I want to see.

"Well," Luke says, forcing me to pull my gaze from Layna's and back to him. He raises his glass in a toast. "On that note, here's to the future. Whatever it holds for each of us, may it be filled with all the happiness and love we can stand."

We all raise our glasses to his toast before drinking. And because I want to more than anything, I actively avoid looking at Layna. Instead, for the rest of the night, I do my best not to let my feelings for her overshadow the celebratory atmosphere. It helps that Michael's name doesn't come up again. The six of us talk and laugh and drink until late into the night, and it feels like old times.

When Linc pulls Harlow out onto the dance floor to dance to some old country song he requested, it doesn't take Luke and Piper long to follow them. Normally, this is where I'd ask Layna to dance. Or to meet me in my office for a quickie. But that was before. I wonder if she'd dance with me if I asked her. Or would that be too weird after all we've been through?

"Come on," Layna says, holding her hand out to me. "We're not going to sit here like the only single losers at the table. Dance with me."

I smile at her tone. It's the same as it's always been. So bossy and sure of herself. It's one of the things I've always loved about her. Standing, I reach out and take her hand.

"Just let me lead this time?" I tease.

"Not a chance," she says.

I know it's a mistake as soon as my hands go to her waist and she leans in close to me. Her hands travel up my chest to rest on my shoulders. The move is flirty and teasing, reminding me of the way things used to be. She inches closer to me as we dance, her body eventually brushing mine as we move. I'm not sure what's happening right now. We've never danced this close before, and we've definitely never touched this way in front of the others.

I know she's been drinking. We both have. I'm nowhere near drunk, but she just might be. I should put more space between us. I know I should. But I've been dreaming of holding her like this since I realized what I feel for her. So, I don't move away from her body. And when she moves even closer, I allow that too. I smooth my hands up her back, the memory of her body still lingering in my fingertips, even after all these weeks of not touching her. I feel as much as hear her sigh in my arms.

"I've missed this," she whispers.

My heart trips in my chest at her words. Does she mean dancing? Or does she mean me? My arms around her? The closeness of our bodies? I want to ask, but I can't seem to find the nerve.

"Me, too," I say, instead.

"I'm glad I didn't lose you, Cole," she whispers.

Is she drunk? Is that what this is? Is this just alcohol talking? Will she even remember this tomorrow? I find myself hoping she does. My heart is pounding so fast as I try to decide what to say. It's not quite a confession, but I try to let the emotion I feel pour into my voice as I speak.

"You could never lose me, Layna. I'm right here. Always."

She leans even closer, her head lowering to my shoulder as we barely sway to the music. I hold her close, allowing myself this one moment to pretend she's mine.

"I knew that last drink was too much."

I look up to see Piper and Luke standing beside us, both looking at Layna with amusement. Piper shakes her head at her sister and I smile sheepishly and shrug.

"I'm not that drunk," Layna says.

I can hear the way her speech is just a little slower than normal and her words lack their usual crispness. Yep. She's drunk.

"Come on," Piper says, reaching for her sister. "We'll drive you home."

Layna raises her head from my shoulder and smiles up at me. She's adorably drunk right now, but I doubt she'll appreciate that in the morning. I smile back, hoping her hangover isn't too brutal tomorrow.

"Your smile's nice," she says, her words slurring a little. "Iss my favorite."

"Thanks," I say, smiling down at her. My voice is gentle when I say, "Time to go home, counselor."

She makes a face before releasing me and turns to put her arm around Piper's shoulders.

"Fine," she grumbles.

I huff out a low laugh as I watch them walk toward the exit, Layna leaning heavily on Piper. Luke turns to me and smiles.

"Thanks for a great night," he says. "See you in Savannah tomorrow?"

I nod, returning the smile. "I'll be a little later. I've got to help with the dinner rush."

He nods before grinning and bouncing a little on his feet. "Dude, I'm getting married!"

His voice is giddy like a kid the night before his birthday. I can't help but laugh as he grabs me and pulls me to him in a back-slapping hug.

"You okay to drive?" I ask, wondering at his odd behavior.

He just laughs. "I only had one beer. I'm high on life."

I make a face. "I can't believe you just uttered those words. Who are you?"

Luke just smiles. "I'm a man in love."

"Get out of my bar and take your future sister-in-law home before she pukes in your car."

Luke's smile falters. "Shit," he says before hurrying toward the exit.

I laugh as I watch him go, shaking my head at my best friend. Who would have thought Luke would be the first of us to tie the knot? Most people probably would have bet on Linc. He's the most steadfast one; the quiet, serious one. But instead, it's Luke. Weird how life works out.

Harlow and Linc depart soon after, their arms wrapped around one another. That just leaves me standing alone in the crowded restaurant thinking about the two minutes I'd held Layna close to me and hoping it won't be the last time I get to do it.

CHAPTER 20

Layna

I wake to a pounding headache and the worst case of dry mouth I've ever had. Why the hell did I drink so much last night? Why did Piper let me? I manage to sit up on the side of my bed without the world spinning around me, so I know it could be worse. I think back over last night, wondering if I did or said anything to make an ass of myself.

I remember talking with the girls about wedding stuff. Someone brought up Michael and everyone seemed to have an opinion on my dating life, which had led to me finishing my first two drinks far faster than I should have. Then Cole had returned with another round of drinks and someone had asked him about his dating life. I remember the way his dark eyes had gone serious and he'd talked about finding the right woman. He'd even said he'd be happy to settle down and get married. My immediate reaction to that had been shock followed by a longing so intense it had nearly knocked the breath out of me. That's when I'd started drinking in earnest.

I don't remember if I ate any of the food Cole ordered from the kitchen. I know for a fact I didn't drink enough water. That explains the headache. I can't remember doing or saying anything embarrassing, though. That's a plus. Try as I might, I can't seem to forget the way Cole looked at me after his big speech. His gaze had lingered on mine for far longer than necessary.

I make my way to the bathroom to brush my teeth and swallow some ibuprofen for my headache. I wish I could stay in bed all day, but today is the day we're all leaving for Savannah for the start of the wedding festivities. No matter how shitty I feel, I need to pull it together for Piper. I walk back into my room to check my phone and see there are a bunch of texts. The first is from Piper.

How's your head? Drink lots of water and rest up this morning because we have a big weekend planned. Love you.

I smile as I type out a quick reply.

I'm alive. Barely. See you at the hotel. Love you.

The next message is from Cole. At the sight of his name, a flash of memory from last night comes back to me in a rush. His arms around me, my head on his shoulder, his hands smoothing up my back as we'd swayed to an old love song. Something in my chest twists at the memory of how right it felt to be held by him. But I know that was just nostalgia for all the times we spent together. That's all it can be, right? It's just because the last time I danced with Cole was back when we were still sleeping together. Of course, it would bring back those feelings. That's all it was. That, and the bourbon. That's

all. I click to read his message and immediately wish I
hadn't.

*Good morning, counselor. I hope you're feeling okay
after last night. If not, here's a photo of your favorite
smile to help you feel better.*

He'd added a smiling selfie, dimples included. Damn
it. Had I really told him his smile was my favorite? What
the fuck? He's never going to let that go. I study the
photo for another moment, annoyed at how handsome
he is. I send him a middle finger emoji and move on.
Before I can click the next message, he replies.

*That's no way to treat the owner of your favorite
smile. But since you're not feeling like yourself today, I'll
forgive you.*

I decide not to respond. It will only encourage him to
keep it up. The next message is from Michael. When I
click the message and read it, my eyes go wide.

"No," I whisper, scrolling higher up in the thread. "No,
no, no, no, no. Fuck!"

There's a message sent from me to him at 11:45pm last
night inviting him to Savannah for my sister's wedding.
What the fuck? I vaguely remember the decision to text
him, but I can't believe I invited him to Piper's wedding.
No more bourbon, ever. It's clearly some kind of poison
sent from Hell to encourage me to ruin my life. I don't
even know how I feel about Michael. I'm definitely not
ready to have him at a family function where stress levels
are already going to be high. I look back to the phone,
reading his response again.

*I'd love to, but I can't stay for the whole weekend. I'm
going to visit my parents Saturday, but I can come to the
rehearsal Friday night.*

What the hell? I'd invited him not only to the wedding but for the entire weekend. Does he think I wanted him to share my hotel room? I read over my drunk texts again, trying to see them as he would.

Hey, cutie! I was thinking if you don't have anything to do this weekend, you could spend it with me at my sister's wedding celebration. I'll be in Savannah all weekend, living it up! Would love to see you there! Bye!

Drunk me sure likes her exclamation points. I'm impressed by my drunk typing skills, to be honest. I guess even when I'm drunk, I hate bad punctuation. I sigh, dropping the phone to the bed. At least he's only coming for one day. I can handle one day. It's not that big of a deal. It's just another place setting at the rehearsal dinner. I'm sure Piper won't mind. On that note, I pick up my phone to call her. She answers on the second ring.

"Happy wedding weekend!" I say in a cheery voice that doesn't match how I feel.

"You sound better than I thought you would," she says.

"Oh, I feel like shit," I admit with a laugh. "But I have a little issue I need to discuss with you."

"Oh god!" Piper's voice is panicked. "Did something happen to the dress? Please tell me you didn't puke on it last night?"

I laugh. "Your dress is fine, Pipes. Calm down."

"Oh, thank god," she breathes. "Whatever it is, I can handle it. Just not that."

"I'm glad you said that," I say. "Because last night, in my drunken state, I managed to text Michael and invite him to your wedding."

There's a moment of quiet before she breaks out laughing. It's so loud I need to move the phone away from my ear because it's making my head hurt more. I wait for her laughter to die down, rubbing my temples with one hand. When she finally quiets, I bring the phone back to my ear.

"Did you get it all out of your system?" I ask in a dry voice.

"Maybe," she says, humor still evident in her voice. "No guarantees. What happened to taking it slow?"

"I don't know, Piper. Maybe someone should have taken my phone from me."

"Oh, no," she says. "You're a grown ass woman. You're not blaming anyone else for your drunk texts."

I sigh. "I know." The misery in my voice isn't exaggerated.

"What did he say?"

"Hold on," I say. "I'll send the screenshot."

I quickly screenshot my text thread with Michael and send it to my sister.

"Got it," she says. "Hang on while I read."

After a few seconds she speaks again.

"Okay, this isn't that bad," she says. "I thought it was going to be super embarrassing. But this doesn't even seem like a drunk text."

"Really?"

"Layna, you didn't even miss a capital letter," she says. "The exclamation points are a bit much, but you just seem excited."

"Ugh," I groan. "He's going to think I'm crazy."

Piper laughs. "He's not going to think that. He's going to think you wanted to spend more time with him. That's a good thing."

"I guess," I mutter.

"You do want to spend more time with him, right?" she asks.

"Yeah," I say. "I mean, not at your wedding though. I'm going to be busy all weekend. I don't think I'm going to have a lot of time to spend with him."

"Then it's a good thing he's only coming for the rehearsal," Piper says.

"About that," I say. "Is it going to be an issue? Adding another person to the dinner?"

"No," she says. "We've got the entire restaurant, remember? It'll be fine. Stop stressing."

I sigh, feeling marginally better. My headache is also starting to fade.

"Thanks, Piper," I say.

"No problem," she says. "Look at it this way, you'll get to see how Michael does around your friends and family. The ultimate test to see if he's boyfriend material."

I laugh. "Maybe you're right."

"Of course, I am," she says. "I can't wait to meet him."

"You will soon enough," I say. "I'll see you later this afternoon."

"Get some rest," she says. "You sound like shit."

"You're supposed to be the sweet sister," I mutter.

"Love you!" she calls in a cheery voice, ignoring me.

"Love you, too," I say before ending the call.

By the time I leave to make the drive to Savannah, I'm feeling much more human. Just showering and eating breakfast helped. I'm still tired, but I'm just happy the headache is gone. My car is loaded with clothes, shoes and a million random things I worried Piper might need this weekend. Though I'm not even sure what she might need. I may have over-packed, but I'd rather have something and not need it than need something and realize it's back at home in Peach Tree.

Hannah, Piper's wedding coordinator, will meet us at the hotel later today. Tomorrow, we have the rehearsal followed by the rehearsal dinner. Saturday morning, I planned a girls-only bridal brunch with all of Piper's girlfriends. Harlow has some kind of top-secret event planned for just the three of us. She wouldn't even tell me what it is, even though it's not my wedding. The bachelorette party will follow that. Then Piper and Luke will get married on Sunday afternoon. It's going to be a busy few days, but I just hope Piper enjoys every second. She deserves to be happy.

When I arrive at the hotel in Savannah later that afternoon, I find the hotel lobby filled with barely organized chaos. I see Piper and Luke amid a large group of strangers. Since Luke is holding a baby on his hip and a petite, dark-haired woman is smiling at the two of them, I figure this must be his sister Mya and his niece. A tall, extremely handsome man is standing next to Mya with his arm protectively around her shoulders. I stand near the door as a valet unloads the massive amount of luggage from my car and I take in the crowd of people. I see Piper hugging a woman with honey-blonde hair, both of them smiling. I've never met this group of people, but I know who they are from hearing my sister and Luke talk about them.

Even if I didn't know this was the King family, it would be obvious they're related. I recognize Van's twin right away. They have the same face and the same dark hair, the same height and build. But that's where the similarities end. Van lacks the long hair and colorful tattoos his brother has. His name is Wyatt, if I remember correctly. There's something slightly disreputable about him that Van doesn't seem to have.

"You get used to the chaos," says a woman's voice from beside me.

Surprised, I turn to see a pretty woman with light brown skin and a wide smile standing there. Beside her is a red-haired woman with pale skin and a mischievous grin.

"Let me know when that happens," the red head says drily. "I was born into it that chaos, and I'm still not used to it."

"Ignore Claire," the first woman says. "I'm Quinn King. You must be Layna?"

I shake the offered hand. "How did you know?"

She laughs. "You look just like your sister."

I smile, pleased by that fact.

"I'm Claire," the red-haired woman says, smiling. "It's nice to meet you."

"You, too," I say. "I've heard a lot about you. All of you."

Claire rolls her eyes. "It's all exaggerated, I promise."

Just then, a boy runs up to Claire and skids to a halt beside her.

"Aunt Claire!" he practically shouts. "There's a pool. With a slide. Can we swim later?"

Claire laughs. "If it's okay with your mom," she says.

"Will you come with me?"

The eager excitement in his voice makes me smile. It's clear this kid loves his aunt.

"Sure," she says, ruffling his hair. Leaning down, she says in low voice, "But only if you stop running in the lobby of this nice hotel like a heathen child from the sticks."

He gives her a sheepish smile. "Yes, ma'am."

The boy walks over to where Piper is standing and starts talking animatedly to the blonde woman who I'm assuming is his mother. Which must make her Hannah. The wedding coordinator. As I look around the room and try to match Piper's description of Luke's extended family with the faces of the strangers before me, I find myself overwhelmed.

"That was Liam," Claire says. "His mom is Hannah."

I nod, looking around at all the people talking and laughing. Coming from a small family, it's a little overwhelming to be surrounded by this many people who are all family.

"How do you keep them all straight?" I say, turning back to Quinn.

She laughs. "It's easy once you get to know them. Finn is the responsible one." She points to the tall, dark-haired man in the button-down shirt and slacks who's standing near Hannah.

"Then there are the twins," she says, pointing to Van first and then Wyatt who's got his arm around a short, dark-haired woman in a pretty sundress.

"They might look like total opposites, but they're practically inseparable," Quinn says.

"I'm surprised they didn't find a set of twins to marry," Claire jokes.

"They settled for two best friends," Quinn says, laughing.

"That just leaves Ronan," Claire says. "The grumpy one."

"Hey!" Quinn says. "That's my husband you're talking about."

Claire eyes her. "Was I telling any lies?"

Quinn rolls her eyes. "He's not grumpy. He's just quiet."

"Hmm," Claire says.

I follow Quinn's gaze to the two men standing near the registration desk. One of them is unmistakably a King. He's got the same nearly black hair and muscular build. A baby with matching dark hair is asleep on his left shoulder, his thumb tucked into his mouth. The man beside him has a stockier build and sandy brown hair. He's got several tattoos on his arms, disappearing under the sleeves of his t-shirt.

"And that's Garrett," Claire says, nodding at the man standing with her brother. "My fiancé."

"Congratulations," I say, smiling at her.

She grins. "Thanks. He's pretty great."

The two men turn as one and I watch Ronan's eyes search the room. Something about his gaze is intimidating. I see what Claire meant when she called him the grumpy one. But when Ronan's gaze lands on Quinn, his entire demeanor shifts. He doesn't smile, but something in his face seems to relax and his eyes soften when he sees her. Even if I didn't know these two people were married, their connection is obvious for anyone to see. When Ronan reaches us, he leans down to give his wife a quick kiss before turning to look at me, a small smile on his lips.

"Ronan, this is Layna, Piper's sister," Quinn says.

His smile widens just a little and he offers me his free hand.

"Nice to meet you, Layna," he says.

"And this is Garrett," she adds.

"Nice to meet you both," I say.

Garrett shakes my hand before wrapping an arm around Claire who leans into his embrace.

"We should get him upstairs," Ronan says, nodding toward the sleeping baby in his arms.

Quinn nods. "Before he wakes up hungry and cranky," she agrees. Turning to me, she smiles. "Layna, it was nice meeting you. Let's find time to hang out for coffee or a drink or something this weekend?"

I nod, smiling. "I'd love that."

"Count me in!" Claire says.

Slowly, the lobby begins to empty enough for me to make my way to the desk to check in. I didn't get a chance to talk to my sister before she and Luke disappeared upstairs, but I'll have plenty of time with her in the next couple of days. For now, I can't wait to get to my room and relax before the celebration starts in full.

CHAPTER 21

Cole

I can't believe she invited him. I know she said she was going to, but I'm still surprised she did it. I also can't believe he accepted. Who brings a date to her sister's rehearsal dinner when she barely knows the guy? And what kind of man agrees to come to something like that after only a couple of weeks of dating? Aren't these things usually reserved for the wedding party and immediate family? I'm not sure if that's true or not, but it feels true. I make a mental note to look it up later.

Not that it matters. *Michael* is still here. Seated next to Layna. Where I should be. Where I could have been if I'd taken Linc's advice and been less of a chicken shit and just told Layna how I felt. Or, she could have turned me down and this would be the world's most awkward rehearsal dinner. I eat my steak in silence while I debate whether that would be better or worse than my current circumstances. Layna laughs at something Michael says and I grind my teeth. This is worse.

After my arrival last night, I'd gone to my room and crashed early. This morning I met my brother and Harlow for breakfast before going for a walk along the riverfront. The city is beautiful this time of year. It's early spring and the flowers are starting to bloom. The oppressive heat and humidity of summer hasn't started up yet and the summertime vacation crowds haven't descended on the city yet.

The ceremony rehearsal had gone perfectly. It hadn't been overly serious with Linc and me cracking jokes to keep the mood light. It hadn't stopped Layna from getting teary-eyed at seeing her sister and Luke standing at the altar, gazing into each other's eyes. Hell, I even felt myself getting a little emotional. Not that I'd let anyone see it. That would threaten to ruin my image.

Now, we're at the rehearsal dinner in the hotel's restaurant. It's closed for our event, but the dining room is filled with people since Luke wanted his entire extended family to join us. I'm glad for the distraction because I'm currently seated at a table with the entire wedding party—plus *Michael*. Why the hell had she invited him? I try to remember if she'd told us about this last night, but I don't remember her mentioning it. Maybe it came up while I was at the bar getting us drinks? Either way, seeing him with his arm around Layna earlier had come as a complete shock. Then I'd had to smile and shake his hand when I secretly wanted to punch his smug face.

He shook my hand and smiled when Layna introduced me as Luke's best friend. Not that she could have introduced me as anything else. What was she supposed to say? "This is Cole, my former orgasm buddy? But don't worry, that's all in the past." I stifle a laugh as I picture his reaction to that. It would wipe the smile off his face, I'm sure.

"Michael, did you grow up in Georgia?" Piper asks, making me grind my teeth in irritation.

She's clearly just trying to be nice to her sister's new *friend*. I refuse to think of him as her boyfriend. They've only been dating for a few weeks. It's too soon for labels like that, right? I didn't hear her introduce him as her boyfriend. But they certainly seem cozy. Too cozy for people who've only been dating a few weeks. I wonder if they're sleeping together. As soon as the thought enters my mind, I push it out. The last thing I need to do is picture Layna with someone else that way. Besides, I tell myself, it's not my business. No matter how I feel about Layna, she made it clear that she doesn't see me that way.

"Near Macon," Michael answers, nodding. "My family still lives there."

"Do you come from a big family?" Harlow asks from the other side of the table.

He nods again, and I saw into my steak with more force than needed.

"I'm the oldest of three brothers," he says. "One is in college in South Carolina and the other just got into medical school."

"Your parents must be so proud," Piper says. "A doctor and a lawyer in the family!"

He chuckles. "They sure are."

I chew my steak without tasting it, trying to focus on anything but Layna's successful lawyer *friend* bragging about his successful family. I'm sure owning a restaurant isn't considered successful in the eyes of someone like him. I briefly wonder if Layna feels the same way. But no. She's not like that. She's never been anything but supportive of Peach Fuzz.

I know she walked away from a successful career as a corporate lawyer in Atlanta, but she's never acted like she's better than anyone in Peach Tree. She's also never made a big deal about her career or her title. If anything, she downplays how amazing she is at her job. Besides, she brags about her sister's coffee shop every chance she gets. It's obvious how proud she is of Piper.

I know it's just my own insecurity making me think things like that. And jealousy. I'm man enough to admit I'm jealous of Michael spending time with Layna. I'm jealous of the fact that he gets to sit near her. I'm jealous of him getting to touch her and put his arms around her. I'm jealous of the fact that she's offering him a bite of pasta off her plate. I look away before I can watch him eat from her fork. There are some things that can't be unseen.

My mind goes back to last night and the way Layna had rested her head on my shoulder. The way she'd sighed as she relaxed her body against mine. The way she said she missed me. The intensity of the longing for her hits me like a punch to the gut and I can't take anymore. Maybe I could use a little fresh air. I smile over at Harlow who's seated across the table from me and excuse myself to use the restroom. I don't actually need to go. I just can't sit here, and watch Layna fall for this guy. Maybe when I get back, it'll be time for dessert, which will be that much closer to this awkward dinner ending.

I stand and turn to walk toward the back of the room where the restrooms are located. I do my best not to look in Layna's direction as I approach her. But I can't seem to help myself. I'm a glutton for punishment, I guess. When I'm almost directly behind her chair, I see Michael hold up his fork for her to taste a bite of his food. What the hell? Now she's sharing eating utensils with the guy? That's not very hygienic. I watch as she leans in, mouth open. That's when I see what's on the fork.

My heart stops and I hear a dull roar in my ears. I don't think. I react before I can speak, reaching out and slapping the fork and its contents out of Michael's hand and away from Layna's open mouth. Every eye in the room turns to me, but I barely notice. I'm focused solely on Layna. I drop to my knees and grab her face, turning her startled gaze to mine.

"Did you eat any of it? Did any of it touch you? How's your breathing?"

"Dude, what the hell?" Michael says, turning an angry glare at me.

I ignore him, along with all the other people at the table who are now staring at me and talking over one another.

"Where's your EpiPen?" I ask, reaching for Layna's purse. "It's in the outside pocket, right?"

I find the pen and hold it up before going back to assessing her. She seems to be breathing okay. She looks a little pale and her eyes are wide, but she doesn't seem to be in distress. I don't see any hives either. It's just beginning to dawn on me that I may have overreacted when she puts her hand on mine to steady it. I hadn't even realized my hands were shaking.

"I'm okay," she says softly.

"The stir fry," I say. "It's made with oyster sauce. Your allergy."

I can barely get the words out. My throat is still clogged with the terror of what could have happened. Ever since Layna told me about her shellfish allergy not long after we met, I've been so careful to make sure it's never around. The kitchen staff at Peach Fuzz has had extensive training on cross-contamination because I've made sure they know that's a mistake I won't forgive. I watch as Layna shakes her head and gives me a small smile. There's some emotion in her eyes that I don't quite recognize.

"It's okay," she says. "Hannah made sure to tell the kitchen to omit anything with shellfish or mollusks. The stir fry tonight isn't made with oyster sauce. It's safe. I'm fine. I promise."

The sudden relief I feel pushes through my terror, and I let out a sigh before pulling in a deep breath. My eyes close for a moment as I think about what could have happened. I don't want to imagine it. I can't. It's too much.

Following quickly on the heels of my relief is a rush of embarrassment and the realization that I may have slightly overreacted. I risk a glance around the table and see that all eyes are still on me. I feel my face go red and hot as I realize the disruption I just caused. Layna was never in any danger. I just caused a massive scene at my best friend's rehearsal dinner for no reason.

"I'm sorry," I whisper to Layna before moving to my feet.

Turning to Michael, I give him a tight smile. "I apologize for my outburst."

He gives me a stiff nod but doesn't return the smile. It's just as well. I don't think he and I are going to be best friends anytime soon. Or ever. Turning to the rest of the table, I give them a sheepish look.

"I apologize for the disruption," I say. Turning to Piper, I say, "Please forgive me for causing a scene."

She shakes her head and waves away my apology. "No need to apologize. You were just looking out for my sister. I'm grateful for that." She smiles. "Besides, it'll be a funny story to tell later."

Everyone at the table laughs and the awkwardness of the moment is broken. I even join in the laughter for a moment. Everyone slowly resumes eating their meal, and a server quietly removes the splatter of food in the center of the white tablecloth. After thanking Piper for her understanding, I excuse myself to continue to the restroom. I don't look back at Layna on my way out of the dining room.

CHAPTER 22

Layna

I watch Cole as he leaves, the tension still visible in the set of his shoulders. I want to go after him and make sure he's okay, but something makes me hesitate. Then Michael says my name, pulling my attention back to dinner and the people around me. I look over at him and see that he's holding my EpiPen in his hand.

"I think he dropped this," Michael says.

I remember Cole dropping it when he'd let out that sigh of—what was that? Was it relief? I can't be sure, but I think it might have been. I take the pen from Michael and slip it back into the outer pocket of my purse where it lives. I haven't needed to use one in years, but I make sure I've always got one with me, just in case. I've got another one in my car and one in my house. Piper even keeps one in her purse in case we're ever out together and I need it.

My mind goes back to Cole and the way he'd held my face in his hands, his eyes wide with panic. I've never seen him look so scared. If I didn't know better, I'd say the look in his eyes before he realized I was okay was one of sheer terror. But that's crazy, right? Cole and I are friends and yes, he knows about my allergy. He knows how serious it can be, but his reaction seemed a little over-the-top.

"I forgot you were allergic to shrimp," Michael says, pulling me back to the present. "I didn't realize it was so serious."

I give a dismissive wave of my hand and smile at him. "No harm done," I say.

I told Michael about my allergy on our first date. I hadn't wanted him to be caught unaware if something happened while we were together. No matter how careful I am about screening what I eat, accidents can happen. But I know for a fact I'd told him that it was an anaphylactic allergic reaction. It's not something I'd fail to mention. But he'd clearly forgotten. Or maybe he'd assumed I was being dramatic. Either way, I find myself slightly hurt that he forgot. It seems like one of those things someone who's dating you would commit to memory.

I try to push aside the slight hurt and focus on enjoying the rest of my meal. My heartrate has finally returned to normal and the conversation around us has resumed. My eyes keep straying to the small stain in the center of the table where the bite of food had landed after Cole knocked it away. I know the scene probably seemed ridiculous to everyone else. And I'm sure Piper was right about it being a funny story later. But I can't stop seeing the look on Cole's ashen face as he'd studied me, verifying that I was truly unharmed. I can't stop feeling like I should have done something more to calm him before he walked out.

My gaze goes to his still-empty chair and his half-eaten steak as I listen to Michael talk about his job to Linc who's seated on his other side. I can't imagine Linc is enjoying the conversation, but he's doing his best to keep up his side of things. How long has Cole been gone? Surely, it's been long enough for him to be back by now. I glance toward the hallway where the restrooms are located. I don't see him walking back this way. After another few minutes of pushing the food around on my plate, I can't take it anymore. Lowering my fork, I smile over at Michael and whisper to him that I'm going to the restroom. He smiles and nods at me before going back to talking to Linc. Satisfied that he won't miss my company while I'm gone, I stand and make my way to the back of the room and the hallway that leads to the restrooms.

I know the restaurant is closed for our private event tonight, but I'm still cautious of running into someone as I loiter around the men's room, waiting for Cole to emerge. When another five minutes pass with no sign of him, I check to see if the coast is clear. Then, I pull open the men's room door and dart inside. I quickly scan the room, making sure it's empty before walking further inside. I've never been in a men's restroom before. It's cleaner than I assumed it would be. Granted, this is an upscale restaurant in Savannah, not a college frat house. But still.

Now that I think of it, I've always heard that women's public restrooms are dirtier than men's. I wonder why people say that. I only have this one bathroom to compare, but so far, I don't see much difference.

Shaking my head at my musings, I return my focus to finding Cole. It doesn't take me long to realize that he's not in here. The bathroom is totally empty. Disappointment settles inside me as I walk to the exit. I don't know why I came looking for him or what I hoped to find, but it's clearly not meant to happen. I reach for the door, but before I can push it open, it swings inward catching me by surprise.

A startled sound escapes me as Luke stands before me, blinking in surprise to find his fiancé's sister in the men's bathroom. He opens his mouth to speak but seems to think better of it. Instead, he just shakes his head and holds the door open for me to exit. I give him a gracious nod and say nothing as I walk past him and back into the empty hallway. I'm curious as to why he thinks I was in the men's bathroom, but I think I'll let this one go for now.

I look back toward the dining area where I know everyone is still eating and laughing. I know I should go back. Back to my date and my sister and our friends. But Cole's chair is still empty. I can't relax and enjoy the night until I know he's okay. Making a quick decision, I turn and begin walking in the opposite direction. I don't know where this hallway leads, but I'm hoping it will lead me to wherever Cole disappeared to. I don't stop to think about why I need to find him or why that look on his face is still etched on my memory. I just need to make sure he's okay. That's what friends do, right?

I don't pass anyone else as I walk down the dimly lit hallway. I don't know if Cole is even down this way. He may have taken a different route back to the dining room. He's had plenty of time to go back by now. But I keep walking, hoping I'll find him. The truth is, I don't want to go back to my seat next to Michael and listen while he drones on about his job and his fancy condo in Atlanta. I feel guilty because I want to be there for my sister, but it's becoming more clear that my drunken text inviting Michael to the wedding was a mistake. It's becoming more and more obvious that he and I aren't going to work. On paper, it seemed like he was the perfect match for me, but now I'm starting to doubt that. He fits all the things I wanted in a man back when I lived in Atlanta and worked in corporate law. But now? Living in Peach Tree? I'm not sure what I want. But I don't think it's him.

The hallway abruptly ends in a set of French doors, and I come to a stop. I cup my hands over my eyes and lean close to the glass, trying to see out. The night outside is dark and makes it impossible to see anything but inky black. Pulling back, I hesitate for a moment. What if Cole isn't out here? What if this is a fire exit and I set off the alarm by opening the door? But I don't see any signage indicating that. What if someone else is out here trying to enjoy a private moment on the balcony? I don't want to interrupt some lovers' tryst.

But I do want to find Cole and make sure he's okay. Isn't that the whole reason I came out here? I can't turn back now. That thought is enough to make me reach for the door handle. As the door opens, I peer out, trying to quickly ascertain if anyone is on the balcony—hopefully without interrupting a make out session. But a pair of broad shoulders dominate my view. I follow them as they taper down to a lean waist and long legs. It's Cole. He's got his back to me, bent forward as he rests his hands on the balcony railing, his head falling forward, but I'd know that tall, lean frame anywhere.

He doesn't move as I step out onto the balcony and quietly close the door behind me. I stand there frozen, trying to decide what to say. I had the whole walk down the hallway to figure out what to say to him, but now that I'm standing here with him, my mind is blank. It takes me several seconds to work up the nerve to say his name. At the sound of my voice, Cole's head jerks upward and he turns to face me. His eyes are wide, and he looks more lost than I've ever seen him. I feel an ache in my chest at the sight of him. I don't know what's going through his mind, but I know I want to be here for him. I take a step closer to where he stands with his back against the railing.

"Layna," he says, his voice low and rough. He clears his throat and speaks again. "What's up? Is everything okay?"

I nod. "I came to find you," I say gently. "I wanted to make sure you were okay. You looked upset. Before, I mean."

He shakes his head, not meeting my gaze. "I'm fine."

I take another step closer until I'm standing directly in front of him. "Are you sure?" I ask. "You don't seem fine."

A faint laugh escapes him, and he shakes his head. "I'm sure. I'm a little embarrassed, but it's nothing I can't handle. I just needed a minute alone."

"Oh," I say, taking a step back.

Of course, he wanted some time to himself. And I tracked him down and invaded his space. I feel like an idiot. I shouldn't be here.

"I'm sorry," I say. "I'll leave you to it."

"No, Layna. Wait." He grabs my arm and I turn back to face him. "You don't need to go. That's not what I meant."

I look down at his hand on my arm and back up to his face. He's cast in shadows, and I can't quite make out his expression, but there's something intense about the way he's looking at me. I know I should pull away from him and go back inside. I should go back to my date and my sister and dinner. Instead, I take a step closer to him. His grip on my arm eases and I feel his thumb lightly stroke the skin of my arm. The memory of last night's dance flits through my mind, of him holding me close for those brief minutes, of his arms around me and his hands smoothing up my back. I'm shocked by the longing I feel at the memory.

"I want you here," he says with a ghost of a smile.

"Why?"

He studies my face for a long moment, his hand still on my arm. It takes him a long time to speak and when he does, I'm surprised by his words.

"You scared me," he whispers.

The pain in his voice brings back the memory of his terror-stricken face as he'd knelt before me, digging through my purse to find my EpiPen. It's clear that for that brief moment he'd been convinced something horrible was happening to me and the idea terrified him.

"I didn't mean to," I whisper.

"Layna," he whispers. "If anything had happened to you..."

His words trail off, but I see that hint of fear in his eyes again as he pulls in a shaky breath. I don't know what any of this means and I'm not sure I want to find out. I'm not

sure I'm ready for whatever emotion is behind his eyes.
I put a hand on his chest, right over his heart, trying to
reassure him that I'm here and I'm whole.

"It didn't," I say, my voice stronger than before. "I'm
okay."

He nods. "But for just a second, I thought..."

He swallows hard as if the words are too painful to
speak. His gaze lingers on mine, and I find that I can't
look away. And I don't want to. There's an ache behind
my breastbone that seems to be growing stronger with
every moment we stand here. I don't know what I'm
feeling right now, but something about the moment feels
charged, almost dangerous.

"Cole," I whisper. "I should go."

He draws in another shaky breath and nods, but I can't
seem to make my feet move to walk away. The moment
spins out between us for several long seconds with
both of us frozen, our gazes locked. I know that every
moment I stand here brings us closer to something we
won't be able to take back. This doesn't feel like all the
times we've touched before. This feels like something
bigger. Something that I'm not sure I'll recover from.

"You should," he whispers, his hand still on my upper
arm.

My eyes drift down to his lips, and I remember the
precise way they feel against my own. I can easily
conjure up the memory of his taste. Without meaning to,
I find myself leaning closer to his warm body. It would
be so easy to kiss him. So easy to close the distance
between us and claim his mouth with mine. And no one
would ever know. It could be another secret we keep
from the rest of the world. I can almost feel his lips on

mine as he dips his head lower. Anticipation coils low in my belly, and I let my hand slide higher on his chest. I don't know if I mean to push him away or pull him closer. But it doesn't matter. I don't get the chance. The door opens behind me, causing Cole and me to spring back from one another. I feel heat creep up my face and neck as I look over and see Linc standing in the open door. His knowing gaze darts back and forth between his brother and me before settling on Cole.

"Am I interrupting?" he asks, his voice carefully neutral.

I paste on a bright smile. "Not at all. I just ran into your brother out here and we were about to come back to the party."

I don't dare look over at Cole. I'm afraid I'll see that expression of longing on his face and I'm not sure I can withstand it a second time. Even with his brother standing here, I'm worried I might throw myself at him. I want to kiss him that much. I want his arms around me, his body against mine. I don't know what's wrong with me. Until I walked out onto this balcony to see him standing there looking so lost, I'd been convinced that I did the right thing by ending things with Cole and trying to move on with my life. But everything that happened tonight has me questioning all my decisions regarding the man standing next to me.

I don't let any of that turmoil show on my face though. I'll spend time unpacking it all later. For now, I need to get back to my sister and my date and try to act normal for the rest of this disastrous dinner. Not to mention, I have a bridal party brunch and a bachelorette party to attend tomorrow.

"Michael was looking for you," Linc says, turning his gaze on me.

Nothing in his tone conveys how he feels about finding me out here with his brother, but I feel guilt burn through me just the same. Not that we'd been doing anything wrong. Not yet anyway. If Linc showed up a few seconds later, we might have. Who am I kidding? I was a millisecond away from kissing Cole when Linc opened that door. He might have just saved us from doing something we'd both regret later.

I smile. "Right. I'll just go find him then. I'll see you both in there?"

I don't wait for an answer as I duck around Linc and walk back inside, closing the door behind me. I take several deep breaths as I make my way back down the hallway to the dining room. I need to look as normal as possible when I go back in. Which means I can't be covered in a head-to-toe blush.

I dart into the women's restroom at the last second and I'm relieved to find it empty. Standing at the sink, I look over my reflection in the mirror. My eyes look brighter than usual and there's still a faint blush on my cheeks, but I don't think anyone will notice the subtle change to my appearance. I take several deep breaths and release them slowly, trying to ease my still racing heart. I bring my hand up, running a finger over my bottom lip. Now that the moment has passed, I can't deny the truth. And that's that there's a part of me that wishes Linc had been a few seconds later with his interruption. It's the same part of me that misses Cole's lips on mine and his arms around me. And I'm starting to worry that it's a feeling that might never go away.

CHAPTER 23

Cole

"Do I want to know?" Linc asks after the door closes behind Layna.

I stand there, staring at the closed door as I fight against the urge to go after her. We'd been moments away from kissing when Linc showed up. I know it. I close my hand into a fist as the memory of touching her arm for those few seconds lingers. I don't know whether to be grateful or angry for my brother's interruption, but judging by the way Layna practically ran back inside to find Michael, I can guess how she feels about it. I shake my head in answer to my Linc's question and turn back to the railing, looking out at the night.

"Nothing happened," I say dismissively.

"Never said it did," he says.

"Your face did," I say.

Linc comes to stand next to me and puts a hand on my shoulder. "You okay?"

I sigh. "Yeah," I say with a nod.

"Are you sure? Because that scene in the dining room tells a different story."

I shrug, trying to sound dismissive. "I overreacted. That's all."

"Hell of an overreaction. You slapped food out of a man's hand."

My lips twitch in amusement. I hadn't seen the look on Michael's face since my focus was solely on Layna, but I can imagine it was a funny sight. I don't regret what I did, even if it was an overreaction on my part.

"Just a misunderstanding," I say, hoping he'll let it go.

He sighs. "Cole, look at me."

I hesitate before turning to face my brother's knowing look. "What?"

"I'm worried about you," he says. "I've never seen you that way."

I roll my eyes and huff out a laugh. "Making an ass of myself? I think you've seen that plenty."

"Don't do that," he says, his voice more serious. "Don't brush it off like it was nothing. Cole, you were terrified that something had happened to Layna."

I shrug. "I was concerned. Is that a crime?"

"You might be able to play that off to everyone else," he says. "But not to me. I know you better than that. So, talk to me."

My grip tightens on the railing until it's almost painful, but I can't let go. Right now, it feels like the lifeline tethering me here. If I let go, I might do something crazy, like run after Layna and kiss her. Or kick her idiot date out of the dinner party. Linc is still waiting for me to speak, but I don't know how to tell him something I can't explain to myself. I grit my teeth against the words I can't say out loud. As if saying them aloud will somehow make them truer. Or more able to hurt me. It's ridiculous, and I know it. But I can't say it. Because tonight, when I thought I could lose her, my whole world seemed to stop. Everything I ever thought I cared about disappeared. Everything but her. And I knew the truth. I don't want to live in a world where she doesn't exist. Even if she isn't with me.

When I don't say anything, Linc speaks.

"Are you in love with her?"

Linc's words cut through my thoughts, silencing them. Of all the things I'd expected him to say, that's not one of them. He's my brother. My best friend, and the one person who knows me better than I know myself. I may have kept mine and Layna's affair from him, but I can't lie to him about something this big. Before I can answer though, Linc dips his head in a single nod.

"I thought so," he says simply. "Then you can't give up on her."

"I'm not giving up," I say. "I'm admitting defeat. There's a difference."

"Not when it comes to love," he says. "Cole, listen to me. I've seen you have flings before. I've seen you have casual hookups. I've even seen you with a serious girlfriend."

"What's your point?" I ask. Does he think reminding me of my sordid past is supposed to convince me I'm good enough to be with Layna?

"My point is that in all that time, I've never seen you in love. Not once. Until now. You can't give up on that."

I give a humorless laugh. "She's dating someone else."

Linc waves a dismissive hand. "It won't last. They're not a good fit. Besides, that guy is boring. Layna needs someone who's more fun. Adventurous. Exciting."

"Someone like me?" I ask sarcastically.

"Not someone *like* you," he says. "She needs *you*. You just need to show her that."

He puts an arm around my shoulder and steers me back toward the doors leading inside.

I sigh. "I don't know how."

"Lucky for you, I know a thing or two about stubborn women," he says, opening the door and leading me inside.

"Let me give you some advice, little brother."

CHAPTER 24

Layna

As I leave the bathroom, I'm calling myself ten different kinds of fool for that scene on the balcony. I shouldn't have gone after Cole. I don't know what I was thinking. It was obvious he was upset. Coupled with my own confused emotions, we were bound to end up... what? Looking into each other's eyes? Almost kissing? I don't even know what that was. The further I get from that balcony and that moment, the less real it all feels. I don't know what to think or feel anymore when it comes to Cole.

I still consider him one of my closest friends. But I've never felt drawn to him the way I'd been on that balcony. Not in all the time we've spent together. Not even while we were in the middle of the best sex of my life. Something shifted between us tonight. Somewhere between Michael holding up that fork to me and Linc interrupting us on the balcony, something changed between me and Cole. And I'm not sure how I feel about it. Part of me wants to ignore it. Pretend it never happened and go back to being friends. But another part of me wonders about this achy feeling in my chest that seems to grow larger with every step I take away from him. What if it means something? Do I want it to mean something? What if it's one-sided?

But then I remember the look in his eyes when he realized I was okay. The way he'd looked at me when I'd found him on the balcony. I've never seen that look in his eyes before. What if he's feeling the same way? What if he's just as confused as I am? I fight the urge to turn around and walk back to him. I can't. Not tonight.

"There you are! I can call off the search party."

I don't know why I'm surprised that Michael is hovering just outside the dining room. He's smiling, but there's a look of mild concern in his eyes.

I force a smile. "No need for that. I just went for some fresh air. The dining room is just so full of people that I needed a moment."

If he has any concerns about my story, he doesn't show it.

"I can understand that," he says. "Feeling better?"

I nod. "Much."

He gestures back toward the dining room that looks mostly the same as I'd left it minutes earlier. I immediately see that Linc's and Cole's chairs are both still empty. I do my best not to stare at Cole's empty chair as I take my seat. Looking up, I can see Piper eyeing me with concern, but I wave it away with a smile. I'm not sure she buys it, but she gives me an answering smile before going back to her dessert. I pick up my own fork, prepared to pretend to enjoy my tiramisu, but I've lost my appetite.

I try to focus on the chatter around me, joining in conversations when appropriate, but my gaze keeps straying to Cole's empty chair on the other side of the table. Where is he? He should have been back by now. I covertly glance down the table toward Harlow and see that Linc is back in his seat beside her. He meets my gaze with one raised eyebrow. Unsure what his expression is meant to convey, I give him a tentative smile. Before I can decipher Linc's strange expression further, I feel Michael's hand on my arm. I find myself slightly annoyed by the interruption, but I force a smile onto my face as I turn back to face him.

He leans in close to my ear. "Would you like to take a walk after dinner? I heard the grounds are lovely."

They are lovely. I'm the one who told him that. They're beautiful. During the day. At night, they're just darkened pathways barely lit by dim lights. You can't see any of the gorgeous flowers at night and there will be no butterflies or hummingbirds darting around. There's not much point to going for a walk out there at night. Unless he's inviting me on a walk as a romantic gesture. Is that what he's doing? I almost heave an exasperated sigh.

It would be a sweet gesture if I were interested in him that way. Earlier tonight, I'd thought for sure I was. But that was before I'd seen that look in Cole's eyes. Before the balcony. Now? Now, I don't know what I feel. But I know that whatever it is, it's not about Michael. As guilty as I feel about that, I know I'd feel even worse if I led him on. I need to end things with him. As soon as possible.

"That's a good idea," I say. "It'll give us time alone to talk."

He smiles. "Exactly."

When dinner finally ends and everyone splits up to go their separate ways, I follow Michael out into the gardens. They're dark, as I'd expected them to be. I hope he isn't bringing me out here for some kind of sexy make-out session. I'm not in the mood for that tonight, even if the thought of kissing Michael didn't feel totally wrong right now.

He reaches out to take my hand in his, lacing our fingers together. I look down at our joined hands. Even this feels wrong. I glance over at the man walking beside me, guilt rushing through me. I might be confused when it comes to what I feel for Cole, but I know one thing for certain. I don't feel anything for Michael. It's not fair for me to keep stringing him along this way.

My steps slow to a halt and he turns to give me a curious look.

"Everything okay?"

I sigh. "Yes. And no. I don't know."

He smiles, but there's confusion in his eyes. Not that I blame him. I'm being as clear as mud right now.

"We need to talk," I say.

He nods. "Okay."

"You're a great guy," I say, trying to let him down easy. "But I think maybe we should put this on pause for a little while."

He looks confused as I untangle my fingers from his.

"I just don't think I'm in the right place to be dating anyone right now," I say, falling back on a classic breakup excuse I used in college. "I thought I was, but I don't think I am. My life is a little stressful and I have a lot going on with work."

Michael turns to me, a faint smile on his lips. "I understand," he says.

I blink in surprise. "You do?"

He nods. "Of course. Layna, I like you. But we've only been dating for a few weeks. It's not that serious. But if you change your mind, you know where I'll be."

I nod. "I do. Thank you for being so nice about this."

He lifts one shoulder in a shrug. "No point in being an ass about it."

"You'd be surprised how many people don't feel that way."

We make our way back inside and walk together through the lobby. I expect him to leave me at the elevator on his way to the exit, but he lingers there beside me as I wait. The silence between us is slightly awkward. Finally, I smile at him.

"I hope you had a nice night," I say. "Before the walk, I mean."

He nods. "I did."

He holds out his arms for a hug and relief goes through me. He's finally getting the hint that I'm ready for him to leave. His arms come around me and I give his back a couple of friendly pats, wondering why this hug seems to be going on for far too long. I pat his back once more, hoping he'll get the hint. Finally, he releases me and slowly eases away.

The kiss catches me completely off-guard. I'd assumed we were on the same page after our talk in the garden. But it seems I was mistaken because as I'd been preparing to tell him goodbye, he was plotting a way to kiss me. I didn't think anything of the hug. Lots of people hug goodbye, especially when they aren't sure they'll see the other person again. I just thought it meant we were parting on good terms. Right up until his lips landed on mine.

My first reaction is shock. His arms are banded tightly around me, holding me against his body. The second reaction is aversion. Up until an hour ago I'd been considering taking our relationship to the next level. And it's not like it's the first time he's kissed me. Each time has been pleasant, and I even felt a hint of desire for him. This is the first time I haven't wanted him to kiss me. And I know the reason. Cole. My hands go to Michael's chest, intending to push him away. A deep voice breaks through my thoughts.

"Excuse me."

I'd know that voice anywhere. It sends a little thrill through me, even as I wish a pit would open and swallow me whole. Regaining my senses, I break off the kiss and try to put some space between Michael and myself. Turning, I see Cole standing a few feet away, his gaze not on me but on something behind me. I take another step back from Michael, unable to look at him.

That's when I realize the elevator door is open behind me and Cole is waiting to enter. Michael and I had been blocking the doors with our little kissing session. My face flames red as I wonder how long we'd been standing there. How must it have looked to Cole? He wouldn't have been able to see that I wasn't a willing participant in that kiss. It's not like I pushed Michael away immediately, after all. From his point of view, I'd been making out with my date before he left me for the evening.

Shit.

The last thing I want is for Cole or Michael to get the wrong idea. *And just what is the right idea, Layna?* I don't know the answer to that question. I need some time and space to think things over. I need to figure out what I'm feeling. And I damned sure can't do it while these two men are standing here looking at me. One looks like he can't wait to kiss me again and the other looks like he wants to hit something. All these thoughts run through my head in the few seconds it takes for Cole to decide he's tired of waiting for us to move out of his way. And my shell-shocked brain is just a little too slow to remember how to make my legs function so that I can stop blocking the freaking elevator.

Instead of walking around me and Michael, Cole opts to walk directly between us. It's rude, but then so is standing in front of the hotel's only elevator and having a make-out session. As Cole turns sideways to pass between us, he shifts to face me. His large body is so close that I can smell his familiar scent. I can see the flecks of gold in his dark eyes as they lock on mine. There's a heat and possessiveness in his gaze that I know I've never seen before. Time seems to slow to a crawl. I forget about everything but his nearness as I fight the urge to reach for him. His mouth curves up into a half-smirk as he brushes past me. Then, he's in the elevator and pressing the button. I can't help but watch him disappear as the doors close.

My heart is pounding, and I know my face is still flushed. But this time it's not from embarrassment. It's not even from the kiss with Michael. It's from whatever the hell I just felt when Cole passed so close to me. The urge to go after him is so intense it's shocking. As many times as he and I have had sex, you'd think I'd have grown immune to his nearness. And I had. Or so I thought. But that was before the scene at dinner earlier. Before whatever that shift was between us. Before the balcony. The sound of Michael clearing his throat brings me back to the present and I remember that he's still standing there.

Double shit.

I turn and give him a questioning look.

"What was that?"

He grins sheepishly. "I just wanted to give you something to think about. Just in case you were on the fence about me." He winks. "Goodnight Layna."

Then he turns and walks away. I watch him until he exits the hotel lobby, wondering how the hell I got myself into this predicament. I'd laugh at the situation if Cole hadn't just seen that kiss. Not that it matters. Cole and I aren't a couple. As far as he knows, I'm still dating Michael. So, it doesn't matter if he saw us kissing.

But later, when I lie awake in my empty bed, it's not Michael I can't stop thinking about. It's not the kiss we shared that consumes my thoughts. It's that two seconds of almost contact I had with Cole before he got on the elevator. It's the way he'd smirked as if he'd known exactly what I'd been thinking. It's every dirty, wicked thing he's ever done to make my body sing. And knowing that I want him to do all of them again.

CHAPTER 25

Layna

The next morning, I'm exhausted after a night of fitful sleep and dreams where Cole kept appearing and disappearing only to reappear, just out of reach. Each time I'd reach for him, he'd shoot me that knowing smirk before vanishing again. I woke up equal parts frustrated and horny with no more understanding of what I want than I'd had last night.

I spend a solid hour getting ready for Piper's bridal brunch. Half of that time is spent on my makeup where I try to hide the evidence of my exhaustion. I'm not sure I succeed, because Piper eyes me with concern when I meet her at the elevator so we can go down to the restaurant together.

"You okay?" she asks.

I smile brightly. "Why wouldn't I be?"

She lifts her shoulder in a shrug. "You just seem a little preoccupied. Are things okay with Michael?"

I wave away her concern. "I'm fine," I say. "Stop worrying about me. Today is all about you. Let's go meet the rest of the girls and have the best day ever."

She still looks unconvinced, but she drops the subject and her lips curve into a smile. "If you say so," she says. "But you'd tell me if you weren't okay, right? If there's something I can help with?"

I smile at my sister. "Of course, I would. But everything is fine. I swear."

She nods as the elevator doors open and we move to step inside. Before we can, however, Cole steps out. He smiles at Piper before his eyes go to mine.

"Good morning, ladies," he says. "You two look beautiful, as always."

Piper smiles. "Such a charmer, Cole," she says. "One of these days you're going to find a woman who's a match for that charm and you won't know what hit you."

Cole grins, his gaze still on me.

"Fingers crossed," he says with a quick wink.

I ignore the flutter low in my belly at the sight of that wink. Not to mention how good he'd looked. I need to pull myself together and stop obsessing over Cole for the rest of the weekend. The next few days are about Piper and Luke, not whatever disaster has befallen my dating life.

Resolved to put Cole and Michael out of my mind, I loop my arm through Piper's as we walk through the lobby. The other women are already there when we arrive. The room is decorated with flowers and balloons and a big banner with "Future Mrs. Wolfe" in big, swirling letters. Piper gasps in surprise as her hands come up to cover her face.

"What is this?" she asks. "This is too much!"

We all laugh.

"You had to know we wouldn't skimp on the decorations," Harlow says, walking over to hand Piper a mimosa.

Taking the glass, she looks around the room in awe. "I didn't expect all this."

"Having Hannah plan your wedding means nothing is too much," Quinn says. "You learn to like it."

"Hey!" Hannah says. "You said you liked it."

"I loved every second of it," Quinn says. "I just like giving you a hard time."

"Bitch," Hannah mutters.

Quinn just shrugs and I laugh. I know I just met these women, but I think I'm going to like them.

"Okay, ladies," Claire says, "These mimosas won't drink themselves!"

I opt to skip alcohol again today. I'm still not over my hangover from two days ago. Hangovers in my 20s used to last until lunchtime. Hangovers in my 30s seem to need 3-5 business days to vanish. That will teach me to drink on an empty stomach. Piper makes the rounds, greeting all the women with hugs before we take our seats.

The morning is filled with laughter and chatting women, champagne, and delicious food. The married women take turns telling stories of their own weddings. Some of the stories are genuinely hilarious. When Claire tells us how she met Garrett and Ronan's reaction to her dating his best friend, I laugh until tears stream from my eyes. Apparently, he hadn't been happy to catch the two of them kissing. Things had escalated until Quinn took it upon herself to spray them all with water.

"He was so pissed!" Quinn says, laughing.

Claire shrugs. "Served him right. He was being an ass."

"It was pretty funny," Hope says, smiling as she finishes her mimosa.

"How long have you and Ronan been married?" I ask Quinn.

She smiles at me. "Just over a year."

I smile at her obvious happiness. "Wow. You two seem so comfortable together. I wouldn't have been surprised if you were high school sweethearts."

She throws back her head and laughs. "Oh, god no! We knew each other for about 6 months before we started hooking up. Honestly, I didn't even like him for most of those first six months. I thought he was boring and uptight. Even after we got together, I was convinced it was just a fling. Nothing serious." She shakes her head, still smiling.

I blink, surprised by this information. "Really? That's hard to believe."

"Why?" she laughs again. "Because we can't keep our hands off each other? How do you think we got the kid?"

I laugh along with her. "That's fair."

I toy with the umbrella in my virgin daquiri, trying to figure out how to word my next question. I don't even know what I'm trying to ask. I just know that I've spent the last two days surrounded by happy couples who seem like they have all the secrets to a perfect relationship. I want to know how they did it. I guess I just want to know if it's possible for me too.

"How long did it take you to fall for him?"

Quinn smiles. "It took me longer than him to figure it out," she says. "Looking back, I think I started falling for him the first time I met him. But I denied the hell out of it for as long as I could. I wasn't looking for anything serious. I damned sure wasn't looking to settle down in a town as small as Oak Hill."

She gazes down at the drink in her hand for a moment before continuing. "I don't know." She shrugs. "Sometimes you just find the right person and all your big plans don't matter anymore. You realize that what you thought you wanted isn't what you need. Life is short. And time is one thing you can't get back. So, if you find the right person, you hold on tight. And you let them know. Every day."

I nod as I take another sip of my drink. I think about Quinn's words, and I try to picture myself as happy as she seems to be. I imagine myself with a husband and a baby and a job I love. I already have the job I love. The husband and the baby are a little harder to conjure in my mind. I try to picture Michael as the man beside me and immediately reject the image. It feels wrong.

I can't picture him doting on me or making any excuse to touch me, picking out baby clothes or changing dirty diapers. He seems like the kind of guy who'd leave that to his wife or to a nanny. I cringe at the thought. I have nothing against people who hire nannies for their kids. But it's not something I want to do. I want the kind of childhood my mom gave me and Piper. She was there for every milestone and every scraped knee. She read us bedtime stories and played dress-up. That's the kind of mom I want to be. And I want a partner who wants to be that kind of dad. I won't settle for less than that.

A memory of Cole playing with his niece and dressing up her dolls pops into my head and I almost smile. I'd gone to visit Harlow one afternoon a few months after I moved to town and Cole had been there. He'd had pink and purple clips stuck all through his dark hair making him look like he had little horns all over his head. He'd been sitting cross-legged on the floor with Ella as she'd orchestrated an entire scene with the dolls. He'd looked up at me and smiled sheepishly and I'd felt something in my chest squeeze almost painfully. Seeing this large man sitting on the floor and looking utterly ridiculous all to make a little girl happy had affected me more than I'd cared to admit.

Of course, I acted like it was nothing. I teased him lightly and complimented Ella on her spectacular work with his hair before going to visit Harlow. But I'd never gotten the image out of my head. And apparently it still affected me, even now. As I sit here, thinking about my future and the imaginary husband and kids I want to someday have, I allow myself the barest moment to picture Cole by my side. I've never dared to let myself think about it before. Knowing how he felt about commitment—not to mention the arrangement we'd had—made it an impossibility. Besides that, he's nearly a decade younger than me. If he were thinking of settling down, he'd probably choose someone his own age or younger.

But those facts don't stop me from picturing it now. I know it can never happen, but for just a moment I can see exactly what it would look like. And it nearly brings me to tears. I can't want him that way. I can't. Wanting a future with Cole Prescott and knowing I'll never have it would break me.

"How did you know it was real?" I ask.

She shakes her head. "I didn't at first. I almost fucked it all up, actually."

"Really?"

She nods. "Yep. I tried to keep things light. I was convinced it was just a fling and that I'd be able to leave once I had enough of him. But he wanted more. When he asked me for it, I froze. I couldn't tell him what he wanted. I didn't know if I could be what he needed. So, I left. But it didn't take me long to figure out that I needed him just as much as he needed me." She shrugs. "So, I came back. And I thank my lucky stars every day that I did."

I'm not sure if hearing Quinn's story makes me feel better or worse. I still don't know what I'm feeling or what I want. If anything, I'm more lost than I was before she told me her story. But I do know one thing I need to do.

"Hey," Quinn says, as if noticing my sudden distress. "You okay?"

I nod, swallowing back a lump in my throat. "Yeah. I'll be right back. I just need to make a phone call."

She gives me a worried look but doesn't push the subject. Instead, she nods. "Okay. I'll cover for you with the bride."

"Thanks," I say, already reaching for my phone as I walk toward the exit.

CHAPTER 26

Layna

"Will you please tell me where we're going?" Piper asks for the third time since we left the hotel.

We're riding in the back of a car being driven by a stoic gentleman who seems content to ignore our conversation. Harlow told us nothing about today's outing. We were told to be in the lobby and ready to leave by 2pm. That's all. Now, we're in the back of a car heading to a part of Savannah I don't recognize. Not that I know the city all that well.

"Nope," Harlow says. "It's a surprise."

Piper looks at me, but I just shrug. "Don't look at me. She's your friend."

"Shut up," Harlow says. "You know you love me."

I laugh. "I do, but sometimes I wonder why."

"Just trust me," she says. "You're going to love this."

"The last time someone asked me to trust them they stole my car," I say.

Piper laughs. "Is it stealing if he was your boyfriend?"

"Yes," I say. "Because it wasn't his fucking car."

"I'd listen to her," Harlow says. "She's a lawyer, so she knows."

"I hate surprises," Piper mutters.

"Too bad," Harlow says. "We're almost there."

"Almost where?" I ask, peering out the tinted window. The car drives up to a nondescript square brick building. The only identifying marker besides the address is a small sign near the door but I'm not close enough to read the words. The driver exits the car and comes to open the door for us to exit. Harlow gives him a smile as she climbs out. I see that she's carrying a large bag, but I hadn't noticed it before.

I smile at the driver as I climb out behind Piper and we stand there, waiting for Harlow to lead the way. She tells the driver to come back in 3 hours. He nods his understanding but says nothing. Come to think of it, I don't think I've heard him speak since we got into the car at the hotel. Is he allowed to speak? Is he contractually obligated to be silent? I try to remember if that's legally enforceable under contract law, but then Harlow is pushing me toward the building.

I read the sign as we pass, but it's just a name with no other information. Jordan Forester. That's it. No indication of who this Jordan person is or why Harlow brought us here. Ignoring the questioning looks Piper and I send her way, Harlow pulls open the door and motions for us to enter. I sigh and lead the way, Piper behind me.

I'm greeted by a brightly lit room with white walls. There are several potted plants scattered around, adding pops of color to all the white. There's a small desk on one side of the room and several photos hung on the walls. It takes me a second to notice the subject of the photos on the walls. They're all women and they're all in various states of undress. One woman is strategically covered by a white sheet and nothing else. There's no visible nudity, but it's clear she's naked. The photo is gorgeous and the woman looks sexy, empowered and happy. Eyes narrowed, I turn to look at Harlow to ask for an explanation as a woman enters from a side door.

"Harlow?" she calls, looking between the three of us.

Harlow smiles and steps forward. "That's me. Hi."

The woman shakes Harlow's hand before turning to look at me and Piper and smiling.

"I'm Jordan," she says. "I'll be taking your photos today. But first, let's get you into hair and makeup. Follow me."

Then she turns to exit through the same door she just entered. Photos? What does she mean? I glance around at the photos on the wall, noticing for the first time one of a woman wearing a nearly translucent negligée. What sort of photos are we taking today? Harlow doesn't say anything. She just motions for us to follow Jordan. She's still clutching the large bag in her hands. I want to know what's in that bag. I eye her suspiciously as I pass, following Jordan down a short hallway until she stops in front of an open doorway. Holding out a hand, she motions for us to enter.

I give her a small smile as my stomach dances with nerves. When I walk into the room, I see three chairs sitting in front of mirrors. Beside each chair, a smiling person stands there as if waiting for us. I turn back to look at Piper who looks just as confused as I feel. Harlow brings up the rear looking totally unbothered.

Jordan looks to Harlow. "Did you bring your own outfits?" she asks.

Harlow nods and hands her the bag. "I wasn't sure what to bring, so I brought a bunch of different colors and styles."

Jordan unzips the bag and peers inside before smiling at Harlow. "I'll take these to the studio and hang them up. You ladies take a seat, and we'll get started."

When she disappears through the door, I shoot Harlow another look. This time, she sighs and her smile falters.

"What is this?" I whisper.

"It's a boudoir photo shoot," she says.

"A what?" I ask.

"Oh, I've heard of these," Piper says, her eyes lighting up in excitement. "You get professional hair and makeup artists to make you look and feel beautiful and a photographer takes pictures of you looking gorgeous and sexy. It's supposed to be really empowering."

I blink at my sister, wondering how she learned about boudoir photo shoots. For that matter, how did Harlow come up with this idea? I doubt there are many boudoir photographers in Peach Tree.

"This is going to be fun!" Piper says.

There's a little bounce in her step as she makes her way over to one of the chairs to introduce herself to her makeup artist. Harlow smiles at me.

"Come on," she says. "I think you're going to love it."

Am I the only one who has reservations about this? It's not that I'm a prude about nudity or sexuality. I just don't know how I feel about meeting someone for the first time and then stripping to my underwear or even getting naked for them to take pictures of me. I don't hate my body, but if I'd known I was taking photos today I might have gone easy on the hashbrowns at breakfast this morning. I'm probably bloated.

"Stop thinking so much," Harlow says. "This is for all of us. I already paid for the photo session. If you don't want to purchase any of the photos afterwards, fine. But do the shoot and see how you feel afterward. Please? Besides, Piper's already loving this."

I look over at my sister and smile. She's chatting it up with her makeup artist who's already applying products to her skin.

"Fine," I sigh. "Let's do it."

"That's the spirit," Harlow says, looping her arm through mine and pulling me over to one of the chairs as though she's worried I might take off running if she lets me out of her sight.

When I finally take my seat between Harlow and Piper, she looks over and smiles at me, her expression filled with excitement. The stylists go to work immediately, making small talk and asking us questions as they work. My stylist introduces herself as Sara and asks me what sort of look I want to achieve. When I tell her I want to keep things realistic and subtle, she smiles and nods knowingly. I begin to feel more relaxed as the minutes pass and think that maybe I can do this. I'll choose a modest outfit and take a few photos and be done with it. No big deal.

"I can tell you're nervous," Piper says as her stylist works on curling her hair into pretty waves down her back.

"Is it that obvious?" I ask, the sarcasm clear in my words.

She laughs. "Only because I know you. Everyone else probably just thinks you're a bitch."

My mouth drops open as Sara works to hide a smile and Harlow laughs out loud.

"I'm not a bitch," I say. I look at Sara. "I'm not. I swear."

She shakes her head. "I have a sister, too. And this is the kind of shit she'd rope me into without telling me. I'm on your side."

"Ha!" I say, sticking my tongue out at my sister.

"To be fair, this was Harlow's idea," Piper says. "Not mine." She shrugs. "But I happen to be on board. Luke is going to flip his shit when he sees these pictures."

"Yes!" Harlow shouts. "Linc won't know what hit him."

I roll my eyes. "I guess I'll save my pictures for when I'm 80 and need to remember that I was hot once."

Piper rolls her eyes. "You're not going to be single forever, Layna. Besides, maybe Michael would like to see them."

Her voice is teasing, but I can't quite muster up a laugh. During this morning's phone call with Michael at brunch, I made it clear to him that he and I weren't going to work out. That ship has sailed. Honestly, I feel relieved about it. He's a nice guy, and easy on the eyes, but there was no real chemistry between us. I know what I said to Cole the night we made my dating profile; that I didn't need all of that. That I'd settle for someone with similar goals. But I don't know. The more I see my sister and Luke, Harlow and Linc, and all the members of the King family; the more I don't want to settle for less. If that means it takes me longer to find the right guy, so be it. But I know he's out there.

"Did something happen with you and Michael?" Piper asks, her voice gentle.

I shake my head, not wanting to go into it right now. Besides, it's not that big of a deal. We were barely even dating.

"I'm not sure Michael is the guy for me," I say. "Too soon to tell."

Piper nods, but she doesn't press. Instead, she says, "I just want you to have what I have, Layna. Someone who sees the real you and loves you for who you are. Someone who drives you crazy in the best way and someone you can't imagine going through life without."

Her words hit me with the force of a sledgehammer blow. My breath catches in my throat, and I work hard to keep my face neutral as I smile.

"Is that all?" I say with a laugh.

She shrugs. "It's what you deserve."

"She's right, you know," Harlow says. "You deserve all that and more. And if Michael isn't those things, cut him loose and find someone who is."

I smile, wondering if I should just tell them I dumped Michael. But I'm so sick of talking about my dating life. I don't want to answer a bunch of questions about how I knew he wasn't right for me or whether I'm okay. *He's not the right guy for you because he's not Cole Prescott*, a voice in my head whispers. That voice has been growing increasingly louder since last night and our moment on the balcony. I've been ignoring it, but I'm worried I won't be able to for much longer.

"Okay, ladies," Piper's stylist says. "Ready to see your finished looks?"

We all nod, smiling as they spin our chairs around to face the mirrors behind us. I don't know what I'm expecting, but when I see myself, I'm slightly stunned by the transformation. The woman in the mirror looks like me, but also different. The makeup is more subtle than I was expecting, but it's a touch more than I wear normally. I can tell that Sara took my own preferences into account when it came to the makeup and hair. I didn't want anything over-the-top. It looks natural, even though I know how much time it took for her to achieve the look. When Piper's eyes meet mine in the mirror, she smiles.

"See?" she says. "We were right."

"I told you to trust me," Harlow says, making me laugh.

All three of us look beautiful. And I'll admit that having my own personal stylist and getting the model treatment was pretty great. I smile at Sara.

"Thank you," I say. "This is perfect."

She grins. "For what it's worth, you don't need to take these pictures for a man. Take them for yourself. You'll be glad you did. I've never seen a single woman leave here feeling bad about herself. They always leave here looking ready to take on the world."

I laugh. "Thanks."

"Have fun with it," Sara says. "And don't stress about the nudity. Think about all the times a doctor you just met has asked you to strip so they can look in all your crevices." She shrugs. "This is less invasive than that. And way more fun."

We all laugh and suddenly I'm feeling less anxious about the whole thing.

"Okay," I say, injecting confidence into the single word. "Let's do it."

The next two hours pass in a blur of smiling, laughing, and posing, all while donning various sexy outfits that it would never have occurred to me to wear if not for this photo shoot. I don't know where Harlow found them or how she guessed mine and Piper's sizes, but they're perfect for today.

Jordan instructs me on how to stand, how to look at the camera, where to look and whether to smile. She does all this while snapping dozens of photos and telling me how amazing I look. It's strange because I've never been overly critical of my body or the way I look, but like most women I've compared myself to the models on magazine covers or the celebrities on television. I've usually felt lacking in that regard. But today? With Jordan's encouragement, I feel every bit as beautiful and confident as one of those women. I realize that if it weren't for Harlow's gift, I might never have felt this.

"Thank you," I say to her as we sit in Jordan's office after our shoots, waiting for her to show us the results on her computer.

Harlow grins over at me. "It was worth it, right?"

I nod, my smile stretching wide across my face. "Definitely."

The elation I feel in that moment seems unmatched. That is, until Jordan shows me my photos. My mouth drops open and I stare in amazement at the woman on the screen. I know it's me because she looks like me and because I just posed for these pictures. But still. Somehow the woman in these photos exudes confidence and sex. She looks into the camera as if she's got a secret. I didn't even know my face could do that.

"Wow," Harlow says.

The image on the screen now is one of me wearing a corset, heels, and thigh-high stockings. It was my favorite of the outfits I wore for the shoot. In this photo, I'm in profile, with my back arched and the curve of my hip visible. My ass is in profile, but it looks amazing at this angle. Is that really what I look like?

"Holy shit," Piper breathes. "You need to buy that picture and frame it."

"It's hot," Jordan agrees. "You photograph well."

"Thank you," I say, feeling a blush heat my cheeks. "Are you sure that camera isn't magic?"

She just laughs. "That's all you, babe."

We spend nearly an hour looking at all the photos Jordan took, each choosing our favorites for our own personal album. I'd nearly choked on my saliva when I found out how much the album costs, but Piper and Harlow convinced me it was an investment. That some day I'll look back at these photos and remember exactly how I felt today. And they'd been right. I'd pulled out my credit card with very little hesitation in the end.

By the time we make our way outside to meet our silent chauffer, it's late in the afternoon. We're supposed to meet the King ladies in a couple of hours for dinner followed by Piper's bachelorette party. It's a good thing we won't need to worry about hair and makeup. Once we're back in the car on our way to the hotel, Harlow hands me a small bag.

"What's this?" I ask, peering inside.

"You looked too hot in that thing to leave it behind," she says. "I asked Jordan if she minded."

Inside the bag, I see black lace and I know immediately that it's the corset from my photo shoot. I look at Harlow and laugh.

"And just when will I have the need to wear a corset?"

She just shrugs. "You never know when one might come in handy."

CHAPTER 27

Cole

I do my best to hide how miserable I am, but I'm not sure how successful I am. I've never been good at pretending. But Luke deserves to have a great time at his bachelor party. Who am I to bring the mood down? Just because the one woman I've ever thought about settling down with has found someone else doesn't mean I can't put on a smile and have fun with my friends, right?

Wrong.

I'm miserable and I don't know how I'm going to keep up the act until this party ends. Linc and I planned it together, so I know it's nowhere near its end. We'll be out until well after midnight, I'm sure. I take a large drink from my glass of bourbon and wince. Not because of the burn, but because it reminds me of her.

Layna.

Bourbon is her drink of choice. She'd been drinking it the night we met. I'd been impressed and surprised by her choice. She looked like a dirty martini kind of girl. Owning a bar means I've gotten skilled at guessing people's drink choice just by their appearance and demeanor, but I'd been wrong about her. When she'd ordered an old fashioned, I'd been pleasantly surprised. And a little turned on.

I sigh at the memory. I don't know why I insist on torturing myself this way. She's clearly moved on. I need to do the same. No matter what I imagined last night on that balcony. I'd just been seeing what I wanted to see. Even if I didn't already know how she felt about me, her making out with Michael in front of the elevator was clear evidence that it's not me she wants. I wonder if she invited him to her room last night after I left. The thought sends a surge of anger through me, though I know I don't have the right. My grip tightens on the glass, and I force myself to relax my hand before I shatter it. Instead, I bring it to my lips and down the rest of the drink in one large gulp. This time I barely feel the burn as it goes down. When the bartender comes over to ask me if I'd like another, I shake my head.

"Just a beer," I say. "I'm sick of bourbon tonight."

He nods and reaches down to grab a bottle from the well beneath the bar. As he sets it on the bar in front of me, I feel a hand on my shoulder.

"Who pissed in your cereal today?" Luke asks.

I turn to him, confused. "What do you mean?"

He shrugs. "You haven't seemed like yourself tonight. You okay?"

I nod. "Yeah, man. I'm good."

"You don't seem good," he says.

I force a laugh. "Why wouldn't I be? My best friend is getting married tomorrow. I'm so happy for you, man.

Stop worrying about me. We're here to celebrate you tonight."

Luke's quiet for several seconds, his gaze on the drink in his hands. "Cole, it's okay if you're going through something. You know I'm here for you, right? If you want to talk, I mean."

The idea of spilling my guts to Luke has some merit, but I don't want tonight's focus to be about me and my problems. Especially since it would take a while to explain the way things with me and Layna went down. I don't want Luke to spend his bachelor party trying to fix my broken heart. That's not what tonight is about.

"I know," I say with a smile. "And I appreciate it more than you know. But I swear I'm good. I'd tell you if I wasn't."

He doesn't look convinced, but he nods. "If you change your mind, I'm here."

"Thanks," I say. "But tonight is about you. So, the question is, are *you* having a good time?"

He grins and looks around the club. It's filled with people dancing and drinking and living it up. Linc and I reserved a private booth for our group and Wyatt and Van have made sure that Luke's hand is never without a drink in it. I think I saw Luke hand at least one of those drinks off to Finn who switched it for a glass of water, but I let it slide. We want him to have a good time, not be so hungover tomorrow that he's miserable at his wedding.

I carry my beer back across the crowded dance floor, weaving my way through the gyrating bodies as I follow Luke back to our booth. As I walk, I resolve to do a better job of pretending I'm not miserable. I'm not sure how to accomplish that, but I know that spending every second thinking about Layna isn't working. I've got to push her from my mind for at least the next few hours. For Luke.

When we get back to the table, I can see a tray of shots waiting and all eyes go to Luke.

"It's about time you came back," Linc says. "These guys were about to drink your shot."

Luke laughs. "I should have stayed gone longer then."

"Nope," Wyatt says. "No getting out of it now."

He reaches down to pick up one of the glasses and hands it to Luke.

"Just one," he says. "It's not a bachelor party without at least one shot and a toast."

Luke sighs as he takes the glass from Wyatt. "Fine," he says. "But I'm not getting shitfaced the night before my wedding. Hangovers and public speaking don't mix well."

Everyone breaks into groans of protest, but Luke just laughs. I know him well enough to know that they're not going to convince him to change his mind. I've known him for years and I can count on one hand the number of times I've seen him drunk. The hangovers had been legendary, too. I watch as all the men seated at the table grab a shot and hold it up in Luke's direction. I follow suit, though the last thing I want is a shot. I don't even know what's in the glass.

"To Luke," Wyatt says. "If you're half as happy as I am, you'll be happier than most."

"Yeah," Finn says. "And if you're half the husband I am, Piper's a lucky woman."

"Hey!" Luke says. "I'll be ten times the husband you are!"

Ronan just rolls his eyes while the twins laugh. Garrett quietly tosses back his shot as if this is a common argument and he's not taking sides. Which, considering he's engaged to their only sister, might be a smart plan. The men all grumble as they drink their shots. No one is looking at me, so I covertly pour mine into one of the glasses of melting ice on the table as I pick up my beer with the other hand. It's a trick I learned years ago and one I've taught to a few Peach Fuzz patrons over the years.

"But seriously," Finn says, clapping a hand on Luke's shoulder. "I want to thank you."

Luke studies Finn, his brows drawn low in confusion. "For what?"

Finn smiles. "For pushing Hannah into my arms."

Wyatt bursts out laughing. "You mean for making you realize you needed to get off your ass and tell her you liked her?"

Finn glares at his brother. "Don't be a dick."

Wyatt just smiles. "Some of us don't need seven years to figure out we want to be with someone. Don't be mad because you're an underachiever."

I don't know exactly what they're talking about, but I remember Luke telling us about how he'd flirted with Hannah when he'd first met her. That was before she and Finn had been a couple. The next time he'd seen Finn and Hannah, they were married. Needless to say, Luke hadn't gotten a heartwarming welcome from Finn that day. But now that a couple of years have passed and everyone can see how much Luke loves Piper, Finn has lightened up on Luke a bit. These days, their teasing is more good-natured than hostile. Which is good, considering they share a niece.

Luke just shrugs. "I'm always happy to help those less fortunate."

The entire table erupts into laughter as Finn just shakes his head, trying not to smile. The night goes on in the same vein with everyone trying to outdo one another's embarrassing stories as the laughter and liquor flow. I refuse more drinks than I accept, though. I count that as a plus by the time everyone is ready to call it a night and I make my way to the bar to close out our tab. Finn is obviously drunk, but he's not obnoxious about it. He's just wearing a goofy grin as he tries to give Luke advice about being married. It's hard to gauge Ronan's level of intoxication. The man is so stoic that I can't properly judge. But I think maybe he's been a little more talkative tonight. Van, however, just might be the drunkest of all. Before I left the table, I saw him on a video chat with Mya, telling her how amazing she is and how much he loves her. Garret had teased him about it, but then he'd tried to push into the shot so he could catch a glimpse of Claire. That's when I'd walked away. I don't want to see what the ladies are up to tonight. I don't want to see her.

I've managed to push her out of my mind for the last few hours, but now she's back. I sigh as I stand there waiting for one of the bartenders to get to me. It's crowded tonight, and the two women are clearly slammed. They're doing an excellent job, though. They've clearly been working together long enough to anticipate the others' moves. As a former bartender and the owner of a bar, it's easy to recognize the skill in their work. I'll make sure to tip them well.

Someone bumps into me from behind, pressing me up against the bar for a brief second. Judging by the size of the person, I'd guess it's a woman. Turning automatically, I see a cute blonde smiling apologetically at me.

"I'm so sorry!" she says. "Someone bumped into me and I lost my balance."

I smile back. "No worries," I say before turning back to wait for the bartender.

"The line is crazy tonight," the woman says from behind me.

I nod. "Uh huh."

"I've been waiting forever just to get a drink."

I hold back my sigh. It's possible I'm imagining it, but it feels like this woman is trying to get me to buy her a drink. In the past, I'd have been excited by the prospect of flirting with a stranger in a bar. I would have bought her a drink and maybe pulled her out onto the dance floor. I might have even ended the night in her bed, though that happened far less than my reputation made it seem. But tonight, I'm not in the mood to flirt and I don't have it in me to pretend to be interested in this woman. She's pretty enough, but she's not the one I want to spend time with.

I can feel her still at my back, standing so close to me that her body is nearly touching mine. Part of me wishes I could forget about Layna and see what this blonde has to offer. I could lose myself in her for a few hours and forget that the one woman I've ever truly cared about is dating someone else. The idea has some merit, but just the thought of kissing someone who isn't Layna is appalling. I almost want to laugh at the ridiculousness of the situation. If the others knew what was going through my head right now, they'd laugh their asses off.

"Listen," the woman says, sliding up between me and the man to my left. Her words are low and I can barely hear them over the thumping music and the crowd.

She's so close I can feel her breasts brushing against my arm as she speaks again. "Don't look over, but that guy bet me 50 bucks I couldn't get you to kiss me."

Confusion lights my features and I tilt my head down to look at the blonde. "Which guy?"

Her eyes dart to the left before she brings her gaze back up to mine and smiles prettily.

"The tall one with the light brown hair," she says. "No tattoos."

Keeping my head tilted down toward hers, I flick my gaze in that direction and see Luke watching me with a grin on his face. I'm going to kill him. I don't care if he is getting married tomorrow. Piper will understand.

"He's drunk," I say.

"He didn't seem drunk," the woman says.

"What's your name?"

"What do you want it to be?"

I can't help it. I laugh.

"Good one," I say.

"It's Ava," she says. "And I'm not really the kind of girl who takes a bet like that. But he said you seemed sad and it was his bachelor party and he wanted to cheer you up."

I sigh. "Ava, I appreciate this. And not so long ago I would have taken you up on that offer and made you fifty dollars richer. But I'm not that guy anymore. And my friend is an ass for involving you in this."

She smiles and shakes her head. "So, he was right. You are sad."

I shake my head. "Sad isn't the right word," I mutter.

"What's her name?" Ava asks.

I laugh again. "It's not important."

"But I was right," she says. "There's a girl."

"Something like that."

She's quiet for several seconds and I feel a little guilty for dismissing her the way I did.

"What are you drinking?" I ask.

She smiles. "Rum and coke."

When the bartender finally approaches, I add Ava's rum and coke to my tab before telling her I'd like to close out for the night.

"Leaving so soon?" Ava asks.

"I've got a groom to strangle and a wedding to ruin. Big night."

She laughs. "Don't be too hard on your friend. He's just looking out for you."

I sigh again because I know she's right. Luke was just trying to make me laugh, and maybe help me hook up. There's no way he can know that I've stopped doing things like that. It's not like we've had wild nights out over the past year or so. And I kept my fling with Layna a secret from everyone. He's just falling back on some of the crazy things we did when we were younger.

"I know," I say. "He's still an ass."

An idea occurs to me. A way to get back at Luke for his little game.

"What were the terms of the bet?" I ask. "The exact wording?"

She thinks for a moment before answering. "He just said, 'I'll give you 50 bucks if you can get that grumpy guy over there to kiss you.'"

"That's all?" I ask. "He didn't say anything else?"

She shakes her head.

"Ava, you're about to be fifty dollars richer," I say, leaning toward her. "Is he still watching?"

She glances over before nodding. "Yeah."

"Good," I say, leaning even closer to her.

Reaching down, I take her hand in mine and lift it to my lips, planting a chaste kiss on her knuckles. At the same time. I turn my head just enough to meet Luke's gaze and flip him the bird with my other hand. He immediately bursts into a fit of laughter.

"Terms have been met," I tell Ava. "Don't forget to collect your money."

She looks up at me, blue eyes wide as she nods. The bartender returns with my card and I sign the slip before handing Ava her drink.

"Have a good night, Ava," I say, giving her upper arm a slight squeeze as I brush past her to return to the table.

When I pass Luke, he's still laughing.

"Give the girl her money," I say.

CHAPTER 28

Layna

I feel like a giant weight has been lifted from my shoulders since breaking things off with Michael this morning. I've felt more like myself than I have in weeks. It's not that he was a bad guy or anything. He just wasn't right for me. He wanted someone more like the old me. Someone more like the woman I was before I moved to Peach Tree. But that's not me anymore. I've changed into this new version of myself, and I need to figure out what she wants. I'm sure Michael will find someone who suits him and wants the same things he does. But that person isn't me. As for myself, I'm going to be patient and wait for the right man to come along at the right time. I even deleted my online dating profile after returning from the boudoir session.

But tonight, I'm not thinking about men or dating. Tonight, I'm going to focus on my sister and celebrating her last night as an unmarried woman. So, when Mya suggests we go to a dance club, I'm the first to raise my hand in favor. Today's photo shoot not only gave me a much-needed boost of self-confidence, but it made me want to celebrate my body and my femininity. I make my way to the front of the party bus and give the driver our new destination. As I make my way back to my seat, Mya hands me a full glass of champagne. I take it without missing a step and smile my thanks.

"To Piper!" Mya shouts. "Though I don't know why anyone would willingly join the Wolfe family, I know I'm happy to have you as my new sister."

Piper laughs. "As long as your father stays far away, I'm happy to have Luke's last name."

"Cheers!" Quinn shouts, raising her glass high.

The rest of us raise our glasses and shout a cheer for the bride before we sip. It's clear that there's no love lost between Mya and her father. Not that it surprises me. Piper told me all about Luke and Mya's father and his callous behavior when he found out he'd fathered a daughter with his mistress. Not to mention the way he raised Luke. It seems to me that they're both better off without him in their lives. I know Luke invited both his parents to the wedding out of familial obligation. Piper told me how relieved he was when only his mother opted to attend. His father had claimed some sort of business emergency, but I think he just didn't want to risk seeing his daughter and realizing what he missed out on by not being there for her. Not that I'm certain he's capable of that depth of emotion. Not even the news that Mya had given birth to his first grandchild had swayed him to mend things with her. Some people are stubborn to the bitter end. I think he might be one of those people.

But it clearly doesn't bother Mya or Luke. They've both managed to find happiness and love despite the lack of it growing up. In fact, Luke has made my sister happier than I've ever seen her. Which makes him one of my favorite people these days.

"To my baby sister," I say, raising my glass again. "The most beautiful bride-to-be I've ever seen. I can't wait to watch you walk down the aisle tomorrow and marry the man of your dreams. Seeing you happy is all I've ever wanted. And I know she'd want the same."

Piper's smile wobbles just a bit before firming again. Maybe I shouldn't have said that last part, but I know her. And I know our mom has been on her mind a lot lately. I just hope I haven't brought down the mood tonight.

"She would," Piper agrees. "And she wouldn't want me to be sad tonight. So, I'm not going to be."

"Good," I say, gesturing toward her glass. "Bottoms up!"

By the time we make it to the dance club, we've finished off two bottles of champagne and it's clear that all the ladies are taking full advantage of our night out. We head immediately for the dance floor, not willing to waste a second of the night. The eight of us dance and laugh until our hearts are pounding and we're out of breath before we find an empty table and Quinn and I head to the bar to order us a round of drinks.

"I needed this," she says as we wait for the bartender to prepare the drinks.

"Me too," I say, smiling. "Not as much as you do, though. I don't have a baby at home."

She laughs. "He's a handful, but I love being a mom."

"Really?" I ask. "You don't miss your independence a little bit?"

She thinks about it for a second and shrugs. "I don't know. Sometimes, I guess. But it's tiny compared to how much I love him and Ronan. They're worth it."

I nod, envying her certainty. When we make our way back to the table, I hear Hope asking Harlow why it took her and Linc so long to figure out they were perfect for each other. I just shake my head as I smile.

"I'd like to hear that one, too," I say. "It was obvious to the rest of us."

Piper laughs. "Especially when you kept freaking out every time he was around."

Harlow glares at her. "I did not *freak out*. I was just nervous. You've seen him. He's intense."

Piper shrugs. "He's a big softie."

"Not always," Harlow mutters, lifting her glass to her lips.

I decide not to ask for clarification on that comment. I get the feeling she was talking about something other than his personality.

It's loud in the club, but Claire must have her phone set to vibrate because she pulls it from her pocket and smiles at the screen before answering the call.

"Hey, Garrett," she says.

"Boo!" Quinn shouts.

"No boys allowed!" Piper calls.

The others chime in with similar comments as I shake my head.

"It's been three hours," Hope says. "He'll see you later."

"Shut up!" Claire says, laughing. "He wants to video chat."

"Do it!" Hannah says. "Let's see what the boys are up to."

It takes a second for Garrett's face to appear on the screen, making Claire smile wider.

"Hey, you," she says.

"I miss you!" Garrett says.

It's clear he's had more than a few drinks tonight. I laugh, along with Hope and Harlow. The others immediately start teasing the big man. Which leads to them teasing Claire about taking a call from a boy during girls' night out.

"You're breaking the rules!" Quinn yells.

"I see Ronan," Claire taunts.

"So?" Quinn says, acting unbothered.

"Who's he talking to?" Claire squints at the screen. "She's cute."

"Hold up!" Quinn says, reaching for the phone. "Let me see this shit."

Claire puts up a slight resistance, but she eventually lets Quinn have the phone, laughing as Garrett says something about motion sickness. Quinn ignores him and studies the screen for a moment before rolling her eyes.

"That's just Wyatt," she says.

Claire shrugs. "Must have been the long hair that threw me off."

"Let me see," Hope says, holding out a hand.

"You all do you know you live with them, right?" I say, shaking my head at their antics.

Harlow shrugs. "So? Let me know if you see Linc," she tells Hope.

Soon, all the women are gathered around the phone in Hope's hand as they shout instructions to Garrett to show them what each man is doing. Even Piper is in on it, waving and smiling at Luke when he shows up on the screen. I roll my eyes at them. A bunch of grown women making fools of themselves on a video call, trying to catch a glimpse of a man who's already theirs. It's silly. But I guess it's sweet. They're all so clearly in love. It makes me wonder if I'll ever find something like that.

"Hey, there's Cole!" Piper says.

"Who's the blonde chick?" Quinn asks.

"Who knows?" Harlow says, laughing.

"Looks like someone might get lucky tonight," Claire teases.

The words hit me like a bullet to the chest. Cole is with another woman. I know I don't have any right to hate that fact, but I do. I hate that he's with someone else. I hate that he might be attracted to her or that he might leave the bar with her. Would he sleep with someone else? It's been six weeks since we ended our fling. That's plenty of time to move on. Haven't I been dating other people this whole time? It's not fair of me to wonder if he's moved on when that's what I've been trying to do this whole time. It wasn't until this morning that I realized how pointless it was. Because I know now that it didn't work. I'm still not over Cole and whatever it is I feel for him. But I'm worried I realized it too late.

I tell myself not to look at the phone screen. It's not my business. And anyway, it won't change anything. If Cole is going to sleep with someone else tonight, I can't stop him. And knowing about it won't change a thing. It will only hurt me more. But what I know I should do wars with my need to see for myself and I give in, leaning over Piper's shoulder to see the phone in her hand.

I spot Cole instantly. He's standing near a bar with some tiny, blonde thing standing entirely too close to him. As I watch, he leans in close to her and I stop breathing. The pain flares in my chest, so fast and so intense that I wish I could look away. He's going to kiss her. He's going to kiss some random girl he met at a bar and I'm going to be stuck watching it. And there's not a damned thing I can do about it. I ignore the little voice saying that he once did far more with me back when I was just some woman he met at a bar.

My eyes are glued to the phone screen as Cole says something to the girl and she smiles up at him adoringly. I've never been a violent person, but the urge to punch something is strong in my mind right now. My teeth are clenched so hard my jaw hurts and there's a dull ache moving up the back of my neck from holding myself so rigid as I stand there watching. Cole's hand wraps around the blonde's and he lifts it to his lips. Then his eyes look beyond the woman to someone off to the left of the camera and his free hand comes up to flip the middle finger at someone. The men all erupt into laughter and jeers as the image on the screen begins to shake. I see the woman walk over to Luke and hold out her hand. He says something that makes her laugh as he reaches into his pocket and hands her something that looks like cash.

"What just happened?" Piper says. "Who is that?"

Garrett is still laughing as he tries to explain in a slightly slurred voice. "Luke bet that girl she couldn't get Cole to kiss her." He laughs again. "But he didn't say where he had to kiss her."

I take a deep breath and relax my jaw as I turn away from the phone and chug an entire bottle of water as the others laugh and talk about what we'd just seen. But I don't want to talk about it. I don't want to think about it. I keep seeing Cole as he'd stood there, his mouth inches from hers, looking for all the world as if he was about to kiss her.

Get a grip, Layna, I tell myself. *Why do you care who he kisses?*

That question plays on repeat in my head for the rest of the night. It's all I can think of as I smile and dance with the others, pretending everything is normal. I ponder it as I gather up everyone at the end of the night and make sure everyone is back on the bus. As we roll through the dark city streets on our way back to the hotel, it's the only question in my mind. When I leave Piper in her hotel room to go back to mine, it's still all I can think of.

Why do you care who he kisses?

As I strip off my clothes and reach for my pajamas, I finally let the answer follow. I finally let myself think the thought I've been hiding from for so long.

Because you still want him.

CHAPTER 29

Layna

I pull the belt of my long coat tighter around my waist as I open the door and peer out into the empty hallway. Blowing out a breath, I try to push out my nerves along with it. I don't know why I'm so nervous. It's not like I'm a simpering virgin. But something about this feels different. Showing up at Cole's door unannounced like this after my earlier revelation feels like the start of something more. I don't want to think too hard about what it might be, so I push it away and focus on keeping my breathing slow and even.

Even if my heart is pounding out of my chest right now, I'm determined that my outward appearance will remain calm and breezy. Cole never needs to know how nervous I am about this. He'd want to know why and I'm not sure I have an answer for that. All I know is that I want him.

After seeing those photos of myself on Michelle's computer screen earlier, I'd felt a surge of confidence and boldness. I'd felt beautiful and bold enough to go after what I want. And what I want tonight is for Cole to fuck me until I come so hard, I see stars. I deserve that, right? It's not too much to ask for. I can worry about what it all means later.

Determined, I stride out into the long hallway, my heels silent on the carpeted floor. I walk purposefully, not allowing myself time to reconsider my actions. I hesitate just long enough to take another steadying breath before I knock on the door and wait. Several long seconds tick by and I start to second-guess myself. What if he's asleep? What if he's not alone after all? Just because I saw him turn away the blonde doesn't mean he couldn't have found someone else after that.

What if he turns me away? I wouldn't blame him. It's after midnight, and he's not expecting me to show up like this. I'm just about to turn and hurry back to my room when the door opens and I'm face-to-face with a pair of confused brown eyes. My nerves vanish at the familiar sight of him.

"Layna? Is something wrong?"

I shake my head, giving him a coy smile. "No," I say.

I step closer and rest a hand on his bare chest, the simple touch grounding me like nothing else ever has.

"Can I come in?" I whisper.

Cole's gaze goes to my hand on his chest and back to my face, but he makes no move to step back from me or to pull me closer.

"Where's Michael?"

Cole's voice is more curious than angry or annoyed. I remind myself that it's a valid question. He doesn't know.

I shake my head. "I don't know. And I don't care. I broke up with him this morning."

Cole looks at me for a long moment, unmoving and silent. I wish I knew what he was thinking.

"Why?" he asks. "I thought he was the perfect boyfriend."

I sigh. "I was wrong about that."

I can tell he wants more of an explanation, but I don't want to do any more thinking tonight. And I damned sure don't want to talk about my mistakes. I trail my hand lower, tracing over the familiar ridges of his muscled abs, stopping just above the waistband of his gym shorts.

"I didn't come here to talk about Michael," I whisper, leaning closer to him.

Cole doesn't move, but I watch his Adam's apple bob as he swallows. "Why did you come here, Layna?"

I let my hand slide down over the front of his shorts, tracing the length of him. I'm not surprised to find that he's already growing hard, and I haven't even made it inside his room.

"I think you know," I say, moving close enough that I can smell his subtle cologne.

Inhaling deeply, I savor the scent of him. God, I've missed that smell. It's something that's so uniquely Cole that I never stopped to wonder about it until I no longer had access to it. I missed it. I missed him. Even though we've spent time together and we've hung out over the past few weeks, I can admit that I've missed this. This closeness, the feel of his skin against mine, the smell of him invading my senses. It feels scary to admit that though. So, I keep the knowledge tucked away for later.

"What if I need you to spell it out for me?" he says.

I can tell he's hesitant, though I'm not sure why. It's not like we're new to having sex with one another. He knows as well as I do how amazing this will be. My hand slides down the length of his rapidly hardening cock with a little more pressure this time as I lean in and press my lips to the side of his neck.

"Can I come in and show you?" I say, my lips moving against his skin.

He sighs out a soft curse and I know he's going to give in even before he pulls me roughly to him and lets the door fall shut behind me. A thrill shoots through me from my nipples down to my toes, concentrating between my legs where I know my thong is already damp from the anticipation of what's about to happen.

Cole's strong arms come around me and he pulls me against his hard body, walking me backward until I'm sandwiched between him and the door. His mouth crushes against mine in a bruising kiss. The emotion that rushes over me at the feel of his lips on mine is one I refuse to call relief, but it's the closest word I can come up with to describe it. The familiar feel of his lips on mine and his arms around me are as close to a feeling of home as I've ever had. That sudden realization has something big and slightly terrifying welling up inside me. It's another of those things I can't think about right now, so I push it away with the others and focus on the pleasure coursing through me.

"Fuck, I've missed this," he groans against my skin just before I feel his teeth skim my neck.

The roughness in his voice coupled with the sting of his teeth on my skin sends a thrill through me and I dig my fingers into the soft strands of his dark hair, holding him against me.

"Me, too," I say, my admission barely above a whisper.

I know he heard me though, because he raises his head to lock that intense gaze on my face. He doesn't say anything as we stand there, locked in some kind of conversation with our eyes. Whatever Cole sees in my gaze must satisfy him because his lips curve into a sexy little half-smile before he lowers his mouth to mine. The intensity of this kiss has somehow ratcheted up a notch from before, leaving me breathless as I cling to him. Why does this feel so right when I know it can't last? I shove that thought from my mind as quickly as it enters, unwilling or unable to unpack that right now. Not when Cole's taste is on my tongue and his hard body is pressed to mine. That's a question for another time when I can think more clearly.

Planting my hands on his chest, I push gently but firmly, easing him back a few inches. When he turns a questioning gaze on me, I smile and reach for the belt tied at my waist. Cole's eyes drift down to my hands, and I can see the heat and excitement in his gaze as he understands. Eagerly, he reaches out to help me, but I push his hands away.

He grins playfully. "I can't unwrap my present?"

I shake my head. "Tonight, I'm in control."

Cole's face loses the playful grin and I see naked desire in his brown eyes when he looks at me. His jaw clenches as he pulls in a ragged breath, and I almost smile at the way he to struggles to hold himself back from reaching for me. He takes another step back so he can see all of me and now I do smile. I know he's letting me take control right now. I also know how hot it makes him when I'm bossy. He loves it when I tell him how to please me. Tonight, I'm going to use that to make sure we both get what we want.

Slowly, I work the knot loose at my waist and let the coat fall open a few inches to reveal a glimpse of what's underneath. I watch Cole's eyes as they travel down the length of my body and see the exact moment when he realizes what I'm wearing. Or, more specifically, what I'm not wearing.

"Holy fuck," he whispers.

The black corset hugs my curves and pushes my cleavage up to a spectacular height. It also gives my body an hourglass shape that I can only dream of having without it. The garters are clipped to black sheer, thigh-high stockings. Between the stockings and corset, a tiny, barely-there lace thong covers my pussy and leaves my ass totally bare. My feet are encased in a pair of 4-inch heels that bring me nearly to Cole's height.

I know I look amazing. I'd seen the photos on Michelle's computer, after all. It had been this outfit that had given me the confidence to stop denying what I wanted. I'd felt bold as I'd looked at those photos. Empowered. Strong. Sexy. I decided right then to stop settling. In my relationships and in my life. Michael was never going to be enough for me. I've known it for a while, even if I'd tried to ignore the fact. But I'm not doing that anymore. Tonight, I'm taking what I want, consequences be damned.

When Cole reaches for me, I shake my head and hold up a hand to stop him. Unsurprisingly, he complies immediately, his body going rigid before me.

"I told you," I say, the heady feeling of power rushing through me. "I'm in control tonight."

He grins. "Yes, ma'am."

Even him calling me ma'am doesn't irritate me tonight. For once, it doesn't feel like a reference to our age difference. Instead, it feels more like him deferring to me. He's acknowledging that he's mine to command. That I'm in charge of what happens between us. It sends a rush of desire through me that has me nearly shaking with anticipation. I'm shocked my voice comes out steady when I speak.

"Take off your clothes and go sit on the edge of the bed," I say, my words an order, rather than a request.

Cole smirks at me before backing slowly toward the bed, keeping his eyes on me the entire time. When the backs of his legs bump up against the bed, he stops, and his hands go to the elastic waistband of his shorts. I watch as he lowers the garment, taking his boxer briefs with them. His thick cock springs free, jutting out toward me and I lick my lips without realizing it. Cole sees it though and I watch as his smirk becomes a full-fledged grin. Slowly, he lowers himself down to sit on the bed, his gaze never leaving mine. I allow my gaze to travel over his naked body, appreciating the beauty of this man. I can admit to myself that I've never seen a more gorgeous male specimen. And tonight, he's all mine to do with as I wish.

"Touch yourself," I say. "Stroke your cock while I watch."

Cole eyes me for only a moment before reaching down to grip his cock in one large hand. He doesn't look away from me as his hand begins to move, sliding up and down his length. I watch for several seconds, mesmerized by the sight of him pleasuring himself. Who knew something like that could be so fucking hot? I let the coat slip down my shoulders and drop to the floor behind me as I step closer, so I have a better view of Cole jacking himself. His eyes roam over my body appreciatively before returning to my face. As I watch, a bead of moisture escapes the tip of his cock, glistening in the low light. I lick my lips again as I watch his hand swipe over it, using it to lubricate his hand as he works his length faster.

"You look so fucking sexy right now, Layna," he says, his voice a raspy whisper. "Just looking at you has me wanting to blow my load."

The smallest whimper escapes me at his words coupled with the erotic sight before me. He gives me a knowing grin, continuing his leisurely strokes. The taut muscles in his forearms strain with each movement, adding to the visual feast. My panties are soaked now, and I wonder if it's possible to orgasm from visual stimulation alone. If so, this scene would do it for me. But we both know it's not enough. Besides, I have no intention of letting him come before I can have him.

"Stop," I order, my voice firm.

Cole immediately goes still, his hand still gripping the base of his cock. Slowly, I walk toward him, my hips swaying with each step. He watches me, his hungry gaze devouring me. When I'm close enough to touch him, I sink down to my knees before him.

"I want a taste," I whisper, looking up at him through my lashes. "Feed me your cock."

He sucks in a ragged breath. This is beyond anything we've done before. Part of me wonders why I'm being so bold tonight, but the rest of me is just eager to have him in my mouth. I've given blowjobs before. I've even enjoyed it on occasion. But I've never been so excited to have a man's cock in my mouth before this moment.

I open my mouth, letting him see my waiting tongue. He hesitates for only a moment before guiding his dick into my waiting mouth. He rests it on my tongue, unsure what to do next. Without taking my eyes off his face, I close my lips around the head and make a little hum of appreciation before swirling my tongue against the underside.

"Shit," he hisses, his body going rigid.

I release him from my mouth. "More," I say.

When he gives me a look of confusion, I reach over to his free hand and place it on the back of my head.

"More," I say again, this time injecting a command into my tone. "I want it all."

I can see the exact moment when understanding dawns and his eyes go dark and hungry with anticipation. Still, he hesitates.

"Are you sure?"

I smile up at him. "I'm in charge, remember?"

He moves to stand, his hand fisting lightly in my hair. "Tap my leg if it's too much," he says.

When I nod, he grips his thick cock at the base and guides it into my waiting mouth. This time, he doesn't stop at just the tip. He pushes slowly, but steadily forward until my mouth is filled with him. I close my lips around his length and suck lightly as he pulls back until just the head of him is between my lips. Then he thrusts back inside my mouth, faster this time. He stops just short of hitting the back of my mouth before repeating the motion. His hand in my hair holds me still for him to thrust into my mouth again and again. It shouldn't be this hot, letting this man fuck my mouth this way. It shouldn't turn me on as much as it does. But even though I'm on my knees for him, we both know he's completely at my mercy.

I hollow my cheeks as I suck harder, swirling my tongue against his flesh as he rocks deeper into my mouth. I can't take his full length. There's no way it would fit without choking me. But I can take more than he's giving me. Relaxing my throat, I push toward him on his next thrust and feel him slip past my gag reflex and down my throat the tiniest bit.

"Fuck," he groans, and I feel the hand in my hair tighten the slightest bit.

Hearing and feeling how much what I'm doing affects him sends a surge of arousal through me and I wish I could clench my thighs together for some semblance of relief. I've never been so turned on in my life. When he pulls back and thrusts forward again without hesitation, I let out a moan. Cole shudders as I hold him there, his cock deep in my throat.

"Layna," he grunts. "I'm not going to last long if you keep doing that."

I'd smile if I could, but instead I swallow lightly against him. When he groans again, I can't help myself. I reach down between my legs to my soaked panties and slide my fingers under the lace so I can touch myself. My eyes roll closed at the instant relief as I slide my fingers over my clit. Cole's grip on my hair tightens just to this side of pain, but I love it. It adds an extra layer of sensation that drives me wild. My fingers move faster over my clit, and I know it won't take much more for me to come. But I slow my speed, not wanting to rush my climax.

Cole's legs are trembling now, and I know he's so close. I could stop now, but I don't want to. I want to feel him lose control. I want to know that I did that to him. I pushed him over the edge with nothing but my mouth.

"Shit, Layna," he warns.

I moan again, letting him feel the vibrations all along his length as I push forward, holding him deep in my throat as he begins to come. I swallow quickly as Cole digs both hands in my hair and holds me still. His guttural groan turns me on even more and I push two fingers into my pussy as I swallow the last of his release.

"Fuck," he pants, easing his still semi-hard cock from my mouth. "You're incredible."

His hands stroke my face softly as he looks down at me. I smile up at him, feeling infinitely powerful.

"That was fun," I say, wiping my mouth with one hand.

When Cole notices that my other hand is still between my legs, his expression shifts to one of regret.

"Shit," he says. "I came too fast. I didn't even take care of you."

I stand, pulling my fingers away from my soaked pussy.

"We have all night," I say.

Without taking his eyes off me, Cole reaches for my wrist and brings my hand up to his mouth. He runs his tongue over my fingers before sucking them into his mouth, licking them clean. Damn. That's fucking hot. An idea springs to mind and I nod toward the bed behind him.

"Lie back," I say. "It's my turn."

His mouth quirks up into that sexy grin I love, and he moves to follow my command. When he lies back on the bed, I'm not surprised to see that he's already growing hard again. But he's nowhere near ready for what I need from him. In the meantime, I have other ideas for ways he can please me. Climbing onto the bed beside him, I waste no time moving to straddle his body. His hands go to my thighs, releasing the clips of the garters before sliding higher to my hips. I move higher, bracing myself above his chest. He looks up to meet my gaze and I can tell he understands my intent when he licks his lips.

"I'm going to sit on your face now," I say in a stern voice. "And I'm not getting off until you get me off. Understood?"

He gives me that cocky grin that I shouldn't like, but secretly do.

"Yes, ma'am," he says, already pulling me up toward his face.

I've never done anything like this before. I've certainly never sat on a man's face. I've had guys go down on me. Cole's done it plenty of times. I know he's got an insanely talented mouth when it comes to getting me off. But I've never felt bold enough or confident enough to do something like this. Tonight though, I feel like a different woman. One who's confident enough to demand what she wants. And Cole never backs down from a challenge.

When he has me positioned over his face, he pulls me down until I'm fully seated. I feel like I should hover or something. Surely this is uncomfortable for him, right? Except he doesn't seem to be uncomfortable. Instead, he yanks my panties off to one side and buries his tongue in my pussy.

"Oh, fuck!" I moan, falling forward to grip the headboard.

It's been so long since I've had his mouth on me. I'd almost forgotten how good he is at making me come with his lips and tongue. My eyes fall closed and everything in my body narrows down to a single point of focus between my legs. Cole's mouth is incredible as he licks and sucks at my clit, driving me to the brink faster than I thought possible. Just when I'm sure I'm about to hurtle over the edge, he moves away from my clit and delivers teasing kisses to my thighs.

A frustrated sound escapes me, and I try to move my clit closer to his mouth, but his grip on my thighs is too strong. He holds me exactly where he wants me as he kisses and nuzzles his face against me. Just when I'm about to demand he make me come now, he sucks my clit lightly between his lips and a startled gasp is pulled from me. Just like that, I'm right back on the brink of an orgasm. My breaths come in pants and my thighs are quivering. My hips move as if they have a mind of their own and I rub myself shamelessly against him, riding his face. This time, Cole doesn't stop. His tongue flicks against my clit rapidly and I scream his name as I fall apart.

"Yes, yes, yes, yes, yes," I moan as waves of pleasure roll through me. "Fuck!"

I grind myself against his face, the intensity of my orgasm shocking me as it slams through me. Cole keeps up his attention on my clit, holding me against him until I beg him to stop. I'm shocked by how hard I just came, but holy shit, it was hot. Cole slides out from under me, but I'm too dazed to understand his intentions until he's on his knees behind me gripping my hips.

"Hold on tight," he says.

It's the only warning I get before I feel his hard cock at my entrance. He pushes into me hard and fast before I'm fully recovered from my devastating orgasm. I spasm against his length, gripping it as he fills me. He feels so fucking *good*. I feel every inch of him as he slides out and then back in.

"Shit," he mutters, holding himself still while he's buried deep inside me.

"What?" I ask, looking back at him.

His jaw is clenched tightly and it's obvious he's barely holding onto his control. "No condom," he says through gritted teeth. "No wonder you feel so fucking good."

His hips flex the tiniest bit and my eyes roll shut at the pleasure it sends through me. Fuck. Cole's inside me with no barrier. We've always used condoms. For that matter, I've always used them with any partner I've had. It's one of the rules I've never broken with anyone. I should make him stop and get one. It's the smart thing to do. But I don't want to stop. I love the feeling of him inside me with nothing between us. Skin to skin. Flesh to flesh. It's intimate and sexy and I don't want to break that connection.

"I'm on birth control," I whisper.

Cole's gaze shoots to mine and I feel his fingers grip my hips just a little tighter. "I've only been with you since we met. And I got tested after that first night."

"So did I," I manage as I roll my hips against him. Fuck, that feels good.

"Layna," he whispers, needing to hear me say the words.

"Don't stop," I say.

I try to make it sound like a command, but I'm close to begging. I need this. I need him.

"Fuck me, Cole."

As if my words were the permission he needed to continue, Cole pulls back before plunging back in, filling me over and over with his hard length. The knowledge that there's nothing between us shouldn't be as sexy as it is, but it's all I can think about as he moves inside me. He keeps up a punishing pace, thrusting in and out until our bodies make lewd slapping sounds as they come together. I grip the headboard like a lifeline as Cole pounds into my body.

He delivers a stinging slap to my ass that makes me cry out. The mix of pleasure from his fucking me and the sharp sting of the slap make me even wetter. I can hear the sloppy sounds our bodies are making. It should make me self-conscious, but it just turns me on more.

"That's it baby," he says through clenched teeth. "Look at you. So fucking dirty. So wet. On your knees for me. Getting filled up by this cock. You love it, don't you?"

"Yes," I say on a moan, surprised I'm coherent enough to speak at all.

"I know you do," he says. "You like to be bad."

He slaps my ass again, this time on the other cheek and I moan. I shouldn't like it so much, but the truth is, I love it when he's rough with me. And he knows that.

"Look at this ass," he says, pulling me hard against him with every thrust. "Bouncing back against me while I fuck your pretty cunt. So fucking sexy."

Another slap to my ass is all it takes to send me flying over the edge.

"I'm coming!" I shout, feeling my pussy spasm around him.

Cole doesn't slow his movements as I come. He keeps thrusting, filling me with his cock again and again while I moan incoherently.

"You feel so fucking good," he grits out as his movements slow just a little. "Coming on my cock like a good girl. Squeezing me so tight. Your pussy was made for my cock."

His filthy words have always shocked me and turned me on. Tonight, they send me flying on a second, smaller wave of pleasure and I moan his name. He slows even more, sliding in and out at a glacial pace as I come down from my earth-shattering orgasms. I can feel my arms shaking, ready to give out when Cole eases out of me and flips me onto my back before immediately filling me again.

It's a new angle and I can see his intense gaze now. He captures my mouth with his as he begins to move again. This feels more intimate than before and part of me wants to close my eyes to hide from it. But I can't seem to look away from Cole's face. There's a look of intense concentration, but there's something else there that I can't define. My hands grip his arms where he's braced above me. It's as if touching him grounds me and helps me feel tethered to my body.

His movements are slow and purposeful as he slides in and out of me. This isn't like before. Before, he was focused solely on making me come with his body and his filthy words. Even the slaps on my ass had been as much for me as for him. But this? Now? This is something different. This is more intense and focused, and I'm so completely caught up in this moment.

"Layna."

He whispers my name as his hand comes up to cup my cheek. The gentle touch wrecks me more than anything he's done to my body so far and I let my eyes fall closed against the rush of emotion. It wasn't supposed to be this way. I was never supposed to feel this intense need for anyone, let alone a man who can never truly be mine. I swallow against the lump of emotion welling up in my throat and try to focus on the pleasure instead.

"Look at me," Cole says, the command in his voice making my eyes snap open.

He's gazing down at me as his body rocks into mine slowly. I don't recognize the look I see in his brown eyes, but something about it scares me. I want to look away, but his gaze has a hold on me, and I find myself unable to break eye contact.

"Stay with me," he whispers.

He pushes deeper inside me, and I gasp, my fingernails digging into his arms. He reaches back and pulls my leg higher, deepening the angle even further. When I cry out in pleasure at the new sensation, he smiles, grinding his pelvis against me. My mouth drops open on a silent moan and I feel myself slip silently over the edge into oblivion, my orgasm building slowly until it swells into a wave of pleasure so intense that tears spring to my eyes.

Cole lowers his head to kiss me, and I pour everything into that kiss, loving the added connection to him as I spiral. Kissing me when he's coming has always been his thing. I've never understood the need for it. Until now. Right now, I need to feel him surrounding me, encompassing me. Even as he fills me with his own release. I wrap my arms around his neck and pull him down to cover me completely as he groans into my mouth. The weight of him on my body, his lips on mine, my arms holding him tight against me; it's something I never knew I could need so much. The idea terrifies me, but I can't seem to release my hold on him, even after he goes still, and I can feel him softening inside me. I'll let go soon. I just need a few more minutes of oblivion.

CHAPTER 30

Cole

"Shit."

The muffled curse pulls me from one of the best nights of sleep I've ever had, bringing me to confused consciousness. The curtains are drawn shut, keeping the room cast in shadows and making it impossible for me to guess the time. I hear a scuffling sound and look in that direction to see Layna bent over, searching for something on the floor. A glance at the clock tells me it's later in the morning than I thought. But there's still plenty of time before we're needed for the wedding festivities.

"Hey."

My low whisper startles Layna and she jumps, turning to look at me.

"What are you doing?"

"Go back to sleep," she whispers. "I'm just trying to find my clothes."

I grin when I remember that she hadn't been wearing clothes last night. "What clothes?" I tease.

My eyes have adjusted, and I can make out Layna's form better now. She doesn't smile at my joke, but that doesn't surprise me. She's caught up in her search. I reach over and flip the switch on the bedside lamp, squinting at the sudden brightness.

"Let me help you look," I say, climbing out of bed.

"You don't need to," Layna objects.

"I want to."

She sighs and moves to pick up a discarded stocking, making me grin. I still don't know why she'd come here last night. Not the real reason, anyway. I have a hard time buying that she just wanted to scratch an itch. We haven't had sex in weeks—not since she started dating other people. I push away my irritation at that memory. Regardless of her reason for showing up last night, I'm happy she did. It had been the most spectacular sex of my life. And she'd looked so hot in that corset thing. Speaking of, I eye the garment where it sticks out from under the blankets at the foot of the bed. Smiling, I hold it out to her.

"Not that I'm complaining," I say as she takes the piece from me. "But why were you wearing that last night?"

As soon as the words leave my mouth, I want to call them back. What if she'd been wearing it for Michael, but something happened to cause them to break up before she could make use of it with him? That would make me her second choice. *Duh, idiot. You've never been her choice.* That thought stings more than I care to admit, so I do my best not to think about it.

Layna waves away my question. "It was Harlow's idea," she says. "A boudoir photo shoot for Piper the night before her wedding."

I blink. "A what?"

"It's one of those things where you get hair and makeup done and you wear all these sexy outfits and have a professional photo shoot," she says as if that makes all the sense in the world.

"That's a thing?" I ask. "Sexy photo shoots?"

My dick stirs to life when I remember how Layna had looked in that outfit. Come to think of it, her hair and makeup had looked a little different too. Not that she isn't always beautiful. But there had been something different about her last night. I'd been too distracted by her actions and what was under that coat to focus on it at the time.

"Yep," she says, still moving around the room, collecting bits of fabric.

"Wait," I say. "Does that mean there are photos of you wearing that? Because if so, I need a copy."

She shakes her head, smiling at me. "If you must know, yes. I ordered a few photos in different outfits and poses. That just happened to be my favorite outfit."

My imagination is full of possibilities, and I want to ask her more about these outfits and poses, but instead I hold out one black high heel toward her. When she moves to take it from me, I pull her against me instead of releasing it. Her hand goes to my chest as if to push me away, but the attempt is half-hearted at best.

"Cole, I need to go," she whispers. "The wedding is..."

"Hours away," I argue, looking down at her. "Stay a little longer. We'll order breakfast. We can try out my giant shower. I'll have you back to your room in plenty of time to be there for Piper."

She still looks hesitant, so I lean down to kiss her lips. "Please?" I murmur the word against her mouth.

She sighs and I feel some of the tension leaving her body. I smile and kiss her again, lingering this time. The hand on my chest slides higher, wrapping around my neck as her lips soften, and she melts against me. I smile, feeling something in my chest swell almost painfully at the realization that she's going to stay a little longer. I'm surprised I managed to convince her, especially after last night. We'd broken more than one of her rules.

Speaking of rules, Layna slept with me last night. It may have only been for a few hours, but she'd stayed in my bed and slept beside me. That had been a first. She's never even allowed herself to doze off beside me in the past, but last night she'd let me pull her back against me as she'd fallen asleep. And it's the best sleep I've had in years. I want to ask her what this means, but I'm not an idiot. I know what would happen if I did that. She'd shut me out so fast my head would spin. I need to play this carefully.

So, I order room service and pull her into the massive, tiled shower while we wait for the food to be delivered. I keep things light, flirting and teasing her as we wash. I try to help her wash her hair, but she swats me away until I leave her to it. Instead, I deliver teasing touches to her body while her hands are occupied. She grins and rolls her eyes at me but doesn't push me away.

When we emerge from the bathroom, clean and dressed in fluffy bathrobes, we help ourselves to the food that was delivered while we were showering.

We eat as we talk about the coming day and all the last-minute wedding preparations. It all feels so blissfully normal that I feel a pang in my chest. This is what I want. I want to wake up with Layna in my bed every morning. I want to talk about our upcoming days over breakfast. I want to know that at the end of the day she'll be there when I come home. I want to hear about her day at work and fall into bed with her each night. I want to share all the little moments as well as the big ones. But I can't tell her any of that.

I think about my brother's words. Him telling me to stop being a chicken shit and just tell Layna how I feel. Then I remember all the times she's pushed me away, citing our age difference or my reputation, and I hesitate. If I knew how she'd react, I'd spill my guts right now. I'd tell her everything. But I don't know, and that's what scares me. Her rejecting me is a strong possibility. Just because she spent the night with me doesn't mean she sees me as boyfriend material. She hasn't said or done anything to indicate she's changed her mind about me.

"I should go soon," she says, pulling my mind back to the present.

She's seated at the vanity, using my hairbrush on her damp hair. I've never seen her so relaxed. Her face is free of makeup and her hair is drying in soft waves down her back. She's wearing a bathrobe and her bare feet are tucked underneath her. I have the sudden thought that I could easily spend the rest of my life with this woman. The idea should terrify me, but it doesn't. The only thing that scares me is not knowing if she can see a future with the guy who started out as just a fling.

"Stay a little longer," I say, catching her gaze in the mirror.

"Cole, I need to get dressed," she says. "Piper and Harlow are expecting me in an hour for hair and makeup."

"How long does it take for hair and makeup? The wedding isn't for hours."

She laughs. "Oh, what a sweet, naïve man. Hair and makeup can take hours. Plus, there are photos and champagne and possible tears. And then fixing the makeup that the tears mess up. It's a whole process."

I don't like the idea of her crying, but I know women tend to cry at weddings. Piper is her only family. She's bound to be emotional about her getting married.

"What time is Piper expecting you?" I ask.

"I told you. In an hour," she says.

"So, stay with me for another half hour and I'll walk you to your door myself," I say.

"Cole..."

"Layna..."

She sighs. "I still don't have any clothes here."

"So, wear some of mine," I say.

"I can't wear your clothes."

"Why not?" I ask. "It's either the bathrobe, last night's incredibly sexy lingerie, or my clothes. I vote for the lingerie. But just know that if you put that back on, I can't guarantee you'll make it to your sister in an hour."

She laughs, shaking her head. "Have you ever worn a corset? They're not the easiest things to put on."

"I'll take your word for it," I say. "So, no corset. That leaves the bathrobe or my clothes. Which is it? And don't worry. I'll walk you right to your door. If anyone gives you a weird look, I promise to intimidate them with my manly glare."

"Cole, you don't have to do that," she says. "I can make it to my room."

"I know you can. But I want to."

"Why?"

Because I'm looking for any excuse to spend just a few more minutes alone with you. But I don't say that. Because I'm not ready to say it aloud. And I don't think she's ready to hear it. And I'm scared she'll tell me it's just sex again. I don't know if I can stomach hearing that again. Not after last night.

"Because I want to," I say lamely.

She holds my gaze in the mirror for a long moment but doesn't speak.

"Why won't you ever let anyone take care of you?" I ask.

She gives me a playful smile, not realizing that my question was serious. "Why?" she asks. "Do you want to?"

"Yeah." I nod. "Why is that such a crazy idea?"

She turns back to the mirror, running the brush through her hair and scoffs. I don't know why I need to press the issue now, of all times. My best friend is getting married in just a few hours and we're both in the wedding party. The last thing I need to do is make things awkward between us now. But something in me won't let this go until I know.

"Seriously," I say. "Tell me why you keep pushing me away but not Michael? You were going to try to have a relationship with him, but you won't even consider it with me. Why?"

Her hand stills and she lowers the brush to the table, but she doesn't turn to look at me. I know I'm about to say things I can't take back. I know whatever happens next, I might just be signing the death certificate on whatever is happening between me and Layna. But I can't seem to stop myself.

"And don't think I don't know better," I say. "You didn't really want him. You were never going to be happy with someone like that. So, why him? Why him and not me?"

I watch as Layna takes in a shuddering breath before lifting her gaze to focus on me in the mirror. When she speaks, her voice is low.

"Because he was safe," she says. "Because you were right. I never need anyone. The only person I ever needed left me. And it wasn't her fault, but she did it. And that broke something in me. Maybe it broke me altogether. I don't know. But I couldn't show that. Because then I was the one who was needed. I couldn't fall apart. I had to be strong for Piper. I had to show her that we'd be okay. I had to be a mom when I still needed mine."

Her voice breaks on the last word and my heart breaks in my chest for the eighteen-year-old girl who lost her mom so suddenly.

"Layna, I can't imagine what that was like. I wish I knew what to do or say to fix that hole in your life."

She shakes her head, still looking into the mirror instead of turning to face me.

"That's just it," she says, her tone careful. "I never wanted someone to fill that hole in my life. I never wanted to fall in love with anyone. I just wanted someone safe to build a life with. Someone I could marry and have kids with. Someone who—"

I can't stop the derisive laugh that comes out. "Someone not me, I guess."

She shakes her head, opening her mouth to speak as she finally turns to face me. But I'm filled with a sudden anger at her 'explanation' and I find I don't want to hear the rest of it. This is her way of telling me, yet again, why I'm not right for her. I'm too young. I'm too wild. I'm not 'safe enough', whatever that means.

"I don't know why I'm surprised," I let out another humorless laugh. "You do this every time. I don't know why I thought it was different this time. But I can't even blame you. Not really. You're the same woman you've always been. The same Layna who just wanted a fling with the small-town guy you thought you'd never see again. You've never pretended to be more. This is my fault for expecting things to be different just because I—"

I clamp my mouth shut against the words I wish I could say.

"Cole, I'm sorry—"

"Don't be," I say, my voice hard.

There's something in her expression that might be pain, but I don't trust my own thoughts and feelings where she's concerned. It's too easy to imagine what I want to see and hear. All at once, fury surges inside me and I need to get out of here before I say something I can't take back.

"I get it. You can't change who you are, right? But don't expect me to wait around for you to figure your shit out. I'm done. This was the last time. I hope it was worth it."

"Cole, wait." She reaches for me, but I pull away before she can touch me.

"Damn it, Layna," I bite off. "Don't."

She goes still, and I wait to see if she'll say or do anything to stop me from leaving. When she just looks at me, her brown eyes shining with unshed tears, I feel my anger burn even brighter.

"I can't just be the person you fuck when you're too afraid to feel something," I say, my voice icy.

She recoils as if I struck her and part of me wants to call back the words. But I don't. I meant them, even if they hurt. So, no matter how much that stricken look in her eyes haunts me, I don't apologize. Instead, I turn and walk away, leaving her alone in my hotel room.

CHAPTER 31

Layna

I sit, unmoving for several long minutes after the door closes behind Cole, replaying his last words over and over in my head. I've never heard him sound so hard and cold. I've never seen him so angry. He could barely even look at me. It's my fault. I did that to him. He'd been carefree, charming, and kind when I met him. Now, I can't stop seeing the cold anger in his eyes before he'd walked out.

I can't just be the person you fuck when you're too afraid to feel something.

That's not what I did, is it? That's not what this was between us. It was supposed to be fun, a way for two friends to let off steam. It was never supposed to turn into something that could cause the kind of anger I'd seen in his eyes. It was never supposed to hurt this badly when it ended. I was never supposed to feel this way about him.

I swallow back the lump in my throat. I can't start crying now. If I start, I'm worried I'll never stop. I look around the room, memories of last night crashing through my mind, overlapping with the fight we just had. It's too much. All of a sudden, it's too much. I need to get out of this room that smells like him and holds all his things. Away from the bed where I'd let him hold me while we slept. A tear escapes and I sniff against it, swiping it away as I move around the room, gathering my things. I don't bother putting on the heels, or even changing from the fluffy robe into my long black coat. My arms full of clothes and shoes, I leave the room, prepared to make the short run down the hallway to my own room. Instead, I run smack into a wall of muscle.

Strong hands wrap around my upper arms, steadying me.

"Whoa," a familiar male voice says. "You okay?"

I feel my face flush red as I look up into the face of Cole's brother. *Shit.* This is the last thing I needed this morning. My eyes are still threatening to release a flood of tears and I know how I must look right now. Walking out of his brother's room in the morning in nothing but a bathrobe, carrying a pile of clothes. I glance down covertly to make sure the lingerie is all wrapped up inside the coat. Thankfully, it is.

I give Linc what I hope is a convincing smile and nod.

"Fine," I say, my voice barely a squeak.

Whatever he sees on my face must not be convincing, because his brows furrow in concern and he sighs.

"I guess it finally happened," he says.

He looks a little disappointed, but not surprised to see me here.

"What did?" I try to make my words sound light and breezy, but the lump growing in my throat makes it impossible.

"Cole finally talked to you," Linc says. "And I'm guessing it didn't go well?"

I have no idea what he's talking about, but the sound of Cole's name sends a fresh wave of pain through me, and I find I don't have it in me to ask.

"I need to go," I whisper.

I cannot break down crying in the hallway. I can't. And I especially can't do it in front of Cole's brother. I also don't have a room key to get back into Cole's room. I need to get to my own room so I can take five minutes to wallow. I can't fall apart right now. To his credit, Linc doesn't ask more questions. He just nods.

"I'll walk you to your room," he says.

I want to argue that I don't need an escort to take me down the hall and around the corner, but I know it would take more time to argue than to just let him walk with me. He's always been a gentleman. I doubt his southern manners would allow him to let me just leave that way. So, I give him a single nod and start walking in the direction of my room.

Linc doesn't say anything as we walk and I'm grateful for his silence. I'm not sure I'd be able to speak right now without turning into a blubbering mess. When we reach my room, I turn to face him.

"Thank you," I say.

"It's no trouble," he says, his voice gentle.

I expect him to turn and walk back toward the elevator only a few feet away, but instead, he sighs. Not meeting my gaze, he rubs the back of his neck as if he's uncomfortable.

"Listen, Layna," he says. "I don't know what happened between you two, but I hope you can work things out."

I nod, managing to hold it together. He can't know how much I wish that was a possibility.

"For what it's worth, I've never seen him this way about another woman. Never."

Linc's words hit me with the force of a sledge hammer, and I feel my breath leave me. He puts a hand on my shoulder and gives me a comforting squeeze. That's all it takes for the dam to burst. A sob escapes me, and I bury my face in my hands. I can't breathe. I can't speak. I can't do anything but stand there and cry as the wave of pain washes over me. I feel arms come around me and hear soft murmurs as Linc tries to comfort me, but it doesn't matter. Those aren't the arms I need around me, and that's not the voice I need to hear right now.

"How long was I gone for coffee?"

I feel Linc's entire body go rigid at the sound of Harlow's amused voice. He immediately moves to distance himself from me, shifting to face her.

"This isn't what it looks like," he says.

"I know," Harlow says. "But the look on your face is hilarious."

If I weren't so destroyed, I might find the situation amusing. I turn and see Harlow standing there, a cup of coffee in each hand as she eyes me and her boyfriend. I edge a little further away from Linc and try to wipe away the tears streaming down my face. It's no use, though. They just keep coming. I open my mouth to speak, to try to explain the situation, but a strangled sob emerges instead. I cover my mouth with my hands, letting my coat, the heels and my lingerie fall to the floor.

Harlow steps forward, handing the cups to Linc and putting an arm around my shoulder.

"I've got this, big guy," she says. "Get the door, please."

I can't even summon up any embarrassment at the fact that Linc is rummaging through my coat pockets to find my room key, pushing aside my thong and one stocking to find it. To his credit, he doesn't say anything. He just stands and opens the door so Harlow can lead me inside. Then he gathers up the pile of clothing and follows behind us.

Harlow leads me over to the small couch and sits with me, keeping her arm around my shoulders. She murmurs something that I know is meant to console me, but it's no use. I can't seem to stop the tears and the sobs from wracking my body.

"Where should I put this?" Linc asks.

I glance up to see him standing there, awkwardly holding my coat and lingerie, one high heel dangling from his fingertip. I have an insane urge to laugh, but I'm crying too hard for that to be a possibility.

"Just throw it in the trash," I manage. "I don't ever want to see it again."

"Is that from the photo shoot?" Harlow asks. She narrows her eyes at Linc. "Do not throw that away! That outfit was *hot*!"

"Um," Linc says. "I feel like I should go. Do you still need me here?"

"You can both go," I say. "I'll be fine."

A fresh round of sobs wracks my body and I bury my face in my hands.

"Fuck that," Harlow says. "I'm not going anywhere. Linc, get me a box of tissues and call Piper. Get her over here."

"No!" I shout. "Do not call her!"

Harlow eyes me carefully. "Layna, honey, you're a hot mess. Clearly something happened to you. And while I'm more than happy to be the shoulder you cry on for as long as you need it, your sister would be really upset if you needed her and she wasn't here. We're calling her. That's not a request."

I realize all at once that there's no way I'm getting out of this without involving my sister. The second I ran into Linc outside Cole's hotel room, my fate was sealed. I try to stem the flow of tears, but it's no use. The truth is, I do want my sister right now. I want her to hug me and tell me it's going to be okay. I want her to comfort me and tell me I screwed up but it's not the end of the world.

But the last thing I want to do is add to her stress on her wedding day. As her maid of honor and her older sister, it's my job to protect her peace today. Not to fuck it up. And finding out that I've been sleeping with the groom's best friend and that I might have ruined all future group outings from now until we die? Well, that might just fuck up her peace.

"It's her wedding day," I whisper. "I don't want to ruin anything."

"You're her sister," Harlow says gently. "She loves you. She'd want to be here for you. Even on her wedding day."

It's no use, I realize. And besides, I'm tired of pretending to be strong.

"Okay," I whisper.

Linc already has his cell phone pressed to his ear and is talking to someone. I hadn't even noticed he'd made a phone call. I listen as he speaks.

"Yeah, man," he says, turning back to eye me carefully. "Just send her to Layna's room. It's urgent."

He pauses as he listens for a moment, nodding.

"Have you seen Cole this morning?" he asks.

My heart clenches at the sound of his name, even as I hate myself for that reaction.

Linc sighs and rubs the back of his neck as he paces the room. "No, it's fine. Nothing to worry about. I'll see you in a couple hours."

He ends the call and looks over to me briefly before turning to look at Harlow.

"Piper will be here soon," he says. "Do you need me to stay?"

She shakes her head. "We can take it from here."

He nods. "Good. I need to go find my brother."

At Harlow's confused expression, Linc gives me a meaningful look. It takes less than a second for Harlow's mouth to drop open and for her to turn her shocked expression on me. I swipe at the stray tears still leaking from my eyes and try not to meet her gaze. Luckily for me, she turns an accusatory glare at her boyfriend.

"You knew about this and didn't tell me?! How long have you known?"

Linc immediately holds up his hands in surrender. "Harlow, listen," he says, "I wanted to tell you, but it wasn't my secret to tell. I swear, I hated not telling you."

She narrows her eyes even further. "Just how long have you known about this?"

"A while," he says, a sheepish expression on his face.

Her brows go up and she turns to look at me. "Just how long has this been going on? *What,* exactly, is going on, anyway? Will someone tell me what the fuck is happening?"

I open my mouth to answer her, unsure of just what I should or shouldn't say. But I'm saved by a knock on the door. My relief is short-lived, however, when I hear my sister's worried voice on the other side of the door.

"Layna? I'm here. What's wrong?"

I sigh as my eyes fill with tears again.

The worry and fear on my sister's face is the first thing I see. I know it's not something I'll forget for a long time. She rushes into the room, pushing open the door as soon as Linc turns the door handle.

"Layna? What happened?"

She's at my side in an instant, sitting beside me on the couch and wrapping her arm around me. I see Linc and Harlow exchange a meaningful look that says he's going to have a lot of explaining to do later. Then he sneaks quietly from the room. When it's just the three of us left in the room, Piper shifts to face me, handing me another tissue. She pushes the hair from my face and tries to tuck it behind my ears, but it keeps falling forward.

"Talk to me," she says in a gentle voice that nearly breaks me all over again. "You never cry. Are you hurt? Did something happen?

I shake my head. "Not physically," I whisper.

"Tell me," Piper says. "I love you, and I'm here for you. No matter what."

CHAPTER 32

Cole

After storming out of my hotel room, it doesn't take me long to realize I don't have anywhere to go. I don't have a plan. It's not like I have another hotel room to go to and I can't exactly go home. I have a wedding to attend in a few hours. I don't even know why I left, but I know I can't go back now. I need to get as far away from Layna as possible before I say something even more horrible to her. Not that what I already said isn't bad enough. I doubt she'll forgive me for that. I push that thought aside. I don't want to think about her right now. I'll deal with it later. For now, I need to decide where to go.

I look down at myself as I walk. I'm wearing a pair of gym shorts, an old t-shirt with the bar's logo on it and carrying my shoes. I never thought a person could do a walk of shame from their own hotel room, but that's exactly what I'm doing right now. I make my way to the elevator, pleased when it opens as soon as I press the button. I push the button for the lobby before leaning against the back wall to put my shoes on. I still don't allow myself to think about Layna or the fight we just had. I especially don't let myself think about last night.

I make my way to the hotel's restaurant, intending to find some coffee or maybe something for breakfast, but I remember I'm wearing gym attire and they probably won't let me in here like this. It's early, but this isn't the kind of place that overlooks decorum. Already, I can see the curious stares of people in the lobby. Okay, change of plans. I turn toward the exit, intending to walk until I find some place that will serve coffee to someone in gym shorts. There's got to be some kind of coffee shop around here, right?

I exit the hotel and turn left at random. I don't even have my cellphone, so I can't look up a nearby coffee shop. I'll just have to hope I'm walking in the right direction. The realization that I don't have my phone reminds me that I also don't have my wallet. Sighing, I stop walking and look up at the sky.

"Shit," I mutter.

"Rough morning?" a voice asks from beside me.

I turn and see Wyatt King standing there, looking as disreputable as ever, his long hair falling around his shoulders and his tattooed arms exposed. His expression is a mixture of concern and humor.

"Too much partying last night?" he asks, smiling at me.

I sigh and shake my head. "I wish a hangover was my biggest problem. I was trying to find coffee, but I left my room without my wallet or my phone."

He nods, though he looks like he wants to ask more questions. "I was on my way to the coffee shop around the corner," he says. "Come on. I'll buy you a cup."

I give him a relieved smile. "Thanks, man. I'll owe you."

He waves that away as we start walking. "Nah. I put my drinks on your tab last night."

When I just nod, he gives me a look through narrowed eyes. "You sure you're okay?"

"Yeah," I say. "Fine."

We walk in silence for a full minute before Wyatt speaks again.

"I don't mean to be rude," he says. "But I think you're full of shit."

This time I do laugh. It's quick, but it makes Wyatt smile in answer. We reach the coffee shop, and he opens the door, motioning for me to enter ahead of him.

As we join the line to order, he says, "You can tell me if I'm overstepping. I'll leave you to your misery. But if you need to talk, I'm a good listener."

I glance over at him. I only met this guy two days ago. I barely know him. I know Luke considers him family, along with the rest of the Kings. It's why he invited them all to his wedding. Which means they're probably good people. Luke is an excellent judge of character. He also told me and Linc how the King family welcomed him as one of them as soon as they found out he was Mya's brother. For a man who grew up with the kind of family Luke did, I know it meant a lot to him to have people who cared about him without any conditions.

I think about Wyatt's offer as we stand in the slow-moving line. He doesn't know anything about me or Layna. He's an impartial party. Maybe that's just what

I need right now. Linc is my brother and I know he has my back, no matter what. But he's also biased in my favor. He can't be trusted not to tell me what I want to hear. Maybe I should talk to Wyatt. Get an outsider's opinion. I don't have to give Layna's name. I can keep it vague.

"Yeah," I say. "Maybe it would be good to talk about it."

Wyatt flashes me a smile. "Good. So many people avoid talking about their issues. You'd be surprised how much can be resolved by a simple conversation."

I nod, thinking of how I might have avoided this whole situation with Layna if I'd just told her how I felt months ago. But Linc was right. I was too much of a chicken shit to put myself out there. But I don't say any of that to Wyatt. Instead, I nod as we step forward to place our coffee orders. When we have our coffee in hand and Wyatt has a cream cheese Danish, we make our way over to a table in the corner. He bites into his pastry and sighs as he chews. I sip my coffee and wait. Finally, he stops chewing and looks at me.

"Okay, go," he says. "What's got you looking so rumpled this morning?"

I sigh, trying to think of where to start. Finally, I decide to start at the beginning.

"There's this girl," I begin.

"There always is," he says.

"Right," I agree. "Well, she and I have been doing a kind of friends-with-benefits thing for a while."

"Oof," he winces. "Friends-with-benefits never works out."

I feel slightly annoyed by the interruption. Especially if he's just going to interrupt to tell me what I already know. I shoot him a pointed look.

"I thought you were a good listener."

He grins. "I am. I swear. No more interruptions, I promise. Continue."

I narrow my eyes at him for a moment, but I've come this far. I can't stop now.

"Well, it's been going on for a while, like I said. Neither of us wanted anything serious. We both knew that going in. But then she decided she wanted to end it so she could give dating a try."

I look at Wyatt, expecting him to interrupt again, but he keeps quiet. He does look as if he's trying to hold back a comment, though. I decide to ignore it and keep talking.

"So, I backed off. Gave her my blessing," I say. "But the truth is, I've always wanted more with her. I just never told her. I figured she'd go on a couple of dates and realize she missed me and that she maybe wanted to give dating me a shot."

Wyatt's expression shifts to one of sympathy. "I'm guessing that's not what happened?"

I shake my head. "She started dating someone. It looked like things were getting serious. I tried to launch a plan to show her she should be with me, but it didn't work."

I take a breath as I try to decide how to explain last night and this morning in a tactful way. I finally decide that there's no way I can explain without Wyatt understanding exactly what happened between me and Layna. So, I just plow ahead.

"But last night she showed up at my hotel room," I say. "She said she dumped the guy. That he wasn't right for her. And she was dressed for *'benefits'*, if you know what I mean."

He nods, his smile knowing. "I do."

"Right. So, she spent the night in my room. And keep in mind, she's never slept in the same bed with me. Not once. So, this morning I woke up thinking this was it. She finally realized she wants me. We can be a real couple, right?"

I sigh as I remember the argument and the stupid way it started. Then I remember what I said to her as I walked out and there's a sick feeling in my gut.

"What happened?" Wyatt asks.

I shrug. "I wimped out. Again. Instead, I yelled at her for not letting me help her. We argued. I stormed out. You found me."

"Looking like a lost puppy on the sidewalk?" he supplies, smiling.

I glare at him and his smile fades.

"Right," he says, leaning back in his chair and picking up his coffee. "You need to tell her how you feel."

I sigh, my eyes rolling toward the ceiling. "If she wanted me, she would have said so. She had every chance to do it this morning."

"Maybe she thinks the same thing about you."

"Then why was she dating someone else?"

He shrugs. "I don't know, man. Women aren't always easy to understand." He leans forward over the table and points a finger at me. "But I'll tell you one thing. If you love this girl, you can't keep being a pussy about it. You need to tell her."

I stare at my coffee cup without replying as Wyatt finishes off the rest of his pastry. I think back to two days ago when the King family arrived at the hotel. They'd been full of noisy laughter, inside jokes and big hugs. I think about the petite brunette I'd seen with Wyatt. She'd looked as different from him as someone could be. Her shoulder-length hair was lightly curled. She'd been wearing a sundress with a floral print. She'd also been standing serenely by his side while he and most of the other Kings had been loudly greeting Luke and Piper in the hotel lobby. I look over at the tattoos and long hair, the disreputable image Wyatt portrays.

"Can I ask you something?" I say.

He nods. "Shoot."

"You and Hope," I say.

Wyatt's face changes completely at the mention of his wife's name. His smile goes soft and almost dream-like and even his eyes seem different. He loses the carefree demeanor of before and for once, he looks serious.

"You want to know what she sees in a bum like me?" he asks.

I laugh. "I wasn't going to say that."

He waves away my words. "Nah, you're good. Everyone wonders about us. From the outside, we seem like total opposites. Everyone says so. You should have seen her mom when she first met me." He laughs before his expression turns serious again.

"I really don't know what she sees in me," he says. "But I knew as soon as I met her that she was something worth holding onto. She didn't see it that way. She thought what everyone else thinks about me. But I was persistent. I eventually managed to convince her that I wasn't a total shithead. We became friends. And then, more. She kept telling me it was temporary. A fling. But I knew I never wanted it to end."

I smile. "How did you convince her?"

He laughs. "Well, she thought she caught me cheating and ran way to another state." He lifts his coffee cup to his lips and downs the last of it. "I had to chase her down and convince her of the truth. It's a long story."

I open my mouth to ask for clarification, but then think better of it.

"So, what are you going to do about your lady?" he asks as we stand and head for the exit.

I think about Wyatt's advice and everything he told me about him and Hope. It sounds like he and I have more in common than I originally thought. Maybe he's right and I should just tell Layna I'm in love with her. I remember everything she said this morning about wanting someone safe and easy and my heart clenches in my chest. I don't know if my heart can take hearing her say aloud that she doesn't want me.

"I don't know," I say. "Hope she sees something in me worth sticking around for."

He claps me on the shoulder as we leave walk. "If not, go after her. It worked for me."

"I'll keep that in mind."

CHAPTER 33

Layna

Once I start talking, I can't seem to stop. I tell Piper and Harlow everything. I tell them how I'd had sex with Cole the night we met and how we had sex again every time I came into town to visit Piper. I tell them about our conversations and how we both agreed it was just sex. Friends with benefits and nothing more.

I tell them about how I ended it over a month ago, before I started dating again. I even tell them about Cole agreeing to be my wingman the night we created my online dating profile, and how he'd rescued me from Dillon. My words finally trail off as I try to decide how to explain the events of last night. The last thing they knew, I was still dating Michael and planning to take him to the wedding. The thought is repellent now.

I glance back and forth between Harlow and Piper, surprised and grateful that neither of them has interrupted me to ask questions the entire time I've been talking. Beyond the twin looks of shock on their faces when they'd realized just how long I've been lying to them, they've kept even their opinions to themselves. Taking a deep breath, I go on.

"I broke up with Michael last night. After the boudoir shoot."

When even this news doesn't gain a response, I turn to Piper.

"You don't have anything to say?"

"Michael was never the guy for you," she says with a shrug.

My mouth drops open. "That's it? *That's* what you're choosing to focus on right now?"

"She's right, though," Harlow says. "He's nice enough, and not bad to look at. But he's boring. And he doesn't want what you want."

I turn to face Harlow now. "What do you mean, he doesn't want what I want? How do you know?"

She makes a face. "He was always going on and on about how much he loves his place in the city. How much he loves his job and his car. It was slightly obnoxious. Plus, he didn't seem to mind it when you weren't around."

"What does that mean?" I ask.

She shrugs. "Just that, when you weren't around, he wasn't wondering where you were. He didn't ask when you'd be back. Most people in a new relationship who are suddenly thrown into a new group of friends will want to stick beside their partner. They're uncomfortable in the new dynamic and want to be near the person they know best. But Michael didn't seem to care. It just seemed like he was networking all the time." She shakes her head. "I don't know. But you can definitely do better than that guy."

I smile for the first time since that disastrous fight with Cole. "Thanks, Harlow."

"Breaking up with Michael isn't what had you crying this morning," Piper says. We're both aware that it's not a question.

I shake my head. "No. It's not."

I suck in a deep breath and tell them the rest of it. I leave out the more sordid details from last night, but there's no mistaking what happened between me and Cole.

"But then this morning we had a fight," I say, my voice breaking on the words.

Had I thought I was finished crying? Turns out there are more tears left in me, after all. Piper's arm comes around my shoulders, and she hugs me against her.

"It's going to be okay," she murmurs.

I know it's what I wanted to hear, but somehow the words make me cry harder. Because she's wrong. I don't think I can fix what I broke this time.

"I don't know," I say. "I think I fucked things up for good."

"Why don't you tell us what happened, and we'll be the judge of whether or not it's fucked up," Harlow says.

I recount the argument with Cole, including his angry words just before he'd stormed out. When I look up to meet Harlow's gaze, she looks more thoughtful than shocked by Cole's behavior.

"What?" I ask, nervous to hear what she thinks.

She sighs. "Well, that's definitely out of character for Cole. I don't know that I've ever seen him truly angry."

The sinking feeling in the pit of my stomach grows larger, threatening to swallow me whole. Harlow has known Cole since they were children and she's never seen him angry enough to shout the things he shouted at me this morning.

"I broke him," I say. "I took a perfectly good man and broke him. With my vagina. What kind of a person does that?"

Harlow snorts out a laugh, but I'm feeling far from amused.

"You didn't break anyone with your vagina," Piper says. "Stop being so dramatic."

"She's right," Harlow says. "He's not broken. He's just pissed off. And he has every right to be."

My mouth drops open. "What? Why?"

Harlow gives me a knowing look before rolling her eyes. "Do I need to spell it out for you? Fine. You both agreed to be fuck buddies, right?"

I'm not sure I like the crude phrasing, but I nod.

"But then you became friends, right?" Harlow asks.

I nod again. "Right."

"And then, maybe something more?" Piper asks, her voice gentler than Harlow's.

I open my mouth to argue, but I can't find the words. Because I think maybe my sister is right.

"You did everything with that man except date him," Harlow says. "You hung out. You watched movies. He knows your favorite ice cream flavor, your food allergies and where you keep your EpiPen. If that's not a man who's smitten, I don't know what is."

Piper's mouth drops open, and she leans around me to look at Harlow. "Oh, my god! You're right. It makes so much more sense now. The way he was panicking when he thought she ate the shrimp! He's totally in love with her."

"You're both delusional," I say, unwilling to consider the validity of their words.

They're both wrong. Of course, they are. There's no way Cole is in love with me. I would know. He would have said something. He would have shown me somehow.

"He's not," I whisper. "He would have told me. He had every chance to tell me."

Piper runs a hand over my hair and sighs. "You want to explain it, or should I?"

"I'll take this one," Harlow says.

She puts her hands on my shoulders and turns me to face her. "If he does love you, can you think of a reason he might not have told you?"

I shake my head, trying to ignore the way my chest feels tight and achy and wrong.

She sighs. "You two did everything that comes with a relationship except go on dates. For over a year. Put yourself in his position. How would you feel if, after all that time together, he came to you and said he was ready to start dating seriously. And he was doing it with someone else. Without even considering you as an option or asking if you were interested. Do you think you would have told him you had feelings for him?"

"But he always said he didn't want anything serious!" I shout. "He said it so many times."

Piper's voice is gentle. "Sometimes people tell you what they think you want to hear. If he'd told you, and you didn't feel the same, you would have ended things, right?"

"Probably," I admit.

I think back to that day in my bedroom and Cole's face when I'd told him it was the last time. The way he'd joked about being chopped liver. He'd played it off as a joke, but what if he was serious? What if he'd wanted more with me and I'd pushed him away? What if he could have been mine this whole time, but I fucked it all up?

"Oh, shit," I whisper, my hand coming up to cover my mouth.

Memories of the past year run in a loop through my head. A hundred different things Cole said or did to make me happy. His sexy grin and the way his eyes light up when he laughs. All the ways he went out of his way to be there for me, even as I'd fought him every step of the way. Why had I done that? He was right this morning. I never let anyone help me, even when I so clearly need help. I'm always pushing people away just so I can prove I'm capable of doing it myself. For what? What's the point?

"What did I do?"

Tears fill my eyes again and I pull in a ragged breath.

"Oh, no," Harlow says. "Enough of the crying shit. Crying time is over. Now is the time to make a plan to fix this shit show. Preferably before the wedding."

CHAPTER 34

Layna

The ceremony is perfect. I don't know how Hannah worked such magic, but everything flows smoothly. I manage to hold back my tears when I walk Piper down the aisle and even when I hand her off to Luke. I don't even cry when Luke recites his vows to her. It isn't until they turn to face the crowd and they're announced as Mr. and Mrs. Lucas Wolfe that tears fill my eyes.

I'd wondered if I had any tears left in me after this morning, but it seems there are still a few reserves. Still, I manage to rein them in before I turn into a watery mess. I remind myself that this is a celebration. It's the happiest day of my sister's life. Just because my heart is breaking in my chest doesn't mean I can't be happy for her. I do my best not to look at Cole as Linc holds out an arm for me to escort me back down the aisle and out of the ceremony room.

"You okay?" he asks, his voice pitched so low only I can hear it.

"Yeah," I whisper. "Thanks for this morning."

"No problem. I'm glad I was there."

"Me too."

He's silent for several seconds as we make our way to the door. When we're almost there, he speaks again.

"Don't give up on him. He's hurt and being stubborn, but he'll come around."

It's the first time he's said anything to me about the situation. Until now, I was worried he was angry with me for hurting his brother. Hell, maybe he is. But even if he is, he still hopes we can work it out.

"I never meant to hurt him," I say.

Linc pats my hand where it rests on his arm. It's such a brotherly gesture that I smile.

"I know you didn't. And he knows it too."

I nod. "I hope you're right."

"I am," Linc says simply. "He's my brother."

I understand what he means without any elaboration. Linc knows Cole better than anyone else does. They share a bond, the same way Piper and I do. If he believes Cole will forgive me, I need to have faith that he's right. Besides, the alternative is too painful to consider.

"Thanks," I say. "For everything."

He smiles down at me before releasing my hand and turning to look for Harlow who's being escorted toward us by Cole. I know he's there, but I don't turn around to watch his approach. I can't. After everything that was said between us today, I don't think I can handle seeing that blank look in his eyes when he looks at me. That might actually break me. Instead, I follow Hannah's direction to the room where the wedding party is supposed to meet for photos.

The next half hour is a blur of smiling and posing and pretending every fiber of my being isn't screaming out for Cole. I want so badly to look at him and see that crooked grin directed at me. I want to see his brown eyes locked on mine with that intensity that never fails to take my breath away. But I know that's too much to wish for right now. Right now I'd settle for him looking at me and not looking right through me as if I'm not there.

By the time we make our way into the reception hall and Piper has her first dance with her new husband, I'm overly emotional and somewhat drained from pretending I'm okay. But I do my best to focus on my sister and how happy she is. I take dozens of photos with my phone, even though I know the photographer is doing a fantastic job. I can't help myself. I'm so happy for her even while my heart is breaking over Cole. It's strange to feel these conflicting emotions at once.

I'm worried I won't be able to keep up this happy mask for the rest of the night, but I won't do anything to ruin Piper's day. She keeps glancing at me, a question in her eyes. I know she's asking if I'm okay, so I nod and smile each time, trying to reassure her. I'm not sure how well it works though. An hour into the reception, Harlow walks over and grabs my hand, pulling me out onto the dance floor.

"Come on," she says. "You haven't danced once tonight."

"I don't feel like dancing," I say, tugging back against her hold on my hand.

"Too bad," Piper says from behind me.

She grabs my other hand and helps Harlow pull me with her.

"You're dancing, whether you like it or not," Piper says.

"Now who's the bridezilla," I mutter.

But I stop fighting them. I know they're just trying to cheer me up. I'm not sure they'll be able to manage it, but I appreciate the gesture. Once we're all out on the floor, I let myself move to the music, dancing with my sister and our friend. Eventually, I find myself smiling a smile that isn't forced and it surprises me to realize I'm having fun. Even with this great big hole in my heart, I can still have fun. I give myself over to the music and the joy of dancing with these women I love so much. I push thoughts of Cole and the future out of my mind and let myself just be present in the moment.

But eventually, the song comes to an end and the dance is over. We're all out of breath and giddy with endorphins. As the music shifts to some slow love song, Luke walks over and pulls Piper against him for a dance. All around me, couples are gathering on the dance floor, holding one another close. My gaze lands Cole where he's standing on the other side of the dance floor next to his brother.

As I watch, Harlow walks in their direction. I can see her intent before she reaches them and a plan forms in my mind. I don't know if it's smart or crazy to do this now. But I need to talk to Cole. I need to tell him everything. And I can't do that if he won't talk to me. Maybe I should wait until after the wedding. Maybe he'll turn me away and cause a scene rather than spend 3 minutes on the dance floor with me, but I've got to try. I hurry to catch up to Harlow before she reaches the two men.

"Wait for me," I say, grabbing her arm.

"What's up?"

I shake my head. "Remember that time we danced together at Peach Fuzz and Linc ended up spending the night at your apartment?"

She smiles. "Oh, do I."

"Good. Because I need a favor."

I begin to explain to Harlow what I need her to do, but I don't get far before she smiles at me and waves away my words.

"Say no more. I've got this."

She turns and continues her walk toward Linc and Cole, leaving me to follow behind her. When she reaches the two men, Linc's smile grows wide and I see his hand move as if to reach for her, but she gives a tiny shake of her head before turning to look at Cole.

"I think I need to dance with the one who brought me," she says in a teasing tone.

Cole looks from Layna to his brother, a confused expression on his face.

"You know he's not your date, right?" Linc says. "He just escorted you down the aisle."

Harlow shrugs. "Details."

Then she grabs Cole's hand and pulls him out onto the floor. I'm not sure if everyone else can see that it's against his will, but it's obvious to me. I'd laugh if I weren't so anxious about this plan of mine.

"I knew she was pissed at me for not telling her about you and Cole, but this seems extreme," Linc says.

I turn back to look at him and smile, holding out a hand.

"Actually, this is my idea," I say. "Dance?"

Linc's eyes narrow in suspicion, but he only hesitates for a moment before taking my hand and leading me out onto the floor.

"Do I get to know the plan?" Linc asks as we sway slowly to the music.

I look around, trying to spot Cole and Harlow on the dance floor.

"Uh huh," I say. "We just need to find your girlfriend."

Linc uses our joined hands to point. "She's right over there."

I yank his hand back down. "Don't be obvious!" I hiss.

"How about you tell me the plan," he says.

I try to direct our movements closer to Harlow and Cole, but Linc is definitely used to leading when it comes to dancing.

"Dance us over to where they are," I say.

"You know we look crazy right now, right?" he asks.

"Who cares? Just get closer to them. And then you're going to cut in."

He laughs softly. "And Cole will have no choice but to dance with you or look like an asshole."

"Exactly," I say. "His good southern manners will force him to dance with me. That's my chance to force him to listen to me. It's my only shot."

"What if he's too mad to be polite?" he asks.

I give him a pointed look. "You know him best. Does that sound like him?"

He sighs but says nothing. Instead, he steers us awkwardly over to where Cole and Harlow are dancing.

"Oh, look who it is!" Harlow says in a bubbly voice.

She's not an actor, that's for sure.

"Oh, wow," Linc says in a flat tone. "What a coincidence."

I want to kick his shin, but that would be even more obvious than their terrible acting.

"May I cut in?" Harlow asks, looking at me.

"Oh, of course," I say, gesturing toward Linc who just rolls his eyes and mumbles something under his breath as he takes her hand.

Cole stands there, not looking at me. His jaw is clenched and I can tell he's still angry.

"What do you say?" I ask, my voice small.

He looks around the dance floor at the other couples who are moving around us as we stand there frozen.

"I don't have much of a choice, do I?" he mutters.

Before I can respond, he reaches for me. His hand on my waist is barely there. It's as if he can't stand touching me. His hand holds mine, but I'd be a fool to believe he's not pissed to be tricked into this dance.

"I'm sorry," I say.

"Let's not do this right now," he says, his voice hard.

I sigh, wondering if maybe Linc was wrong and Cole will never listen to me. I don't know if I can take living in Peach Tree with him hating me. Seeing him all the time but knowing he'll never be mine isn't something I'm prepared to do. After a few seconds of silence, I decide to try a different tactic.

"Do you remember that case? The one I've been fighting for weeks?"

Cole's quiet for so long that I wonder if he's going to spend the rest of this dance acting like I don't exist. But he eventually speaks, though he won't look at me.

"The one with the kid?"

The relief I feel when he speaks is enough to steal my breath, but I try to keep my excitement hidden.

"Yeah," I say, nodding.

"What about it?" he asks, even though I can tell he doesn't really want to talk to me right now.

Not that I can blame him after what I've put him through. I may have forced him to dance with me, but he's only here to avoid causing a scene. He keeps his head deliberately turned away from me so he won't have to meet my gaze while we sway to the music. He's also keeping me at arm's length. Literally. If he were holding me any further away from his body, I don't think I'd even be able to put my hands on his shoulders. I can't imagine how we look to anyone who happens to glance our way.

The distance between us is my fault, I know. I did this to us by letting my fear dictate my actions. I was convinced that he and I could never work, so I never gave it a chance. Now, I've lost him, and I don't know if there's anything I can say to win him back. But I know I need to try.

"Well, I did it," I say. "I got the charges dismissed. I knew he wasn't guilty. I knew it, but the red tape took forever to wade through. I found out today that it's official. He's free to live his life now."

"That's great, Layna," he says, his voice carefully neutral. "I'm happy for you."

Cole's voice lacks his usual upbeat tone and charm. I know it's my fault. A choked sound escapes me, and I try to make it sound more like a laugh than a sob. I pull in a deep breath and let it out, fighting the urge to cry. I asked him to dance for a reason. I need to focus. The song is already half over.

"All I could think was, 'I can't wait to tell Cole.'"

I try to meet his gaze, wondering if he can see my feelings on my face. But it's no use. He still won't look at me. A muscle in his jaw ticks and I can tell he's not as unaffected by me as he'd like me to think. I keep talking, determined to break through his barriers.

"Today, something good happened," I say, trying to close the distance between us. "The first person I wanted to tell was you. Not Piper. Not Harlow. Not my stupid friends back in Atlanta. You."

I take a deep breath before continuing.

"You were wrong this morning," I say. "When I said I wanted someone safe to build a life with. You thought that was me saying I don't want to be with you, but that's not it at all. That's what I was trying to tell you before, but I messed it up. The truth is that I've been scared my whole adult life. Scared to let someone in. Scared to fall in love. Scared to lose someone else. I didn't want someone to mean so much to me that losing them would break me."

Another choked laugh escapes me. My heart clenches painfully and I know I need to tell him all of it before I can't get the words out. Taking a deep breath, I try to steady myself for what I'm about to say.

"Cole, somehow, you've become the person I can't live without. I wasn't looking for it and I don't know how it happened or when it happened. And honestly, it scares the shit out of me. But you're the person I want beside me when all my dreams come true. Or when my whole world falls apart. Because I know you'll help me put it back together again. I know, without even asking, that you'll be right there beside me."

I focus on a spot somewhere over his left shoulder, unable to look at his face to gauge his expression. I realize my words are coming too fast, but I can't seem to stop them from spilling out. But I know if I don't get this out, I might never work up the nerve to try again. So, I keep talking.

"I didn't get it at first," I say. "Not for a long time. I didn't understand what that deep faith in another person meant. But I do now. I know what I said before. That I don't need anyone. That I'd be fine on my own. And maybe that's true. Maybe I'll be fine on my own. But I don't want to be fine, Cole. I don't want to settle for fine just because it's easier and safer and less scary. I want more than that. And the truth is that I don't think I can be happy without you.

"Just being around you makes me smile. You're like the sun and I couldn't help but be pulled into your gravitational field. I'm drawn to you. I always have been. Since that first night. And I know that sounds crazy and I know you're going to tell me it was just sex. It's always been just sex with us. And I know that was my rule. I know that. But that's not what this is now. Because I need you."

I feel my throat go tight with emotion and I'm worried I won't be able to get the words out before the tears come along to choke me. Swallowing hard, I tell him the truth I've been hiding from for all these months. I hadn't even realized we'd stopped dancing. We're standing still in the middle of the dance floor as other dancers move around us, casting strange looks our way. But I don't look at them. I turn my watery gaze to Cole. He's looking at me now, those intense brown eyes that have always held me captive locked on mine.

"I never need anybody," I whisper as a tear tracks down my cheek. "But I need you. I'm in love with you. And I know I screwed it all up and I know it's probably too late for you to forgive me, but I need you, Cole. I just *need* you. And I—"

He puts a finger over my lips, stopping my words.

"Shh," he says. "Layna, you have me. You always have. I'm sorry for what I said before. I didn't mean it. I was angry and scared. The truth is, I think I've been in love with you since that first night. Back when you thought I was the server and you still flirted with me."

"I didn't flirt with you," I mutter out of habit.

"Liar," he says, giving me that grin I love.

His hand moves to cup my cheek and I'm struck by what I see in his eyes.

"I love you, Layna. I always have. I've just been waiting for you to catch up."

My heart stutters in my chest as his words finally sink in. Shock steals my breath and I stand there blinking at the man I love. The man who just told me he loves me. The man who's loved me all along. It's so unbelievable.

"Are you sure?" I whisper as more tears fill my eyes and spill over.

His smile grows even wider.

"I'm sure," he says as he lowers his lips to mine.

The kiss is unlike any other kiss we've shared. It's tender, almost reverent. His lips are soft and slow against mine. There's no rush, no reason to hurry to get to the next step. There's only this moment.

Right now.

And it's perfect.

CHAPTER 35

Cole

As the song ends and a more upbeat one begins playing, I lead Layna off the dance floor intending to drag her back to my room for some privacy. But we're barely five feet from the dance floor when my brother and Harlow step into our path. They're both grinning at us from ear to ear and I know exactly what's about to happen.

"It's about time you two figured your shit out," Linc says.

Harlow points a finger at him. "Don't think I'm not still pissed at you for not telling me about this."

Linc sighs. "I said I was sorry, baby. I couldn't break my word."

"It's my fault," I say. "I was too much of a chicken shit to tell Layna how I felt, and I put him in the middle of it. I made him swear not to tell you. Don't be mad at him."

Layna is watching this byplay with interest. I know she's probably wondering what I told Linc and when.

And I'll tell her everything. Later. When I can get her alone and out of that dress.

"I just like giving him a hard time," Harlow says with a wink. "I'm happy for you two."

I lift mine and Layna's joined hands and plant a kiss on the back of hers.

"Thank you," Layna says, leaning her head on my shoulder.

"What do you mean you just like giving me a hard time?" Linc shoots an accusatory glare at Harlow.

She just smiles prettily and shrugs as he towers over her.

"You're going to pay for that later," he warns in a low voice.

"I'm counting on it," Harlow whispers.

As they walk away, Layna and I exchange glances.

"I don't think we were supposed to hear that last part," she says.

"I really wish I hadn't," I say.

We both laugh and I pull Layna to me for a kiss. I can't help myself. I keep looking for excuses to touch her, to kiss her. I still can't believe she's mine. I think I must be in shock. When Harlow pulled me out onto the floor for that dance, I didn't know what to expect. And after she and Linc had left me standing there with Layna, I'd known it was planned. I'd assumed Layna would apologize and try to explain once again why we weren't right for each other. I figured she would use the public venue to get me to talk to her without causing a scene. I never expected her to tell me she's in love with me. I still can't quite believe it.

"What?" Layna asks, her brows lowered in confusion. "You're staring at me."

I smile and shake my head. "Nothing. Just trying to wrap my head around it all."

She steps closer and wraps her arms around my waist. "It's a lot to take in."

I gaze down at this woman who, until only a few minutes ago, I'd thought I'd lost for good. Her expression is so full of happiness. So different from the way I left her this morning, in my hotel room, her eyes shining with unshed tears. When I remember the words I said to her just before I'd left, shame washes over me.

"I'm sorry," I say.

"For what?" she asks, confusion wrinkling her brow.

"This morning. I shouldn't have said that. I was angry and hurting."

She shakes her head. "Cole, stop. You were right to say it. As much as it hurt to hear, you weren't exactly wrong. I kept you at a distance because I was scared. I didn't want to risk falling for you. I didn't want to fall for anyone. But especially not you. Because I knew how easy it would be to love you. And how much it would hurt if you didn't feel the same way. So, I kept things light. I told you again and again that we were just friends. I kept reminding myself of all the reasons we shouldn't be together. All the ways it might not work out. And all the while I was ignoring the way I felt about you. Pretending I wasn't falling for you."

Her eyes close for a moment and she takes a deep breath. When she looks at me again, her eyes shine with unshed tears.

"Cole, I'm scared of what I feel for you," she whispers. "What if it doesn't work out? What if—"

I bring my hands up to cup her face and silence her with a kiss.

Pressing my forehead to hers, I whisper, "I'm scared too. I've never felt this before. I don't know how to do this. But I know I want to try. With you. So, let's be scared together."

"I love you," she whispers.

I smile. I don't think I'll ever get tired of hearing her say those words.

"I love you, too."

The next hour drags slowly by. Every time I try to lure Layna away from the reception, it seems like someone comes over to chat with us. When it's time for the wedding toasts, we take our seats with the rest of the wedding party. Layna and I are separated since the bride's attendants are on one side and the groom's are on the other. I can tell that Linc is just as annoyed by this as I am. But when Layna stands to give her toast to her sister, I feel a sense of pride welling up inside me. She stands tall and beautiful as she speaks, her voice only cracking at the end when she dabs at her eyes. I glance around the room and see that most of the women in the crowd are doing the same. Some of the men are covertly blinking shining eyes as well.

When she finishes, she turns to look at me, giving me a smile that's meant just for me. My heart trips in my chest almost painfully. I return the smile, wishing she weren't so far away from me right now. How long do we need to sit in these assigned seats? Someone should have talked to Piper about this before the wedding. I watch as Layna turns to walk back to her chair. She takes two steps in that direction before turning back to face me and walking directly over to where I'm seated.

"Can I sit here?" she asks, one eyebrow raised in challenge.

My smile grows wider, and I shift my chair away from the table intending to stand. Before I can, Layna lowers herself to sit in my lap, bringing one arm around the back of my neck. My arms immediately move to encircle her waist and I lean forward to kiss her cheek. I'm surprised by her boldness in front of a room full of people, but I admit I'm not upset about it.

"I didn't take you for a public display of affection kind of girl," I whisper.

"I'm not usually," she says. "But I don't want to be way over there when you're over here. We spent enough time apart."

God damn, I love this woman.

"You were fucking amazing up there," I whisper.

"That was more nerve-wracking than convincing a jury to acquit a guilty client," she mutters. "Allegedly."

My shoulders shake with laughter, and I try to hide my face in her shoulder.

"I'll take your word for it," I say. "I'm glad it was Linc and not me."

My brother being the best man instead of me is something I harassed Luke about constantly in the months leading up to the wedding. Not that I really wanted the job. I hate public speaking, but I know my brother hates it more. So, watching him stand in front of this crowd of people and give a heartfelt toast to our best friend is payment enough for Luke not picking me.

By the time the toasts are done, and the cake is cut, I'm beyond ready to throw Layna over my shoulder and carry her to my room. Why the hell do wedding receptions last so long, anyway? I know it's a celebration, but aren't the bride and groom ready to be alone after all this? I know I would be. At that thought, I find my eyes drifting to Layna where she's now seated in her own chair beside me talking with Harlow. I wonder if she wants a big wedding. I bet she'd make a gorgeous bride.

Whoa. Slow down.

We've only just decided to see where this goes. Granted, I'm madly in love with her and we've practically been a couple for the last year. Minus the actual dating part, of course. For some reason, the idea of settling down with her doesn't scare me a bit. The only thing that scares me is the idea of life without her. When the hell did I grow up to be this guy? I'm not sure, but I think I like him.

"Can we sneak out now?" Layna's voice whispers in my ear.

"I've been waiting for you to ask," I say, moving to my feet as the words leave my mouth.

Layna puts her hand in mine, and I pull her to her feet. We're both stifling our laughter as I lead her toward the exit. Before we can make it there, however, I hear Piper call her name. She pulls to a stop and we both turn to see Piper and Luke walking our way. Piper looks beautiful in her white gown. I smile at the happy couple as Layna and I walk toward them, hand-in-hand.

"Where are you two off to in such a hurry?" Piper asks, her gaze going to our joined hands before moving back to my face.

"We were just going to get some fresh air," Layna says.

I nod in agreement.

"That's weird," Luke says. "Because the balcony is in the opposite direction." He points behind him with one thumb.

"Is it?" Layna says. "I didn't know that."

"Liar," Piper says with a grin.

"Bitch," Layna says, her mouth turning up into a smile.

"I'm happy for you," Piper says. Then, turning to me, her face turns serious. "If you hurt her, I'll stuff you in my trunk and help the search party look for you. I'll even work up some tears for effect."

My mouth drops open as Luke bursts out laughing. I turn to him.

"You're laughing? She just threatened to kidnap me!"

He just shrugs. "I don't think they can make me testify against my wife."

"He's right," Layna says, wrapping her arms around my waist. "It's in the constitution."

I look at her, eyes narrowed. "I guess I'm stuck with you, then."

She gives me the biggest smile I've ever seen. "I guess so."

"Lucky me," I say, leaning down to kiss her.

It's late by the time Layna and I can leave the reception. I'm not upset by the delay, though. It gives us time to dance again without me being an ass the whole time. I savor every second of her in my arms, holding her close to me as we sway to the music. I even manage to kiss her on the dance floor, complete with a dramatic dip that makes her laugh. I can't seem to help myself. I'll never get tired of touching her, kissing her, making her smile.

Being with Layna in public, where everyone can see us together, is such a novelty that it seems neither of us is in a real hurry to end it. We spent a year in the dark, hiding away with stolen touches and quick interludes. Now, we have all the time in the world. No more hiding. No more secrets from our friends and family. We'll have plenty of time to be alone. Tonight, we get to enjoy showing the world how we feel.

CHAPTER 36

Cole

After going to Layna's room so she can pack her things, I help by shoving everything into her suitcase. I can tell she wants to argue with me about the proper way to pack her things, but she manages to hold back. I almost laugh at the annoyance in her eyes. I'm going to pay for that later, I'm sure. But I don't care. I can't wait to have her in my room. In my bed. Without needing to rush out first thing in the morning. I want to wake up with her in my arms, the way I've never been able to in the past.

The walk to my room feels longer than I remember. The anticipation of getting Layna alone and out of that dress is killing me. As I round the corner to my room, I stop short. My suitcase is sitting next to my door and a man dressed in the hotel's uniform emerges from the open doorway holding a garment bag. My mouth drops open in a question, but I don't get a chance to voice it before the man speaks.

"Ah, Mr. Prescott, sir," he says. "I'm so sorry. We were just finishing up."

Another uniformed man emerges from my room holding another of my bags.

"Finishing up what?" I ask.

"Moving your things to your new room," the first man answers. "We were hoping to have it finished before you retired for the night."

"New room?" I ask.

What the hell is going on?

The man nods. "Top floor, as requested. With a city view. If you'll follow me, I'll take you there. We have all your things packed. Unless you'd like to do a last sweep of the room?"

A new room. On the top floor. I glance over at Layna, but she looks as confused as I feel. Before I can ask what's going on, Layna's phone rings. She glances at the screen and smiles before answering.

"Piper, did you forget something?"

She listens for a moment, her face going soft as her smile widens. "You didn't need to do that," she says. "Then tell Luke thank you from us. I love you too. Enjoy your honeymoon. I love you."

She ends the call and turns back to me.

"This is Luke," she says. "The room upgrade. It's a gift from him."

My confusion must show on my face. "Since when does the guy getting married buy gifts for other people?"

She shrugs. "Groomsman gifts are customary, actually. They're usually not this extravagant. But I say we enjoy it, Mr. Prescott."

She hooks her hand in the crook of my elbow and smiles up at me.

"Okay, counselor," I say. "Let's go see this new room of ours."

We follow the two men back to the elevator, Layna's hand in mine. When we enter, one of the men uses a keycard to access the penthouse level. I look at Layna with a raised brow. She just shrugs. When the doors open, a long hallway stretches out before us. The two men walk to the end of the hallway and one of them uses a keycard to open the door at the end. The other one carries my luggage inside. I lead Layna through the doorway and into the nicest hotel room I've ever been in. My eyes go wide as I try to decide what to look at first.

The hotel employee is giving us a brief rundown of the room, but I'm barely listening. I'm too distracted by the view outside the massive windows. It feels like I can see the entire city from here, though I know this is just one small slice of it. Finally, the two men leave and I'm alone with Layna. She walks up behind me and wraps her arms around my waist, resting her head against my back.

She exhales on a sigh. "Alone, at last."

I turn in her arms and she smiles up at me. She's so beautiful. Her dark hair is falling over her shoulders in waves and her lips are turned up in a smile. I've had sex with this woman more times than I can count. I've taken her and been taken by her in so many ways I can't think of them all. But tonight feels different. Tonight, she's mine and I'm hers. No more lies or secrets. No more pretending for our friends. No more pretending for ourselves. Tonight, I can show her all the ways I've wanted to love her since the night we met.

As if reading my mind, Layna says, "I still can't believe it. I can't believe we're here. Together."

Her eyes go bright and for a moment I'm worried she's going to cry, but she blinks away the tears that threaten.

"I didn't think I could have this," she whispers.

I pull her tight against me, holding her to me as I speak. "I told you once, remember? That you deserve someone who thinks the sun rises and sets in your eyes. Someone who wants to be beside you through everything in life. Remember?"

She nods against my chest.

"I didn't realize it at the time, but I was describing the way I feel about you. The way I've always felt about you. You deserve all of that and more."

"I hate how much time we wasted," she says.

I smile. "We may not have said the right things, but we made good use of that time. At least, I think so."

She laughs in my arms and leans back to look up at me. "True. What do you say we make good use of this fancy ass hotel room?"

I grin. "Yes, ma'am."

She sighs. "I still don't like you calling me ma'am."

"I know."

Her eyes narrow. "So, why do you do it?"

"Because you're cute when you're annoyed."

"You're such a dick," she mutters, but there's no heat behind the words.

"What about my dick?" I ask, my voice dropping lower.

Layna looks up at me through lowered lashes as she speaks. "Oh, I can think of a few things I'd like to do with it."

She pushes lightly against my chest and I take a step backward. She follows, giving me another light push.

"A few things, huh?" I ask, my mind swimming with possibilities.

She nods, still following me as she backs me up another few steps. When my back touches the glass of the floor-to-ceiling window looking out over the city, I stop and give her a questioning look.

"I don't think I can go any further," I say.

She smiles, reaching for my belt. "This is far enough."

It takes me a second to realize her intent, but I feel myself go rock-hard when I do. She uses her hold on my belt to turn me so the window is on my left. To anyone looking in, she and I would be standing in profile. They'd be able to see exactly what's happening. Layna takes me in her hand, gripping lightly as she looks up at me. She gives my cock a slow stroke, sending a jolt of desire through me. Then, she lowers herself to her knees on the plush carpet.

"Layna," I whisper. "The window?"

She shrugs. "Let them look."

Then she opens her mouth and guides my length inside. My mouth drops open as I watch her lick and suck me. The sight is so damned hot. I know I'll never forget the way she looks right now. I love when she takes charge, controlling me, owning my body like it's hers. Because it is. She knows it, too. I risk looking away from her long enough to admire the view out the window. I take in the lights of the city, the cars driving through the streets, the lights from houses, hotels, and apartments, people busy living their lives. If anyone were to look up right now, would they see us? Could they see this beautiful woman kneeling before me, taking my cock in her mouth? The thought is almost enough to make me come in her mouth before we've even gotten started.

She takes me deeper, gripping the base of my cock in one hand as her mouth works me over My hands go to her head, stroking her hair gently as she bobs up and down on me. My thoughts drift to last night and the way she'd taken me down her throat and held me there. The way she'd swallowed every drop of me until I could barely move. It's almost too much. I almost come, right then. Instead, I gently urge her back until her mouth is no longer on me. She's still holding me in one hand, lightly stroking me as she looks up, a question in her eyes.

"Stand up."

There's a hint of challenge in her eyes, but she doesn't argue. Rising to her feet, she stands before me, still wearing the dress she'd worn for the wedding.

"Turn around," I say. "Face the window."

I know she likes being in charge. I worry I might be pushing her too far with my commands, but she doesn't balk. She turns slowly to face the window without comment. Reaching out, my hands find the zipper at her back, and I slowly lower it to expose her to my gaze. As I do, I lower my lips to her neck, kissing the spot I know is most sensitive for her. She shivers and sucks in a breath. I almost smile. I know her body so well after all the time we've spent together. Tonight, I'm going to use that knowledge to make her come as many times as possible.

I slide the dress down her arms until it falls, pooling on the floor at her feet. She steps out of it but keeps her back to me. I unclasp her bra and toss it aside, my fingers smoothing over the marks left on her skin. She's wearing another one of those lacy thongs that never fails to drive me wild. I slide a finger under the strap at her hip, letting my fingers trace against her skin.

"Cole," she whispers. "Stop teasing me."

I grin at the bossiness in her tone.

"We've got all night. I want to take my time with you."

I hear her sharp intake of breath. This is killing her, I know. But I know she's also loving every second of it. I quickly strip off the rest of my clothes before pressing my body against hers, moving her forward until she has to brace herself against the window with her hands.

"Look out there," I whisper, sliding my hands around to cup her breasts.

"Look at all those cars, all those people." I squeeze her nipple, exerting just enough pressure to make her gasp.

"What do you think they'd do if they could see you right now? Pressed up against the glass, my hands all over you?"

I move my hand down to the waistband of her thong, my fingers sliding under the lacy material to touch her. She's already wet for me, but it's not enough. Not yet. I press my hips forward, grinding lightly against her ass, smiling when she pushes back against me.

"Do you think they'd stop to watch?" I murmur. "Should we give them a show?"

She nods. "Yes."

Though she can't see it, I smile. "Spread your legs, baby."

Layna immediately widens her stance, giving me more room to slide my hand down to touch her. She gasps when my fingers brush her clit, making my smile grow wider. She's always so responsive to my touch. Always so needy for more. I love it. I love her. My fingers slide over her clit again, coating my fingers in her arousal before sliding lower to push two fingers inside her. She gasps and her hips buck against my hand. Thrusting slowly, I work my fingers in and out a few more times before bringing them back up to work her clit. Her whole body jerks as I move my fingers over her clit in tight little circles.

"That's it, baby," I say in a low voice. "Come on my hand."

She gasps as her body jerks again. My other arm wraps tightly around her, pulling her back against me as I work her clit even faster, using slightly more pressure as I do.

"Shit," she whispers, her body shaking against mine.

"Look at all those people down there," I say. "Are they watching? Can they see me with my hand on your pretty cunt, working you over?"

"Cole!"

My fingers move faster as I slide my other hand up to cup her breast, lightly squeezing her nipple.

"You're so fucking sexy right now. So wet and writhing against me." I press my hard cock against her ass again. "You feel that? That's how fucking hard you make me. I can't wait to be in this tight pussy, baby."

I can feel the tremors wracking Layna's body. She's so close. I squeeze her nipple again, slightly harder this time. Lowering my head, I kiss that sensitive spot on the back of her neck as my fingers keep up their frantic pace on her clit.

"Come for me, Layna. Let all those people see what they can't have."

Her body goes rigid and her fingers curl into fists against the glass as she cries out. I don't stop circling her clit as she comes.

"That's it, baby."

I kiss her neck, pressing my cock harder against her ass, letting her feel how turned on I am.

"You're so fucking sexy when you come."

She moans something incoherent, and her head falls back against my shoulder.

"God damn, I love those sounds you make."

She answers me with another moan as her hips buck against my hand. I slow my movements, easing the pressure against her clit as she comes down from her orgasm. My lips press kisses to the side of her neck and her hand comes up to tangle in my hair.

"Do you really think people can see us?" she asks.

I look out at the view, considering. "If they are, we should give them a show."

I turn Layna around to face me before reaching to slide her panties down her legs. When she steps out of them, I waste no time wrapping my arms around her and lifting her to press her back against the glass. Her eyes go wide when she realizes that I intend to fuck her against the glass. I give her a second to tell me she doesn't want to, but when she just wraps her legs around my waist and smiles, I know she's all in.

Reaching down, I fit myself against her as she grips my shoulders. Then I grip her ass in both hands as she sinks down, slowly impaling herself on my cock. She lets out a sexy little moan as I fill her, driving me wild.

"I'll never get enough of this," I say, beginning to move. "This pussy was made to take my cock."

She gasps as I pull out and thrust into her again. I move slowly, giving her time to adjust to the position, but she surprises me.

"Faster," she whispers.

"Yes, ma'am."

I tighten my grip on her ass, pulling her down onto me as I thrust up into her. Her mouth falls open as I pound into her, our bodies making slapping sounds with each punishing thrust of our hips. Layna's eyes are locked on mine and she's making these sexy little noises each time I slam into her.

"You like that, baby?" I grunt out.

She nods, an incoherent moan slipping from her lips.

"You like me fucking this pussy where the whole world can see?"

She moans again, louder this time.

"You want them all to see you come on my cock?"

She turns her head to the side so she can see the city below.

"You want them to see how dirty you are? How much you like getting fucked?"

Her cries are getting louder now and her grip tightens on my neck as I feel her begin to pulse around my cock.

"Let me feel you come, baby. Give it to me."

"Oh, god!"

Layna cries out as her body tenses and her pussy clamps down on my cock. I don't stop, thrusting hard and fast inside her as her orgasm consumes her. She moans my name and her nails dig into my shoulders almost painfully, but I don't care. I'm too lost in the moment, caught up in the sight and the feel and the sound of her falling apart around me. She pulls my face down to hers, but hesitates before our lips meet.

"Cole. I love you," she whispers before pressing her lips to mine.

Those three words send me over the edge and I lose the last thread of control I'd been holding onto. My legs threaten to give out as my orgasm hits me hard and fast. The force of my climax steals my breath and it's all I can do to keep standing as I groan against her mouth, filling her with my release. Eventually, I go still, my body spent. I can hear my heart pounding and my breaths are coming in heaving pants. I raise my head to look at Layna. I need to tell her I love her too. But before I can open my mouth to speak, my knees buckle, and we both drop to the floor in a heap.

Layna's immediate laughter lets me know she's not hurt. It's a good thing, too. I don't think I could move to help her if she was. My legs feel like jelly, and I don't think my heartrate will return to normal for a few days. I manage to straighten my legs from where they're bent underneath me so I'm lying flat on my back on the carpet. Chest still heaving, I work to catch my breath.

"Holy shit," Layna gasps from where she's lying on the floor beside me.

"Yeah," I agree.

"That was intense."

"Yeah."

She laughs.

"Don't laugh at a dying man," I wheeze.

"Big baby," she mutters, making me smile. "You're the one who dropped me. What if I was hurt?"

I can't help but laugh now, even though my breathing is still labored.

"Dating you isn't going to be boring, is it?"

She laughs. "Not if I can help it."

That reminds me.

"Layna," her name is a breathless pant.

"Yeah?"

"I have a question."

"It better not require any brain cells, because I don't have the energy to think."

I huff out another laugh and turn my head to look at her where she's sprawled naked beside me on the floor.

"Will you go on a date with me?"

Her smile is wide and instant as she reaches a hand toward me. I twine my fingers through hers.

"I thought you'd never ask."

End of Book 3

A Word From Isla

To say I'm sad to see this series end is an understatement. I've adored creating these characters and telling their stories. I try to write the kinds of characters that people relate to and fall in love with as they read. I hope I've managed to do that with Peach Tree.

I want to take a moment to thank the people who helped me make this series happen. First and foremost is my amazing husband who left me alone for hours on end, even when it meant I was neglecting him and our entire life. He's my real life book boyfriend, even though he made me move across the country. Twice.

Special and forever thanks to Joni. She's always had unwavering faith in my writing. She encourages me when I'm down and makes sure I take care of myself while simultaneously demanding the next book. She's also one of the funniest, most sarcastic women I know. I hope one day I grow up to be just like her.

Thank you to Nika, for being my cheerleader, my therapist and my friend. She helped me with this book more than she knows. She had total faith in me, even when I didn't. Sometimes that's all we need.

Made in the USA
Coppell, TX
18 July 2023